WOUNDED

JASINDA WILDER

To Bex,

love heals all wounds.

Wishing that love for

you.

~Jasinda

Wilder

This is a work of fiction. Names, characters, places, and incidents are either the product of the author's imagination or are used fictitiously. Any resemblance to actual events, places, organizations, or persons, whether living or dead, is entirely coincidental.

WOUNDED

ISBN: 978-0-9882642-6-7

This book is for all the brave men and women of the American armed forces, past and present.

PROLOGUE

The Prayer

First Gulf War; Iraq, 1991

HAIL MARY, FULL OF GRACE, THE LORD IS WITH THEE.

The words were whispered under his breath, his fingers rubbing the beads of the rosary. His eyes were squeezed shut, his hands trembling. He couldn't stand up, could only slump on his knees and lean back against the rough, cool stone of the wall.

He wasn't sure if the silence was real or if his hearing had been blasted away. Whatever the case, the world was silent around him.

A bullet bit into the wall near his head, and he threw himself to the side. He felt a brief spat of pain as his head crashed against the ground. He'd heard no gunshot, so his ears must not have been working. Another bullet, a third and fourth, and then a whole murderous hailstorm impacted the wall and the dirt road, shredding the stone and flecking him with stinging shards of rock. He lunged to his feet, stumbled into a run, and ducked into a doorway. Bullets followed him, thunking into the wood of the door, disappearing into the darkness within, zinging and ricocheting. He let himself fall to the floor, then rolled over and curled into the corner.

Blessed art thou amongst women, and blessed is the fruit of thy womb, Jesus.

His ears rang, popped, and cleared. Immediately, the sound of assault rifle fire filled the air, a harsh *hackhackhack*, a pause…*hackhackhack*; the *whistle-whoosh* of an RPG, followed by a brief, fraught, waiting silence…a deafening crump as the grenade exploded nearby, shaking dust from the ceiling.

A man screamed shrilly in Arabic a few feet away…*"Allah! Allah!"*

Another voice, farther away, screaming curses in English.

Silence.

Silence.

Hackhackhack…an AK-47; *crackcrackcrackcrack*…an American M16A2 returning fire.

He managed to rise to his feet without vomiting or collapsing. He was in no way ready for this—he'd signed up to take pictures, write a story, not to be shot at. He was a journalist, not a soldier. *Stop shooting at me*, he wanted to say but couldn't.

He huddled against the wall and inspected his camera, breathed a sigh of amazed relief to see it intact. A bit miraculous, actually, considering how he'd been throwing himself around. He poked his head around the corner, scanned the scene for a shot.

There: a man in a red-and-white checkered keffiyeh standing on a rooftop firing an AK-47, the stock of an RPG poking up above his head. The photographer swapped lenses, wide-angle for telephoto, focused in on the insurgent—snap—caught him as he lifted the rifle to his shoulder, one eye squinted—snap—again as he lifted the rifle above his head in jubilation. The photographer flopped down to street level, lying prone, *snapsnapsnap*, capturing the dying slump and fall of a Marine, the tortured disbelief on his face, the arms clutched about his red-weeping throat, then *snapsnapsnap* as his buddy knelt in the street beside him to draw bead on the insurgent, *crackcrackcrack…crackcrack*: The *keffiyeh* jerked and was stained pink.

He heard a rustle and whimper from a far corner: a boy and his sister huddled together, holding tightly to one another. The boy stood up slowly, resolve hardening in his eyes. He reached down to the floor, lifted a rifle, and aimed it. The photographer raised his hands to show he was unarmed; the boy jabbered something in Arabic, motioned at the photographer with the muzzle. He shook his head, edged backward, lowered his hands: he had a Beretta 9mm at the small of his back, a precaution he'd hoped he would never have to use.

If he'd learned anything as an embedded journalist, it was the single rule of warfare: kill or be killed.

He was already making justifications, excuses.

The boy began to yell, shrill and angry. The photographer backed up against the wall, hand edging slowly towards the hard lump of the pistol against his spine. He gripped the gun tightly, preparing to jerk and fire. If he had been facing an adult, the move would have been obvious, but this was a boy, just a boy, no more than ten or eleven.

He held the AK like he knew how to use it, however, and the desperate terror in his eyes spoke of a short life lived in a perpetual war zone. He probably had been lulled to sleep by gunfire and explosions as much as mother's song and father's arms. He probably had played with that rifle as a toddler, sitting on his father's lap, lifted it, pretended to shoot it, making the sounds boys make the world over when playing soldier. This boy, though, had actually seen war. He playacted things he'd seen, not just scenes from the imaginations of sheltered children. He had seen uncles and cousins shrouded by old blankets, still and cold, had seen Marines tromp through his village, tall and arrogant.

Maybe he had been given a candy bar by one, a cuff on the head by another, a cold stare by a third. Maybe his father had been killed by an American in desert camo. Maybe he was left alone with his sister. Now, here was an American, and he had a chance to even the score. What did this boy know about rules of engagement, or the dishonor of killing an unarmed noncombatant? Of course, the boy couldn't know anything of this, and of course, the journalist was not unarmed.

Holy Mary, Mother of God, pray for us sinners...

He pulled the pistol as quickly and smoothly as possible, fired once, twice. The boy jerked sideways, left arm blossoming red, dust pattering from the missed second shot. The boy fell in slow motion, blood blooming like a pink, spreading rosette. The look in his eyes was something the photographer would never forget. The boy looked at the American, his expression doleful, accusing, baffled, hurt, as if a toy had been stolen.

His sister was screaming, but the journalist couldn't hear it, his hearing gone out again, but her mouth was opened wide and her chest was heaving and she was leaning over her brother. She turned to the photographer, screaming at him, shaking her head *no no no*.

He lowered the pistol, turned away, head clutched in trembling hands, trying to shake the vision of the boy falling. He didn't see the girl stop screaming and take up the AK-47. She held it as she had seen so many times before: low at her waist, strap hanging like a distended belly, black muzzle-mouth wavering, two fingers on the trigger, scarred and scuffed wooden stock tucked into her underarm.

She pulled the trigger, and it was the roar of the rifle that brought him back to the present. She missed, and he was frozen. He could shoot her brother because he was a boy and would grow into an insurgent by the time he was a teenager, if he wasn't already.

This was just a girl, twelve years old, if that. Maybe she had just begun wearing the *hijab*, maybe she was the only mother the boy had. He couldn't shoot her. He just couldn't.

Couldn't.

She had no such compunction; she did not miss a second time.

Holy Mary, Mother of God, pray for us sinners, now and at the hour of death.

Agony ripped through him as the hot bullets tore apart his chest and stomach. She emptied the entire clip into him, dropping the rifle when it went clickclickclick, empty. She fell to her knees beside her brother, weeping now, limp and sobbing. She did not look at the American as he lay on the ground bleeding out.

Amen.

He was floating now. He saw the girl, far away somehow, thin shoulders shaking. The pain was distant, and he was cold. There was no sound once again, but this time the silence was a welcome respite from the cacophony of hell. The silence was an enveloping cocoon of comfort.

He heard the Hail Mary once again, but he was not thinking it, not saying it. It was a prayer whispered to him across the chasm of eternity:

Hail Mary, full of grace, the Lord is with thee.

Blessed art thou among women, and blessed is the fruit of thy womb, Jesus.

Holy Mary, Mother of God, pray for us sinners, now and at the hour of death.

Amen.

There was heavy significance to the words, but he was too cloaked in slow peace and drifting chill to understand.

Then: *May the Lord Jesus Christ protect you and lead you to eternal life.*

He recognized that...what was it? Where had he heard those words before?

Then it came to him...Chaplain McGillis said them, whispered them to Jimmy Carson when he was gasping his last breath, to Andrew Chavez and to Lucas Haney as they died.

The Last Rites...

The American heard McGillis' voice in his head as he whispered the Eucharist and the Viaticum. Perhaps not in his head. Perhaps next to him, kneeling and kissing his small silver cross, fingers on his forehead.

The silence spread, the cold deepened...peace like a river drowning him in its black embrace...

There was no white light. There was only blackness, and silence, and cold.

ONE
Rania

First Gulf War; Iraq, 1991

THE AMERICAN, HE DIES SLOWLY. Not like Mama, who died instantly, in a spray of pink blood. I remember when Mama died. I tried to wipe the blood from my face, but I only smeared it worse, making my face sticky, like a mud-mask. He does not die like Papa, either, who was killed by a single stray bullet to the head, sudden and silent. The American, he dies like Uncle Ahmed, slowly, and in pain. Something about being shot in the belly, it causes such horrid suffering. Uncle Ahmed, he cried out to Allah to save him, weeping so piteously for so long that I forgot to be sad and just wanted him to die so the awful moaning and cursing and pleading would stop. Allah forgive me, but I did wish it. Not only once, but many times.

This American, however, he is not so noisy. He lies there bleeding from the belly and the chest, making a sucking noise every time he breathes. He does not cry, or scream, or clutch himself, as if trying to hold his life in with weakening arms. He just lies there, muttering to himself quietly, staring up at the ceiling, fingering those little wooden prayer beads. He works the beads as if they give him comfort, as if they, along with the strange words he speaks, could take away the pain.

Hassan, my poor brother, is noisy, moaning and cursing. He stares up at me, trying to breathe slowly, clutching at my arm, mouth working. I weep quietly, put my fingers over his mouth, tell him I love him, tell him he will be fine, he will be fine. I unwrap my hijab, rip a piece from it, and wind the length of fabric tightly around his bleeding arm. Hassan, he only gasps, looking terrified, and holds my gaze and clenches his teeth as I cinch the cloth tight around his wound.

I feel shame and guilt wash over me when I look at the American, dying alone. The anger that took me over, caused me to pick up the gun and shoot him—the anger is gone, and I feel hollow, empty like a water jug. I know Allah will forgive me, but will the American? He does not look evil. He looks kind, and young. He is tall and thin, with bright red hair and a beard that is not quite a beard, the stubble and scruff of a man who has not shaved in many days. His eyes are blue, very bright, startling in their intensity.

He stumbled in upon us, fleeing from the bullets as we had, clutching a camera and breathing as if scared, holding the beads by his chin and praying. I could not understand his words, but I knew he was praying. His eyes were closed, and his mouth was moving, but he was not speaking out loud. Prayer is prayer, even if he was not praying to Allah as he should. *Perhaps Allah will hear him anyway*, I remember thinking. Maybe all gods are the same god, only with different names, and a prayer to one is a prayer to all.

I want that to be true, as I watch the American struggle for breath, clinging stubbornly to life. I want him to have comfort, to have salvation that would carry his soul to heaven. I do not want to have sent him to hell. He looks so afraid, rubbing those wooden beads and praying, bleeding to death.

No one should have to die alone and afraid.

He took some pictures with his camera, braving the storm of bullets, peeking around the door post and popping back in, as I have seen other men do, only they did it with guns instead of a camera. I wonder what his pictures look like. Do they show death in all its many forms? My people dying, his people dying, each killing the other.

I do not know why they fight.

Then the American heard Hassan moving, and Hassan got angry, although he was more afraid than angry. When boys and men are afraid, they turn it into to anger, quickly, in the way the blue hot sky becomes dark with black clouds when a sudden storm rushes in.

Hassan was very afraid. He only wanted to protect me, to be a man, to be brave, and so he made himself very angry, but he was just a boy. The American was not dangerous, not until Hassan pointed Papa's gun at him. I did not want Hassan to shoot, but I was frozen with fear. When I saw the American reaching behind his back, I knew in my stomach and my heart that something bad was going to happen.

And it did, so fast. The American drew his gun, quick as a viper striking, and the air was filled with the thunder of gunfire. Hassan cried out, jerked backward, fell to the dirt floor. The sound was deafening, made my ears ring.

I was overcome by anger then. He was my brother, and we were alone. We were just frightened children. I had to protect my brother. The anger overtook me. I could not help it. It was as if I was dreaming, in the way that I was moving without being able to control what I was doing. I reached down, hearing vaguely the sound of screaming somewhere far away, picked up the heavy rifle, and fired it. I missed, and I thought for a moment that he might shoot me, but he did not. I was glad. I didn't want to die. He shook his head slightly, and I saw some kind of resolve harden there in his vivid blue eyes. Was he resolving to kill me, since I held a gun?

I could not die. Hassan needs me. Aunt Maida needs me. My finger jerked on the trigger, and the American was ripped apart, slumped to the ground.

My legs would not support me any longer, and I knew the screaming was coming from me.

When Hassan quiets and is able to sit up, I let myself cry soft tears, silent tears. I hear the American whispering, hear him sob and sigh a breath, hear the beads clicking together. I stand up, brush the dirt from my knees, and go over to him. He looks at me, but I do not think he sees me. Perhaps he sees someone else, maybe his mother, or a friend, or a wife.

I take his hand in mine. I do not care that he is an infidel, and that I will be unclean from touching a man like that. I only know that Allah would want me to pray for him. So I pray. I pray the prayer to ease his passing into Allah's arms, not knowing whether the god he prays to was like Allah or if the beads themselves were his god, or if he only prayed to his ancestors, like the people I learned about in school, before I stopped going. I pray, and I let myself cry for him, because if he has a mother, or a sister, or a wife, I know they would want someone to weep at his death.

He dies while I pray, and I close his eyes, as I closed Mama's, and Papa's, and Uncle Ahmed's. I fold his hands over his prayer beads. They are smooth and worn from being rubbed so often. I place his camera on his stomach as well, so that when the other Americans find him, they will be able to see his pictures.

I stand up again and go to the doorway, trying not to see the American's body. I feel very grown up as I creep carefully toward Aunt Maida's house, Hassan trailing behind me, clutching his arm, teeth grinding against the pain. I feel old in my heart, tired in my soul.

I am glad I prayed for the American, and I hope his god heard me.

I pray to my god, to Allah, and wonder if he hears me.

The fighting has moved away from where we live, Hassan and Aunt Maida and I. The bombs flash in the night, shaking the earth until dawn. Gunfire rattles and cracks, and there are faint yells and screams. It is the constant sound of death. I hear the *whump-whump-whump* of American helicopters, the high howl of jets, the rumble of tanks and the things that carry many soldiers, like tanks but without the cannons. It is all far away now, though.

Hassan's arm heals slowly, and he burns with anger, and with impatience to join the fighting. "I am a man!" he yells. "I will kill the Americans, as they killed Mama and Papa. As soon as I am well, I will go and kill them."

I beg him to stay here, where it is something like safe. Aunt Maida just sits at the table, staring with blank eyes at the wall, and she does not say anything. After her husband, my Uncle Ahmed, died she began to drift away in her mind, so that she will not have to miss him anymore. She will die soon, I think, and then it will be only me and Hassan in this world.

Aunt and Uncle and Mama and Papa each had very little money, and now it is only Aunt Maida. Life continues, despite the war, despite the death all around. Shops open in the morning to sell food, the stalls with their hawk-eyed vendors. I try to beg for food, to steal it, but I get little. Hassan is hungry, and so am I. Aunt Maida says nothing, does not move, but I think her body is eating itself to keep her alive, and soon there will be no more body to eat, and she will close her eyes forever.

I pray to Allah to save her, to wake her up so she will take care of Hassan and me, because I am just a girl and I do not know how. I pray to Allah to protect Hassan, to keep him away from the fighting. I think of the dying American and how his praying did not save him. Uncle Ahmed called on Allah to save him, and he died. I prayed for Allah to spare Mama and Papa, but they died, too. I am beginning to wonder if Allah hears me. Maybe because I am only a child he does not listen. Perhaps he only hears the prayers of adults.

I do not think I will pray anymore if Aunt Maida dies and leaves us alone.

Iraq, 1993

I wake up to early morning sunlight streaming in through the boarded-up window, piercing the gloomy gray of our small house. It is still, too still. I sit up, adjusting my dress on my shoulders. My head covering, or what is left of it, is on the ground beside me, but I do not put it on yet. My hair is long and loose and tangled, glinting black and almost blue on my shoulder. I should brush it, but I do not have time, because I must continue to search for food for Aunt Maida and Hassan and me.

I look around without standing up. The house is so small I can see it all from where I sit on my bed beneath the window, next to the door. There is the kitchen, a stove and an empty refrigerator. There is the couch, threadbare and ripped, empty. Hassan is gone. I feel panic in my belly, knowing he is too young to understand what he is doing, but I cannot go after him yet.

Something else is wrong. I find Aunt Maida in her chair by the little black and white TV, now always off. She is still sitting straight up, her hands folded in her lap, staring at the wall, but her thin chest does not rise and fall as it has for so many weeks now. I managed to feed her for a while, some soup heated on the stove, then some bread and beans I bought, found, or stole. Then she turned her face away and would not eat anything. She would let me pour water into her mouth, so at least she would not die of thirst, which I think is worse than dying of hunger, although I do not know why I think that.

Perhaps it is because hunger is only a dull ache in your belly, growing sharper as the days move past. You grow more hungry, always more hungry, like a hole in your belly growing ever larger until you think it may swallow your ribs and your heart and your liver and whatever else hides behind the skin of your chest and belly, parts I do not know the name of.

Thirst, however…it is a desperation. You would do anything for one drink of water. To be thirsty is worse than to be hungry. You can eat a bug, or worm, you can snatch a can of beans or a hunk of hard bread from a market stall. But to find water? It is not so easy. A bottle of water is heavy. It does not fit beneath the folds of a dress, or in a sleeve. You get thirstier and thirstier until it is like anger or hatred. Your mouth turns into a desert, dry and sandy and empty, your lips cracked.

I think this is why thirst is worse than hunger.

Aunt Maida dies of hunger, but really of a broken heart. She is old, and she loved my Uncle Ahmed for all of her life, since she was a little girl. He never hit her, like many men do their wives. He loved her. When he died, I think she did, too—it just took a longer time for her body to realize her heart and mind were already dead.

I touch her face, and it is cold, so cold, and hard. Her eyes stare unseeing. She sees Uncle Ahmed in heaven, I think.

"Do you see Allah?" I do not recognize my voice, or why I am asking questions of a dead woman. "Is He there, Aunt Maida? Ask Him why He does not answer me!"

She does not respond, of course, for she is dead.

I am just a girl, only fourteen, and my arms are weak, but Aunt Maida is so small, so thin like a bird that I can drag her from the house, still stiffened into a sitting position. An old woman watches from an open doorway. Her eyes are like brown beads, hard and cold, and she does not move to help me, or ask questions. I have no *hijab* on, and she curls her lip in disapproval. I drag my dead aunt through the street, as far as I can. I do not know where I will put her, what to do with her. There is no one to tell, I think. At least, I do not know who to tell. So I drag her as far as I can until my arms and legs and back are sore and empty of strength, and then I leave her, sitting awkwardly in an alley, amid the heaps of trash.

I stand over her for a moment, wondering what to say to the dead body. In the end, I do not say anything. I whisper, "Goodbye, Aunt Maida," to her spirit, but that is after I am back home.

A dead body is just a dead body. Aunt Maida has been gone for a long time.

I am worried about Hassan. I do not expect him to come back, but I keep hoping. I wrap my tattered and torn hijab around my head as best I can and set out to find Hassan, to bring him home and scold him being a stupid boy.

He spoke of finding a gun.

I think of that day two years ago, in the wrecked building. I do not know where he got that rifle in the first place. I was gone, looking for food, and I found Hassan huddling in a doorway while gunfire racketed in the streets, dust kicking up, shouts echoing, English and Arabic.

I hid in a far corner, waiting for the shooting to stop, and when it did, I ran across the street to where he was hiding, tears drying on his face. He was not hurt, and I held him close when the shooting started up again. He was clutching something to himself against the wall, between his knees and his arms wrapped around it, his little body shaking. I was behind him, my arms around his shoulders, my fingers clutching his sleeves.

An American soldier trotted past us, rifle raised to his cheek. He paused, glanced at us, dismissed us, and continued on, loping away like a wild dog, threat clear in the way he ran, hunched down close to the earth. When he paused, Hassan tensed, and I could feel hate seething from him. They killed Mama and Papa, so he hates them. It is simple, to him.

I know the bullets that took their lives could easily have been ours, however. Stray bullets do not recognize American or Iraqi. They only know soft flesh and red blood. I cannot explain this to Hassan, though, for he will not care. I cannot explain why anyone is killing anyone, for I do not know the answer myself. Iraq has never been a safe place, but when the bombs began to drop, crumping in the distance and flashing like fireworks, it became even deadlier. The streets filled with men with guns, tanks, trucks with *keffiyeh*-clad warriors clutching guns. It was sudden, and it has not stopped.

Death is all around now.

When the American soldier passed on, we ran, and I pulled Hassan behind me, not looking back at him. Guns crashed and bullets buzzed and ricocheted ahead of us, and I jerked Hassan into an empty building, destroyed by a bomb or a rocket. We hid in the corner and waited.

And then the American man with the camera came, and he was not a soldier, but still an American. He saw us, and that was when Hassan stepped forward, a gun in his arms, too big for him. I wanted to yell at him, ask him where he had gotten such a thing, but I could not. My throat was closed, and if I yelled, I was afraid the American might have a gun we could not see and shoot us.

And then the gun went off, the American's hidden gun. And then I killed him.

I heard crying, and I knew it was me. I knew tears would not bring back the dead American. I did not mourn him, for I did not know him. But I mourned his death. I mourned for myself, for having killed him.

I see him even now while I am awake two years later, staring at the spot where he died. His blue eyes are wide and staring into me, but not seeing me. Blood spreads beneath him, seeping from the holes in his belly and chest, pools around him. It stinks, the blood. It smells... coppery, and vaguely of shit.

I let myself think the bad word, since there is no one to care.

I blink, and he is gone, leaving me with the bad taste of memories and waking nightmares, and always the gnawing mouth of hunger.

It is a long walk, and it is well past dark by the time I find anyone. I find a knot of soldiers, black and brown rifles leaning against the wall near their hands, or across their knees. There are seven of them, smoking cigarettes. They talk loudly, proclaim their feats in battle, how many Americans they have killed. They are all liars. I can tell by the way they laugh too loud, laugh through the smoke streaming from their noses.

They stop when they see me, and they drag their rifles closer to hand, even though I am Iraqi, and just a girl.

"What are you doing here, girl?" one of them growls. "It is dangerous. You should be home with your mama and papa."

I ignore their stupid questions. "My brother…" My voice is soft, too soft. I strengthen it. "My brother ran away to fight. He is only twelve years old. I need to find him."

They laugh. One of them does not, and he speaks to me. "I saw a boy. Hours ago. With some other men. He had a rifle, and he was shooting it at the Americans. He hit one, too, I think."

"Stupid boy," I mutter under my breath. "I need to find him," I say, louder.

The one who spoke shrugs. "Good luck. I only saw him the once, very quickly. He was off to the west."

I look around me, having no idea which way is west. "Can you show me?"

He stares at me, then lifts one shoulder. "I could."

The others are watching me, a look in their eyes that makes me nervous. I want to get away from them.

"Please show me? He is just a boy. He should not be fighting."

"If he can shoot a rifle and kill the infidels, he is a man," one of the others says. "You should go home to your mama and let the boy do a man's work."

"We have no mama or papa. They died. He needs me. Please, help me find him."

The strange, hungry look in their eyes strengthens when they realize I am alone, all alone. Their gaze travels down my body, from my ripped hijab to my old dress, my small girl's breasts and my thin legs, the triangle between them visible when a breeze blows my dress flat against me. I know what they want. I know that much. I have seen what men do with women, and I know I do not want it to happen to me with these men.

I edge away, watching them. They do not move, and the one who said he had seen my brother nods, ever so slightly.

"I need a drink!" he says, a little too loudly, and the others forget about me as they head off in search of alcohol.

They traipse off into the night, and the kinder one looks back at me. He is older; perhaps he has—or had—a daughter my age. Perhaps he too knows what would happen to me, and is seeking to spare me in the only way he can. I nod at him, a silent thanks. He flicks his fingers near his knee, a quick, quiet gesture telling me to go.

I turn and run through a side street, turning blindly until the sound of their laughter fades. I stop running, turn in place to find my bearings. The buildings are all the same, tan walls dark in the moonlight, shop fronts shuttered and barred closed. The city is deserted, it seems. It is not, though, not really. People are shut in their homes, where they have at least the illusion of safety.

Alone, lost, I have no such illusion. I walk aimlessly, toward noise, toward the light of fires. I pass clumps of men with the ever-present rifles. I stay away from them this time, searching the groups hunched over orange tips of cigarettes for a smaller figure.

I pray to Allah, even though I promised myself I would not. "Allah, the all-compassionate, the all-merciful, please, let me find Hassan. Let me find him alive, please, Allah."

Perhaps it is luck, perhaps it is Allah answering my prayer, but I find him. He is pretending to be a man, hanging his gun over his shoulder by the strap, the awful weapon almost as tall as he is. He stands with a group of men, laughing at a joke someone has told. He does not get it, though. I can tell by the way he looks around to see if everyone is laughing, stopping when they do.

I march up to him, fear forgotten beneath the river of white-hot anger. I grasp him by the shirt back and haul him around. I snatch the rifle from his thin shoulder and shove it into the arms of the man next to Hassan. I slap Hassan across the face, once, twice, as hard as I can.

"You foolish little boy!" I scream, loud. "You ran away, you little idiot! I have spent the entire day looking for you."

The men are laughing, and Hassan is angry, embarrassed.

"Leave me alone, Rania! I am a man, not a boy. I do not need you for my mother. I am a soldier." He takes the gun back from the man beside him and shoulders it resolutely. "I am a soldier. I have killed a man today. I shot him. I, Hassan. I will drive the infidels from our land, and you cannot stop me."

I take him by the ear and twist it, pulling him into a walk. "You are coming home. You are not a soldier—you are a twelve-year-old boy."

He wrenches free and slaps me across the cheek, hard enough to spin me around. "Fuck off!"

I stop, touching my cheek, stunned. "Hassan! What would Mama say if she heard you talk like that?"

His eyes fill with angry tears. He does not stop them. "I do not care! Mama is dead! Papa is dead! There is only you, and you are a girl. And Aunt Maida, but she will die soon—"

"She died last night. While you were gone. I had to deal with it alone."

He has the decency to look chagrined at least, deflating. "I am sorry, Rania." He sees the relenting in my eyes and puffs back up, dashing the tears from his eyes at last. "She was already dead. She just did not know it. Her body had to catch up to the rest of her. I am still not coming home."

One of the men crosses the circle and draws me aside, speaks to me in low tones. "You will not win this way, girl. You have gotten him angry, and he cannot back down without losing face. Just go home. We will take care of him. He is a good boy. He will be a good soldier."

"I do not *want* him to be a soldier!" I say, too loudly.

The man only shrugs. "You cannot stop it. It is war. He is willing and able to wield a rifle, so he becomes a soldier. If you drag him home now, he will just run away again as soon as you are asleep."

I slump and draw a deep breath. He is right, and I know it. "He is my brother. I have to protect him."

The man shook his head. "You cannot. He will live, or he will die. You cannot change it. At least this way he gets to choose his fate."

"So I am just supposed to walk away and let a twelve-year-old play soldier?"

"He is not playing. He shot real bullets from a real rifle at real soldiers. Real bullets were shot back at him. That makes him a real soldier in any book."

Hassan comes over to me, his hands in his pockets. He looks like a strange cross between a man and a boy. The look in his eyes is serious, with that distance and coldness of men who have seen war. His posture, however, is that of a boy, hands in his pants pockets, foot kicking the dirt with the toe of his battered shoe, yet he has a rifle slung on his shoulder, casually comfortable with the weapon.

"This is my choice, Rania, not yours," he says, not looking at me but at the ground between his feet. "They will feed me and give me somewhere to sleep. Less for you to worry about, right?"

"What will I do?" I hate how petulant I sound.

"Take care of yourself. I do not know." He shrugs, a gesture clearly picked up from these other men. "Stop worrying about me."

He turns away, clapping me on the back as if I was a friend rather than his sister. He is trying so hard to be a grown-up. I push him away.

I am just a girl, dismissed.

I stalk away, not looking back, angry, fighting empty tears for the brother who will likely die soon.

"Rania—" Hassan's voice echoes from behind me. He knows me well enough to see the anger in the set of my shoulders.

 I do not stop, but fling the words over my shoulder, still walking. "Be a soldier, then. Get killed. See if I care."

He does not respond. I hear one of the men slap Hassan on the back. "She will come around, son. Give her time."

I keep walking, knowing the man is wrong. I will not come around. Hassan is right about one thing, though.

Only having to feed myself will make things easier.

I make my way through the dark city, gunfire silenced for now. I am not sure exactly where I am going, but I eventually find my way home. The small box that is my home is dark and smells of death. There is no food, no coffee or tea, only running water in the tap and gas from the stove.

I collapse in bed and let myself cry for my brother.

Days pass. I do not hear from Hassan, or see him. I spend my days looking for work, some way to earn money so I can eat. I find nothing. No stores want to hire a girl, or they simply cannot afford to pay another person. I find an old woman who gives me money to help her do her laundry and clean her house. That sustains me for some months. It is pleasant. She has me come to her house every other day to wash her clothes in her little sink and hang them to dry, and wash the floors and sink and toilet, and then she give me a little money, enough to buy food until the next time I come. I begin to have hope that I will be okay. And then one day I go to her house, and she is lying on her bed, staring at the ceiling. Her dark eyes are cloudy and still, her sagging breasts still, her hands still. I stand in the doorway of her bedroom and stare at her body, yet another person who has died.

I push away my guilt and rummage through her apartment. I find some money, some clothes, some food. I pack it all in a little bag I find in her closet and walk away, leaving her lying on her bed. Guilt draws me back. I knock hesitantly on the door across from hers.

A middle-aged man with a thick beard and a yellow-stained white sleeveless shirt stretching over a fat belly answers the door. "What do you want?"

I reel back from the stench of his body odor. "The woman who lives there," I point at the door behind me, "she died. I washed her laundry for her. I came today, and she was dead. From being old, I think."

"Did you take anything?" he asks, squinting at the bag on my shoulder.

"No," I lie, proud of my calm voice.

"Hmph." The man stares at me. "You are lying. That is her bag. I saw her with it when she visited her daughter in Beirut."

Panic shoots through me. "Please. It is just some food."

He waves his hand at me. "Go. She will not need her food, will she?"

"No, she will not."

The man waves his hand at me again, pushes past me, and closes his door behind him to shuffle across the hall and into the old woman's apartment. I watch him for a moment, then turn and go home.

The money lasts me for a long time. I am able to live off the old woman's money for many months, eating a little, stealing a little where I can to stretch it. And then, one day, the money is gone. I do not know how long it has been since I have seen Hassan, since Aunt Maida died. A year, maybe more? I do not know. I have looked for work, laundry to wash, someone to cook for, someone to clean for, but no one wants any help. They all want to stay in their houses where it is safe. They want to pretend they don't hear the gunfire, see the trucks rumble by with hard-eyed soldiers, hear the airplanes screaming overhead.

I am growing desperate. The hole of hunger in my belly is growing. My house is bare of food again. I have no money; I cannot find any kind of work. I roam the city, stopping in shops to beg for food or work.

No one relents. No one cares. I am just a girl.

I go farther and farther from home, until one day I cannot get back before dark. I huddle in a doorway, watching the darkness seep across the buildings like hungry fingers. I am nearly asleep when the smell of cooking food wafts across my face. I hear laughter, male, loud,

boisterous and drunk. I stand up, scan the streets. I see
the orange flicker of a fire on a rooftop, and before I realize it, I am creeping across the street, through the blackened doorway and up the creaking, rickety stairs at the
back of the building. I do not have a plan, or any idea
what waits for me up here, but the smell of roasting meat
is enough to drive caution from my mind.

There are several men sitting on crates and buckets
and an old couch, all dragged around a fire built inside
an old metal barrel of some kind. There are eight men
that I can see. Their rifles are on the ground or propped
against the half-wall rimming the rooftop. Bottles of
alcohol are being passed around and swigged from. One
of the men half-turns to take a proffered bottle and sees
me. He nudges the man next to me and points at me
with the bottle.

"You should not be here, girl," he says.

"You have food," I say, barely above a whisper. Like it
explains everything.

"Yes, we do," he says.

"I am hungry. Please, can you give me some?" I do
not step forward when he extends a foil packet to me. I
can see meat in it, and my stomach growls loudly.

"Come get it," he says. "I will not hurt you."

I am not sure I believe him. He has the hungry look
in his eyes, the raking glance over my body. I want to
turn and run, but the hunger in my belly holds sway over
me. I inch forward. The other men have gone still and

silent, bottles set down, eyes narrowed and watching the exchange. They do not even seem to be breathing.

One of them tightens his fingers in the fabric of his pants by his knees. They are all watching me. Fear pounds in my heart, but I cannot turn away. The foil with the roasted meat is within my grasp. I need it. I have not eaten in days. My stomach growls again, loudly enough for them all to hear, and the one holding the food smiles. It is not a humorous smile, a laughing smile, but a triumphant one.

I reach for the packet, and he lets me take it. I want to gobble all the succulent, juicy meat down as fast as I can, like an animal, but I force myself to go slowly, nibble, watching the men. I take a bite, chew carefully, nearly moaning in relief. Another, and I almost forget about the men.

Almost.

A hard, big hand latches around my wrist. "Nothing is free, girl." The voice is low and rough and hard.

I look up to see beady brown eyes leering down at me.

"I have no…no money." I hand back the packet, although it takes a huge effort to do so. "Take it back—I cannot pay. I am sorry."

"I said nothing about money." He chuckles like something is funny, but I do not know what.

One of the others speaks up. "She is too young, Malik. No."

The one with the packet of meat—whose name seems to be Malik—glances back at the other one in disgust. "She is plenty old enough. You do not have to join in." He looks at me. "Have you bled?"

I am confused. "What? Bled?" I try to pull away.

His grip on my arms tightens. "Yes, girl. Bled. Your monthly blood. Woman's blood."

I feel horror and embarrassment pulse through me. "Y-yes. More than a year now."

He turns to the other men, grinning. "See? She is a woman."

I am beginning to understand what is about to occur. I shake my head and try to pull free. "Please, no. No."

Malik does not let go. His grin widens. "Yes, girl. Yes. You ate my food. Now you pay me. It will not hurt too much. I am not a monster. I will not share you."

"Yes, you will," someone says, threat in his voice.

Malik growls, lifts his rifle from the ground without letting go of my arm. "No, I will *not*. She ate **my** food."

"You do not need to be this way," the one who first protested says. "She is just a girl. I will buy you more food. Let her go."

Malik spits on the ground, swaying a little. "You are weak, Mohammed."

He tugs me away from the fire, towards a black patch of shadows hiding the stairs. I stumble after him, fear pounding through me wildly now. The stairs creak under his weight, and in my fear-blindness I miss a stair, stumbling. Malik catches me, holds me up by the wrist and tugs me to my feet. There is a pallet of blankets on the floor in a corner, an empty bottle of booze, a box of shells, a cardboard box with cans and other food items in it, and next to the bed are some magazines with a picture of naked American women on the front.

I struggle, pull away, and try to kick him. He darts out of reach and then slaps me across the face, hard enough that stars burst across my eyes and my ears ring.

I smell his breath as he thrusts his face close to mine. "Listen, girl. It is a fair trade. You need to eat, and nothing is free."

"I had one bite," I whisper. "Please, let me go."

Malik tugs my ripped hijab from my head and tosses it to the ground, pulling hair loose in the process, but I barely feel it. "I will make you a deal. If you cooperate quietly, I will give you more food, and some money. It has been weeks since I have had a woman, and you are very pretty. I am feeling generous. If you keep struggling, I might be forced to hurt you, and I do not want to do that. Not to such a pretty little face like yours."

Everything in me shrinks away from him, but my need for food, my need to survive moves my mouth. "Food? And money?"

He laughs. "That got your attention."

He does not let go of me, but pushes me to the blankets. I stumble and fall to my back, scramble away from him, but he kneels near the foot end of the blankets to rummage in the box. He pulls out several cans of food, a packet of jerked meat, and a bottle of liquor. He sets these things on the floor, and then reaches in his pocket and pulls out a wad of money, peels off a few bills, and adds it to the pile.

"There. I think that is more than generous." Malik grins at me, and I realize he is drunk.

I cower against the wall, staring at the food and the money, well aware that what he is offering will keep me alive for at least a month, if I'm careful. But what he is suggesting I do to get it…I cannot. I just cannot. My knees tighten, and my arms cross over my chest.

"I…I do not—" my voice cracks.

I need the food, but I do not know how to agree. Fear boils through me, disgust at the sweat-stained armpits of his shirt, the scraggly beard on his chin, the hard brown eyes, the acne scars on his forehead.

"It will be over quick, girl."

He moves to kneel over me, pushes my dress up over my hips with rough hands. He unbuttons the front, and my heart hammers as he bares my breasts, my privates. My eyes are closed, my body trembling. My stomach growls, gnaws, fueling my desperation. Hard fingers claw at my breasts, and I whimper. Hard fingers rip away my thin cotton panties, and dig into my soft privates. I cry out loud, but he ignores me.

I try to pull away, but he holds me in place with a hand on my shoulder. A belt jingles, and that sound becomes seared into my soul. A zipper goes *zzzhrip*, and then his weight is above me. I squeeze my eyes closed tighter, try to close my knees, but he is already between my legs and something hard is pressing against my privates. I whimper again, and then something pinches, sharp and painful, and then pops.

I weep quietly for my virginity.

It is over quickly, and his weight is gone. Something hot and wet is on my leg. A piece of cloth is dropped onto my chest, and then I cannot feel his presence or smell him. I open my eyes, and see that I am alone.

Allah, what have I done?

I have not prayed to Allah in a very long time, and I do not know why I do so now.

I take the rag and wipe myself. There is thick, sticky white fluid dripping down my thighs, mixed with blood. I nearly vomit but have nothing in my stomach to bring up, so I only dry-heave and taste acid. I take the cans and wrap them in my *hijab*. The money I clutch in my damp palm.

I run home. I do not cry until I am in my bed. I bathe in the morning, but do not feel clean, even after scrubbing until my skin is raw. I look at the wealth of food, the money that can feed me, and I feel a bit better. It was awful, but it kept me alive.

I eat, and push away my self-loathing, my disgust, my worry for what I will do when this is gone.

TWO

Hunter

Operation Iraqi Freedom; Des Moines, Iowa, 2003

THE BAR IS DIM AND BLURRY AND SPINNING as I finish my beer. I've lost count by now. Ten? Twelve? There might have been a few shots in there, too. It doesn't matter. Derek is next to me, perched on the stool with one foot on the scratched wood floor, flirting with a tall brown-haired girl with huge round breasts. He's close to scoring, I'm pretty sure. He's been working this girl for over an hour, playing up his best war stories from the last tour. We've been back for a month, and we're not due to ship back to Iraq for another month, but Derek has gotten plenty of mileage out of his experiences. And by mileage, I mean ass.

This girl, for instance, is hanging off his every word, leaning closer and closer to him, arching her back to make her already-impressive rack even bigger. She's stroking his knee absently, and he's pretending not to notice, all the while inching his own hand up her knee toward her thigh, which is bare almost to her hip bones in the little khaki shorts she's wearing.

I wish him well. I've got my own piece of heaven waiting at home...well, *her* home. It's where I've been staying since I got back Stateside. Lani Cutler has been my girlfriend since my sophomore year of high school, and she waited for me through Basic, gave me somewhere to stay until I shipped out, and then gave me one hell of a warrior's send-off...for three days straight. And now I'm back and she's here still, giving me a warrior's welcome and a warm bed. I don't know what else it is between us, exactly, which is part of the reason I've tied one on tonight. Things are different, difficult, and confused.

I keep trying to start the conversation with her, but she always avoids it.

I was gone for over a year, and I know better than to ask what—or who—she did while I was gone, since I never demanded she wait for me. She's a good girl, sweet, beautiful, smart, from a good family. Too good for the likes of me, but she doesn't seem to know that. She claims to love me, and I believe her. I've been thinking of asking her to marry me, to make sure I've always got someone to come home to, permanently. I love her, I think. I think about her when I'm gone, miss her. I can see us together.

I've even bought the ring. Little thing, not real expensive, but it's something.

But I have doubts.

At some point, my beer disappears and is replaced by a glass of water with four wedges of lemon. A rocks glass full of pretzel nuggets is in front of me, and suddenly, nothing has ever tasted so good as those yeasty little balls of crunchy goodness.

Derek laughs at something the girl—whom I've named The Rack—says and stands up. "We're gonna get out of here, Hunt. You good?"

I nod. "Yep. 'M good. Not a far walk from here."

Derek frowns. "Sure you're in any kind of condition to walk, bro? You look three sheets to the wind."

I shrug. "Maybe two sheets. But I'm good."

"Dude, don't be a dickhead. You're hammered. Get in the cab with us."

"Fuck you," I mumble.

"You first, asshat." Derek is laughing at me, but I'm too dizzy to care.

"Oh, be nice to your friend," The Rack says. "Can't you see he's pining over a girl?"

Derek laughs. "Sweetheart, that's not pining. He's gonna stumble home and fuck her sideways."

I blear at the girl, wondering if I'm that obvious. "Shuddup, Derek," I slur. "'Sides. I'm pretty sure that's all it is. Fuckin'. Just fuckin'. No love. Just sex."

"See?" The girl slaps Derek's shoulder. "He's pining. He loves her, but she doesn't love him. I'm a bartender. I know that look. Now, get your friend home, and then take me to your place."

Then I'm stumbling outside into the bitter Iowa winter, hunching against the driving wind. I'd forgotten it was winter, for a minute. I've been in the desert so long I find the chill unbearable now. Before I shipped out, I'd have been out in this in a T-shirt, playing tackle football with Derek and the guys. This little flurry storm wouldn't have stopped us from playing ball. We never even bothered with coats until it was single digits.

I'm sliding into the cab, The Rack next to me, her slim, soft arm pressing against mine. I mean, I know she's going home with Derek, and I've got Lani waiting for me, but I'm drunk and I don't mind her proximity.

"You smell nice, like vanilla," I say.

Oops. I hadn't meant to say that. Kind of a creeper thing to say. Fortunately, the Rack is amiable enough and experienced enough with drunk people to not take me seriously.

"Thanks," she giggles, and her boobs bounce pleasantly. I try not to stare.

I focus out the window on the shards of snow whipping past, the trees and the buildings of suburban Des Moines. She giggles again at something Derek says, and now that I don't have her bouncing tits to distract me, the sound of her giggle is actually fairly obnoxious, but I can't place why. Something about it irritates me, rubs me the wrong way.

Oh, god, I'm entering the dickhead phase of my drunk. I sigh at myself and concentrate on trying to see single objects rather than double.

We pull into Lani's apartment complex, and I hand Derek a couple of random bills from my pocket to cover the bar tab and the cab fare.

"Thanks for the ride," I say. I wink at them, or try to. I think I actually just closed both eyes.

Derek laughs. "Yeah, dude, no problem. Get some sleep. We'll hit the gym tomorrow."

I nod and extend my hand. Derek slaps my palm and grabs my hand as if we're about to arm wrestle, and then lets go. I get out and stumble to the door, peering unsteadily at the number to make sure it's the right one. It is, and I go inside, finding the apartment dark and silent. There's a single candle burning on the kitchen counter, one of the crazy scented ones Lani likes so much. Cherry butterscotch buttered coconut rum, or some stupid shit like that. I blow it out, because Lani tends to leave them lit all night, which is a fire hazard, even though she acts like it's not.

I lean against the counter, breathing in the scent of extinguished candle. I've always wished they'd make a candle that smells like a blown-out candle. The clock on the microwave says one-fifty-five, and I know it's probably unlikely that I'll see any action with Lani tonight. She's a receptionist at a doctor's office and has to get up pretty early to be at work, so she goes to bed early. It doesn't bother me, usually, since I'm an early riser myself, having been in the Marine Corps for such a long time. But tonight, I'm horny. I'm worked up.

Now that I'm home and away from the familiar comfort of the bar, being drunk is a little unpleasant, dizzy and disorienting. I want to sleep, but I know I won't be able to. I want to make love to Lani, but that's not going to happen, either. She might wake up, she might even respond enough to let me do what I want, but she won't really wake up, she'll just move a little, make some partially fake moaning sounds, and then go back to sleep.

I crack open a Dr. Pepper from the fridge, grab a box of Cheez-Its, and plop in front of the TV, grabbing the remote and flicking it on. I click through channels aimlessly, munching and sipping, stopping on a few minutes of Purdue-Clemson game, but it doesn't hold my interest. A few more channels, and then I land on CNN, coverage from the war. I try to change the channel, but it doesn't happen. My finger won't press the button.

I see the flashes, the tracers, hear clip footage of the *hack-hack...hackhackhack* of AK fire, and suddenly I'm transported, kneeling beside an open door, M16 tucked into my shoulder, kicking as I blast triple bursts at a red-and-white-checked *keffiyeh* visible on a rooftop.

My head aches, my chest clenches, and my fists tighten until I hear the plastic remote cracking in my hand, and then the segment ends and a commercial for Tide detergent shakes me out of it. I flick on the TV and scan the DVDs on the shelf, but nothing seems interesting.

There's an Xbox, here for when Lani's younger brother comes over after school on Thursday afternoons. Some games, mostly sports, a role-playing game, and then the latest *Call of Duty*. I haven't played that one yet. We don't get the new games over there very often. I pop it in and change the channel to the correct TV input. The opening screens cycle, and then I'm in, quick play option. It's scarily realistic. The sounds are dead on, filtered through speakers, but enough to crash into my head and call up the real thing.

I'm racking up kills like crazy, biting it and respawning, and the controller is slippery with sweat and I'm leaning forward, teeth grinding. Certain parts are realistic, others aren't. The sounds are the most realistic.

I feel small soft hands on my shoulders, sliding down my arms to take the controller from me. I let her take it.

"Hunter? What are you doing, baby?" Lani's voice is muzzy with sleep.

I turn away from the TV and look at her. She's so beautiful, wavy blonde hair sleep-mussed, blue eyes squinting at the light. She's wearing one of my T-shirts, a Slipknot concert shirt, and it comes to mid-thigh, her small, perky breasts poking the cotton.

"Got back from the bar with Derek and couldn't sleep," I say.

"I never felt you come back to bed."

I shrug. "I didn't. I knew I wouldn't be able to sleep."

She circles the couch and sits next to me. "Isn't that game a little...difficult for you to play?"

I don't answer right away. I shrug, eventually. "Yeah, guess so. Just curious."

"You okay?" she asks.

I hesitate, then decide now isn't the right time to address what's on my mind. I'm half-drunk, and she's half-asleep. "Nah. Just coming down and getting tired."

"Well, why don't you come to bed?" Lani slips her hand around my bicep.

"Yeah, I'll be right in."

Lani laughs, a breathy giggle, and that's when I realize why the Rack's giggle irritated me: it was like Lani's. I push the thought away and turn to her.

"What's funny?" I ask.

She scratches her nails up my arm. "I meant, come to bed…" and the tone of her voice suggests what she's getting at.

"Don't you have to wake up for work in a few hours?"

I ask myself why I'm arguing and don't come up with an answer.

"It's only two-thirty," she says. "I don't have to be up till seven. We have time." She stands up and backs toward the bedroom.

I sit and watch her, feeling the zipper of my jeans tighten as she peels her shirt off, revealing her naked curves. I stand up and follow after her, shedding my shirt and pants as I go. I'm hard and ready, and she's crawling backward across the bed, her hair splaying across the pillow, her hand reaching for me as I climb up between her legs.

Sex with Lani never fails to be spectacular. She's passionate and vocal, crying out when she comes, moaning my name as I plunge into her, soft hands clutching my shoulders.

Her eyes, though, when I glance at her, reveal a distance as they look at me. A kind of disguised apathy. As if she's acting. The thought bothers me, and I push it away. I release with a soft grunt, my face buried in her neck.

I wish she would put her hand on my head when I bury my face against her like this. She never does, though, and I always find myself wishing she would. I never say anything, because she'd do it, but only since I asked her to. It's a little thing, insignificant, but somehow it always seems to hit me like this. She does what she thinks I want. She knows I get horny when I'm drunk, so she has sex with me when I get back from the bar. I'm not sure she wants to, though. Not really.

She's asleep again, turned away from me, still naked, beautiful, and it seems for a moment as if we're in different realities. The absurdity of the thought makes me snort. I roll over behind her and slip my arm over her hip. She's warm and soft and present here with me.

A glow of affection for Lani spreads through me, replacing my doubts. She loves me, and I love her. All is well with my world, in this moment, at least.

A tiny voice in the very bottom-most, shadowy part of my heart speaks up.

Right?

And then I fall asleep without answering that question.

The next few weeks pass somewhat awkwardly. Lani is increasingly distant. She usually is in the days and weeks prior to my shipping out, but this is different. More pronounced. We don't have sex again.

She's on her phone a lot, texting nonstop. She plugs it in next to her bed and puts in on silent. Sometimes it's under her pillow. It's always in her hand or in her purse, or in her back pocket. It's never, ever where I can see it. If I approach her while she's texting, or on call, she pauses until I go away, putting the phone against her chest.

I ignore it as best I can, but warning bells are going off. I ignore those, too. Nothing's going on, right? I mean, I'm about to ship out in a week, for Christ's sake. She would wait till I'm gone to start anything, right?

I go to the gym three days before my plane leaves Des Moines. I'm only there for about half an hour before I feel something in my shoulder pull and decide to call it a day. Usually I'm at the gym for an hour or two, which how it's been since high school.

The gym is a couple miles away from Lani's apartment, and I walk the distance, huddled in a thick coat and sweatpants, feeling the wind bite through the cotton to freeze the sweat on my legs. As I approach the apartment complex, my heart begins to hammer in my chest. There's no reason for it, but it's a feeling I've learned to recognize. It's foreboding. Premonition, maybe. A gut feeling. I've learned to recognize these feelings and trust them. Something is wrong. I don't feel the prickling of my skin, the crawling of my flesh and the cold sweat of fear, so I don't think it's a danger situation, but something is off.

I approach Lani's front door and slip in, silently. The hinges don't squeak, and the knob doesn't scrape. My footfalls are stealthy on the carpet. I don't know why I'm doing this. I'm in a tactical crouch, and my hands are clutched in front of me automatically, as if I'm holding a rifle. It's habit, reflex. Every sense is attuned.

I shrug out of my coat and drape it across a chair back. My skin tightens with apprehension. Is Lani hurt? I don't smell blood. I smell…sweat? Bodies. I smell sex.

Then I hear it: a sigh, gentle, brief, and female. It's a sound I know all too well. It's the sound Lani makes when she comes. She doesn't scream or cry out; she clutches me close, arms around my neck, and sighs—almost a whimper—into my ear. I can almost feel her arms, hear the sigh, but I'm not in that bedroom. She's not making that sound for me. I wait, crouched outside her door and listen, just to make sure I'm not mistaken. Maybe she's pleasuring herself. I don't like that idea much more, since why would she need to do that if she has me? But…no. I hear him. A deeper sigh. A grunt. Murmured words, her laugh, a male moan.

She's having sex, and it's not me.

Fuck.

Anger ripples through me, turning my sight red, making my hands shake. I breathe, hard and deep and fast. I wait, force my blood to slow, force my hands to unfist. I can't afford mistakes. I can't afford to lose my temper. I've been too careful about it for too long to mess up now. Juvie was bad enough. I'm not going to jail. I'm not going to get court-martialed.

When I'm as calm as I can get under the circumstances, I fling open the bedroom door. There she is. Naked and beautiful, underneath Douglas Pearson. Doug. Skinny little Doug, nerdy, introverted, acne-scarred, works at an insurance agency Doug motherfucking Pearson.

I resist the urge to throw him out the first-story window.

"Get the fuck out, Doug." My voice is a whisper. Calm and deadly. "Get the fuck out, *now*. I'll be gone in a minute, and you can have her back. I just need to talk to her."

Doug scrambles off the bed and dresses in record time. He stops in front of me, his eyes wide with terror, his nostrils flaring, reeking of fear. But he stops in front of me and faces me. I give him credit for having some balls. "You won't...you won't hurt her? If you're going to hurt someone, hurt me."

I laugh. It's not an amused sound. "Don't tempt me, pencil-dick. No. I'm not going to hurt anyone. Except you if you don't get the *fuck* out of my face."

He gets out. Lani clutches the bed sheet around her chest, as if I haven't seen her naked a million times before.

As if we didn't lose our virginity together at fifteen. As if I didn't have a ring in my duffel bag. That act, the shielding herself from my view, tells me all I need to know.

"Three days, Lani. Three goddamn days. You couldn't wait *three* motherfucking days?" I turn away from her and talk to the door. I'm too pissed to trust myself facing her. "I don't get it. If you didn't want me, why the fuck didn't you tell me? I mean, *fuck*."

"Stop saying that word, Hunter. I don't like it."

I whirl. "Fuck you, Lani. I'm a goddamn Marine. I've got a dirty fucking mouth, and I'm pissed off. You *cheated* on me." I force myself to take two long steps across the room away from her. "I've never asked. I come back, and I don't ask you any questions. I'm gone for a long time, and I've never asked what you do while I'm gone. But… while I'm here, I kind of expected you to be faithful. Is that too much to ask?"

Lani doesn't answer.

"How long?" I ask. "How long has this been going on with that little prick?"

"Don't talk about Doug like that, Hunter. He's a good man. He—"

"I didn't ask about him. I don't care. *How…long*." It doesn't come out as a question.

"I first started seeing him about two months after you left the last time." She lowers her eyes away from mine.

That's a full year. More.

She's ashamed, and she should be.

"And you've been going behind me with him all the time I've been back?"

She nods, a tiny jerk of her chin.

"Fuck." I want to hit something. My fist balls and I lift it to punch through the wall or the door, but I don't. "Un-fucking-believable, Lani. If you don't love me, have the balls to say so."

She moves forward off the bed, sheet trailing behind her, clutched to her chest. "It's not that I don't love you, Hunter. I do. But...I'm not *in love* with you."

"What's the difference?"

She reaches for me and I pull away. She lowers her hand. Her vivid blue eyes shimmer. "There's a huge difference."

I collapse backward against the wall, anger fading to confusion and hurt. Without the anger to prop me up, I'm limp. "Then explain it."

She pulls clothes from the drawers, glances at me, and hesitates.

"What?" I ask. "Like I haven't seen you naked before?"

"It's not that," she says. "It's...I don't know. I just feel weird about it. Just turn around and give me a second, okay? Please?"

I turn and stare out the window at the wind-driven drifts of snow. I ignore the rustle of skin and cloth, resist the urge to turn and watch her dress. It will only hurt more.

"Okay," she says. "I'm ready."

I slip out of the room to the kitchen without looking back at her. "I need a drink."

She follows me. I open a pair of beers and hand her one. She holds it without drinking.

"Hunter, listen. I do care about you. I love you. I've loved you since the tenth grade. But…things change. You're gone. You're fighting, and you're not here. That's really it. It's hard to stay in love with you when you're thousands of miles away for months at a time. I was lonely. Doug was there. I…love him, too. I'm *in love* with him. I'm so sorry. I can't image how that must hurt to hear, but you deserve the truth."

"I deserved the truth months ago, Lani."

She winces. "I know. I feel terrible. It's just…he's good to me. He takes care of me. He's there for me."

Something dawns on me. "He knew about this? He knew about us? You and me? And he was okay with it?"

She has the decency to look chagrined. "Yeah. I know how that must seem, and he…he hated it, but I told him it would only be for a little bit. Just until you left again."

"How long were you planning on stringing me along?" My beer is gone and I get another. I need it for fortification against the rage.

"I was going to send you a letter." Her voice is tiny.

"God, really? A Dear John? You were actually gonna send me a real Dear John letter? Fuck, Lani. That's the cruelest shit you could've done. There's nothing worse." Suddenly that second beer is gone and a third is cracked open.

"Slow down, Hunter. Please. I can't have this conversation with you if you're drunk."

"We'll have this conversation however the fuck I want. You owe me that much."

On impulse I go get my duffel bag, move around the apartment shoving my things into it, and then rummage until I find the ring. I drop the duffel on the floor by the front door, put my coat on, and turn to Lani. I open the ring box and set it on the counter by the front door.

"For your information, I had something I've been keeping from you, too. I was going to—I loved you, Lani. I was always faithful to you. All the time I was gone, I never hooked up. Never. All the other guys went to the brothels and the bars and shit, and I never did. I waited for you. Because I love you. Because I was *in love* with you."

Lani crosses the room to examine the ring. "Damn it, Hunter. Goddamn it." She never swears. "You aren't in love with me. You're in love with the idea of me. You've never been with anyone else. I'm comfortable for you. I'm what you know. That's it. That's all it ever was and all it ever will be."

I hesitate, gathering my voice so it doesn't crack. "You're all I had, Lani. Now I don't even have that. I have no one else…" I look down, stare at my shoes, tighten my control. "Maybe you're right. But if you didn't love me, you should've told me. Broken up with me."

She cries now, slow, quiet tears. "I'm sorry. I didn't want to hurt you. I didn't want to have to see you in pain."

I let her see the agony in my eyes. "Well, you fucked that up."

I pick up my duffel bag and walk out, pushing down the emotion until there's nothing left but emptiness. No anger, no hurt. Nothing.

I walk away, my coat buttoned up tight, duffel slung across my back. It's frigid out. Evening. Seven, maybe eight o'clock. Full dark. Snow drifts, not really falling, just blown around by the knife-like wind. I don't know where I'm going, where I'm walking. I can't see much in the dark with the snow stinging my eyes. I don't care. I welcome the pain of the cold right now. It distracts me from my anger.

I'm pissed that she cheated on me for so long, pissed that she didn't have the goddamn balls to tell me she didn't love me.

Mainly, I'm pissed that she's right. We lost our virginity together, explored our sexuality together. I've never even dated anyone else. Never kissed or held or fucked anyone else. Never even considered it. I've held on to her for so long because she's familiar and comforting. She's what I have.

Had.

I try not to think about being alone, but it's inevitable. I'm shuffling down a sidewalk, skeins of snow skirling around my feet as I pass through pools of streetlamp light. And then, suddenly, I'm seventeen again. In school. Sitting in trig, doodling instead of paying attention to the lecture since I hate math because it's boring and easy. The principal, Mr. Boyd, comes in and announces that he'd like to see me outside for a moment. And then tells me to grab my bag. My heart suddenly pounds and my palms sweat and something is wrong, wrong, wrong.

I hear the words from Mr. Boyd, crackling and static-y and broken up by disbelief: "Car accident...killed on impact...critical condition...ride to the hospital..."

I follow numbly through the hallways, backpack hanging from one shoulder. The hospital is quiet, orderlies and nurses bustling past on squeaky sneakers, doctors in lab coats with clipboards and file folders. I'm in a room, curtained off. Monitors beep. Antiseptic and cleaners and death and sickness assault my nostrils.

Mom, bruised, broken, bleeding. Dying. A tubes is in her mouth and an oxygen cannula in her nose. Bandages on her head. Someone is pulling me away to explain about internal bleeding, cranial swelling.

"Will she die?" I ask, cutting off the explanation.

A male voice, deep, calm, soothing. I don't look at him. "It's hard to tell. It doesn't look good, though, son. I'm sorry. We're doing all we can."

"My dad?"

Silence.

Another voice, and face, stepping in front of my blank stare. A policeman. "Son, I'm sorry, but your father didn't make it. He was killed on impact." The policeman rests his hand on my shoulder briefly and then drops it. "Is there anyone we can call for you, son?"

A brief spike of rage pulses through me. "I'm not your son. I'm *her* son." I jab my finger at the door. "My name is Hunter."

The policeman nods. "Sure thing, Hunter. Sorry. It's just a habit, didn't mean anything by it. So, do you have a relative we could call for you?"

I shake my head. "No. There's no one else."

The officer seems shocked. "No one at all? No sisters or aunts or grandparents?"

I choke down the urge to punch his face. "No, ass-hole. That's what 'no one' means. My grandparents are all dead. I'm an only child."

"Watch it, son."

"*You* watch it, *Officer*. I'm about to be an orphan. I think I'm allowed to be upset."

He relents. "You're right. I'm sorry. So where are you going to go?"

I shrug. "My girlfriend's parents might be able to help. I don't know."

I'm shaken out of the memory and back into the present by a car skidding to a stop in the road next to me. It's Doug, talking through the rolled-down window of his sensible Mercury four-door sedan. "Hunter, look, I know you don't want to see me, of all people, but let me drop off you somewhere. It's below zero out here and dropping fast, man. You'll get hypothermia."

I ignore him and keep walking. He pulls the car over and jumps out, the car facing away from me, door open, lights on to illuminate a swath of thickly falling snow.

"Hunter, dude, listen—"

I try to keep walking past him, but he keeps pace and steps in front of me. Big fucking mistake. I stop, glare for about three heartbeats while I wait for him to move, then jerk my fist from my coat pocket and swing. I connect with his jaw and send him flying. He's just a little guy, no meat, no muscle, no experience with fights. He crumples hard. I step over to him to make sure he's not seriously hurt. He's not, just stunned unconscious. He wakes immediately to see me standing over him, fists clenched. He scrambles away.

"Hunter, please, listen. I was just—"

I move away. "Fuck off. I don't want a ride. If I see you again, I'll break your skinny fucking neck."

He stumbles to his car, clutching his jaw, and drives off. The heat of anger keeps me warm for a while. I finally remember my cell phone.

It rings six times before Derek picks up, out of breath. "Dude, what's up? I'm…unnhh…god*damn*, Maggie!… I'm busy." I hear a woman moaning in the background.

"Sorry, bro. Listen, I caught Lani in bed with Doug Pearson. I need you to pick me up. It's fucking cold out here."

I hear Derek's breath catch and he stifles a groan, and the woman gasps softly. Only Derek would stay on the phone during sex.

"Sure thing, man. Be right there." I hear Maggie's moaning voice start to get loud just as he hangs up.

I shake my head in bemusement. Derek is a dog. The man gets more pussy than a cat licking itself. I don't get it, but it's his thing. I keep walking, head ducked down, shoulders hunched up in that odd, useless gesture we do when we're cold. I make it another half mile or so before Derek's borrowed red F-150 swings around in an illegal U-turn and skids to a stop next to me. There's a tarp over some construction tools in the bed. I toss my duffel bag under the tarp and get in the truck.

Derek pulls away towards his parents' house. "So. Bitch be trippin', huh?"

I rub my hands together and hold them in front of the heater vent. "Yeah. Got back from the gym and walked in on them." I groan and flop my head back on the ripped cloth seat back. "Fuck, man. With Doug Pearson. *Doug*, of all people."

"Isn't he, like, an insurance salesman or something?" Derek asks.

"Yeah. Something like that."

Derek shakes his head. "Fucked up, man. Cheating on a beast like you with a skinny little shit like Doug?"

I scrub my hand over my wet, buzz-cut scalp. "No shit. Don't remind me."

We went to high school with Doug Pearson. Graduated with him. He was the geek who sat alone in the corner while Derek and I sat a table filled with our lettermen jock buddies. Doug was valedictorian, NHS, school band, all that. And now he sells insurance. Won't ever leave Des Moines, probably.

But he got the girl, didn't he?

Fuck.

"Hey, man, don't sweat it. She's a ho. Her loss. Now you can get some real hookups goin' on. Fuck a real bitch. Lani's always been stuck up. You're better off."

I remind myself that he means well.

"I was gonna ask her to marry me, D." My voice is quiet.

Derek cocks an eyebrow at me, incredulous. "Dude, thank god you didn't. You don't need her. I know you've been with her forever, but that don't make her right for you. I never said anything 'cause you wouldn't have listened, but I never liked her. She's hot and all that, but I never got the sense she loved you as much as you loved her."

I slug Derek's arm hard. "Next time say something, fucker."

"Hopefully there won't *be* a next time." He grins at me. "Lets go get fucked up. I've got a bottle of Johnny with our name on it back at my folks' place."

"Sounds good." It does sound good, in that moment.

I want nothing more than to forget Lani for a while. It won't change anything or erase the pain, but it'll let me forget. I learned the hard way after my parents died that no amount of booze or pot or anything else will take away the pain. I quit trying to bury the hurt and just dealt with it. Good thing I've got practice, because I can feel the pain spreading cracks through my heart.

This is going to take some time to heal.

Good thing we ship out soon.

THREE
Rania

Iraq, 1993

I CLUTCH MY STOMACH AND TRY NOT TO MOAN. The food and money I got from the soldier lasted me more than two months. Now it is gone, and I am hungry again. Desperation ripples through me.

I hunch against the wall as a troop of uniformed Iraqi soldiers march past. Official government soldiers. Hard-eyed, rough, merciless. I hate them.

My home is gone. A stray bomb or mortar or something. I have nowhere to sleep. Nowhere to go. No one to help me. Hassan is nowhere to be found. I have looked. I do not feel in my heart that he is dead; he has just found a better life for himself.

An idea is percolating in the bottom of my belly. I have ignored it for days. I cannot do it. I will not do it.

But my hunger, my thirst, my need to survive, to not give up, this drives me. I wait for dawn and then sneak across the city, looking for a specific building. I find it, eventually. I huddle in an alley across the street, watching, hoping they will be there, hoping they will not be.

Night falls. My stomach growls and rumbles and expands, empty, gnawing at my ribs.

I see him, striding down the street, cigarette tip glowing like a moving orange star through the shadows. My legs are moving before my brain has time to stop me. He sees me coming. His eyes are not unkind, but he still eyes me with the hungry, lustful look that I have come to understand.

"You should not be here, girl." He sips his cigarette and speaks between puffs of acrid gray. "What do you want?"

"I…" Words fail me. "What you gave me, it is gone. I am hungry."

He frowns. "You made it last all this time? Girl, that wasn't enough to feed a rat for a week."

"I do not need much."

"What do you want from me? I do not have enough to just give you food or money all the time."

I do not know how to say it. The words will not come. Instead, I reach up and unwrap my hijab. I shake my hair out and look up at him through the waves of black. "Please?"

He sighs and flicks his cigarette away. "No. That was a one-time thing. I was drunk. I did not mean to turn you into a prostitute."

I shrug. "I do not know how else to get food. No one will give me a job. I have looked. I almost got caught stealing. He almost cut off my hand."

"It is no way for a girl to live." He looks uncomfortable. "I felt bad, after you left."

"What choice do I have? Should I just lie down and die? I do not want to do this, you know. But I do not see how else to survive."

He blows a breath out through his teeth. "All right. Fine. Where do you live?"

I shift uncomfortably. "Nowhere. My house got destroyed."

He curses. "There are plenty of abandoned houses around here, girl. Come on. I'll find you something."

He stalks ahead of me, mumbling something to himself. Eventually he finds a house that is empty and in reasonable condition. It is next to a bombed-out mosque. The window has no glass, the door is broken off its hinges, and the electricity does not work. But there is running water. A real shower. A real toilet. The soldier fidgets around the house. I do not know what he is doing, so I get to work clearing the dirt and debris. The kitchen, living room, and bedroom are all one room. The kitchen part has some cabinets, a stove, an empty refrigerator. I hear a crackle and a hum, and then the single bare light bulb in the ceiling flickers to life.

He comes back, wiping his hands on his pants. I stare at the bulb in awe.

"I was an electrician before the war started," he says by way of explanation.

"Thank you."

He shrugs. He fixes the door, then stares around at the little room. "It is not much, but it is something. The mosque next door is not used, obviously. You could… work there. Sleep here. It helps to have somewhere safe to go."

I laugh. "Safe? What is safe?"

He laughs, too. "True. But it is better than the streets."

The silence is awkward. I do not know what to do. Neither does he.

"Are you serious about this?" he asks. "Once you start, I do not think it will be very easy to stop."

"Do you have a better idea for me?" I say. "I told you, I do not want to do this. It makes me sick to think about. But…I don't have any other choice. I have tried everything else. I have not eaten in a week. I stole a piece of bread a few days ago, and almost got my hand chopped off for it. No one will help me. I do not know what else to do. You…you gave me money and food for—for that. Maybe someone else will, too."

He rubs his face with both hands. "What's your name?"

"Rania."

"Rania, I'm Malik." He takes a step closer. "You are a very pretty girl, Rania. I am not your father or your brother or your husband. I cannot tell you what to do.

I am just a soldier. I would not want a girl in my family to do this."

"You would help her, though. If she was desperate."

"Yes, I would."

"There is no one to help me. You have helped me. I do not want to, but I have to, to eat."

"I guess I get that. I wish it did not come to this for you. I like you. You have spirit. You are very beautiful."

He takes another step, and I force myself to hold still. His eyes look me over, head to toes. His hand drifts up to touch my hip. I refuse to shudder. He is nice about it. Not forceful, not moving to make me before I am ready.

"I do not know what to do," I say.

"You will learn, I guess."

I hear it, the sound that will become my life: a belt jingling.

It is not so bad this time. It does not hurt like it did the first time. He is gentler now that he is sober. I close my eyes and hold still. It is over quickly.

He gives me money before he leaves. He stops and looks at me. "Rania, if you are going to make money doing this, you have to pretend to like it. It will go better for you." He rubs his face like he did before. "I will send someone to you, for work. A client."

He turns away.

"Thank you for helping me, Malik."

He shrugs. "I will not be back. I have no conscience left, I thought, but this…it is too strange for me. I did what I could for you. Perhaps Allah will forgive me, perhaps he will not."

"Do you believe in Allah? I do not think I do."

"I do not know," he says. "I want to, but the things I have seen make me wonder. I do not want to think an Allah who loved us would let a nice girl like you have to resort to such things as this."

"That is why I do not believe. I was a good girl. I went to mosque. I prayed facing Mecca. I wore the hijab. I respected my parents. But here I am. A prostitute, now." It hurts to say those words. I say them again to make it hurt less. "I am a whore."

Malik cringes. "Yes, I suppose you are." He looks at his dirty thumbnail rather than me. "There are worse things to be."

I stare at him. "Like what?"

"A soldier. A killer." He pauses, staring at his dirty thumbnail. "It is worse to be dead, too." He is gone, then.

I buy food, blankets. I set up a little nest in a corner of the mosque, in the shadows. It is dark, so I find candles. Malik is true to his word and sends a friend, an officer in the government army. He is not so nice as Malik. He is not so gentle. I try to pretend to like it, although I am pretending to do something I do not know anything about. He does not seem to notice, and he gives me money. As he leaves, he tells me how much I should charge for the next time, since I did not ask, and the amount seems a lot. The next man who comes, another officer, I charge him that amount, and he pays it without complaining.

I am no longer hungry.

Now I only wear the *hijab* when I go out, so people do not ask me any questions. I feel like everyone who sees me knows what I am. As if it is written on my forehead in bold black ink.

Perhaps it is written on my soul, now, and they can see it in my eyes, those windows to my soul.

I do not see Hassan for a very long time.

I am sitting outside my home, waiting for my next client, as I call them. I have told the clients my name is Sabah. No one has heard the name Rania in a long time now, for there is no one who knows me except as Sabah.

My hair is down, now. Long black waves hiding my face. I see the man striding down the street, a young man, youthful, skinny, confident. I do not look at him, but take his hand in mine and lead him to the mosque. Something about the feel of his hand in mine seems strangely familiar. I turn to peek at him and my heart stops.

We are at the nest of blankets and I can feel his hard manhood pressed against my hip. My flesh crawls in disgust, and I move away from him. I turn, push my hair back away from my face.

Hassan curses, eyes wide. "Rania? What the—what the fuck is this? I thought—Sabah…"

I tilt my head up, refusing to be ashamed. "I am Sabah."

"No. No. You…you cannot be. I have heard the officers talking about Sabah. How…what they did with you." He seems about to vomit.

"And you thought you would try her for yourself." I push past him and walk back toward my home next door. "Go away, Hassan. Forget you saw me."

He follows me. "How could you do this? Rania, this is wrong, you are my sister, you should not be—I cannot let—"

I spin around and slap him across the face. Rage is boiling in me. "You turned your back on me, Hassan. You chose to be a soldier. I was starving. I had to survive somehow. This is how. Go away."

"No, Rania. I cannot believe…"

"There is nothing to believe. Can you afford to keep me alive? Can you give me enough money to let me stop?"

He frowns, seems about to cry. He is still only fifteen, after all. "No…no. I cannot."

"Then go away. Do not tell anyone you know me, or my name. Do not come back." I keep walking. "I am not Rania, anymore. I am Sabah."

He turns and stumbles away. He looks back at me over his shoulder, confusion and horror and pain and a welter of emotions too many to name cross his face. I watch him, hiding my shame behind impassive eyes.

When he is gone, I let a tear slide down, for Hassan.

For the family that I had. I know I will not see my brother again.

Rania...she is no more. She did not die; she just does not exist anymore. I am Sabah now. Sabah is strong. Sabah knows what men like and how to give it to them.

I have money enough, now. Enough to eat, to have clothes. I buy some hair dye and turn my hair yellow, like an American girl. When I am done, I do not recognize myself. I have found a broken mirror and taped the sharpened edges, fixed it to the wall. Men pay more if I wear makeup, so I wear makeup. Men pay more if I wear clothes that show my flesh, so I wear a harlot's garb.

In the mirror now, I see only Sabah, the prostitute. Slender waist, full breasts shown by a sleeveless shirt, hips flaring and legs long and bare beneath a tiny American-style miniskirt. No panties, because whores do not need them. I am not a Muslim girl anymore. I am not an Arab girl anymore. I am only a prostitute, without religion, without any god but money. It is to survive, I tell myself.

It is not because I enjoy what I do. I hate it. I mask my utter disgust every time I draw an officer or soldier into my work nest. My skin crawls when they touch me. My heart shrivels into a smaller, harder knot of callous hate every time they leave and I must clean myself and pretend to smile for the next one.

They love me. Sabah...Sabah. She is confident, smiling a seductive smile. It is a game. An act. I hate them all. I would as soon kill them as do what I do. I cannot think the words. I do it, but I cannot speak of it, think of it.

I am paid for sex. Ugh. My stomach clenches as I think the words, sitting at my glassless window, waiting. I am Sabah, the prostitute. Flaxen-haired, naked on the nest of blankets, surrounded by candles, a scruff-bearded officer kneeling above me, soft, fleshy body touching mine, his flabby belly on my thighs, his slimy hands on my breasts, his rough manhood striking into my soft, dry womanhood. I am Sabah, near to vomiting as he finishes and tosses a sweat-wet wad of money on the bed next to me, striding away with an arrogant, satisfied swagger. Grinning. Laughing, clapping his companion on the back as the next enters, fumbles with his buckle.

That motion, that moment, it is always the worst. I feel always the surge of disgust and fear when the client first fumbles with his belt, hating the jangle of metal on metal, forcing my writhe of disgust into a sensuous, seductive pose.

Operation Iraqi Freedom; Iraq, 2003

War is coming once more. Many years have passed.

I hate still and even more vehemently than ever what I do to survive, but Malik was right...all too right. It is impossible to stop now. Even if I wear the hijab to hide my blonde hair, they seem to know, as if I do indeed have "whore" tattooed on my forehead. They know and turn me away, unless it is to spend my whore money in their store. Never to work. Never to earn "honest" money. I have tried, a thousand times. Begged for work. Explained how desperate I am to find another trade, another job. No one will employ me, so I am forced to entertain clients to eat.

War is coming. I feel it. Another war. More death. More soldiers.

I venture out less frequently now. Fighting has come, ambushes, American soldiers, and some from other countries. Car bombs detonate. Bombs go off and men scream, curse in half a dozen languages, but mostly English. Sudden bursts of gunfire break the silence of night and the cacophony of day.

With the return of war comes the return of fear.

I am afraid. I refuse to show it, but it is there.

Like a boy, fear makes me angry.

Then the unthinkable happens: I am on the way home from buying food when I see Hassan. He is with a group of rebels, rifle on his shoulder. He sees me. Then one of them in the front lurches to the side, drops to his knee, jerks his gun to his shoulder, and fires at something I cannot see. Shouts echo, gunfire rattles, deafens. I kneel beside a door, watching Hassan scramble for cover, firing. I peer out and see a file of American soldiers, a patrol, accompanied by an armored car of some kind. The Americans are outnumbered, although I do not think they realize it yet. There are about twenty Americans that I see, and Hassan's troop is at least fifty, spread out. I watch them find positions, waiting for the patrol of Americans.

The American soldiers advance, doorway by doorway. Each motion is precise, each man covered by several others. My brother's men, by contrast, operate more as a group of individuals, no cohesion, no teamwork, no real leader. They find their own cover, fire in wild, undisciplined bursts. The Americans fire three shots, pause, shoot three more. They pick targets and aim. Hassan and his men fire almost randomly. Some come close to their targets, but most miss by a large margin.

I watch as one American falls. Then another. Hassan's men—I think of them as his men, although he is but one of many rather than any kind of leader—are dropping, dropping, dropping.

I hear the harsh voice of an AK-47 near me, *hack-hackhackhachack*—then the crisper sound of an American rifle, the name of which I do not know, answering, *crackcrackcrack*. Bullets patter and spatter in the dirt, and against the wall inches from my head. I suppress a scream, huddle closer to the ground.

I peer out, the need to watch winning over terror: Hassan is out there.

The AK speaks again, the sound moving closer, and then I see him, Hassan, crouching in the doorway, rifle kicking at his thin shoulder, one eye closed to aim. He glances at me, grins a lopsided, too-casual smile, then goes back to shooting.

Time slows. My stomach coils into a knot, my blood freezes, and I know what will happen. I want to scream, but cannot. A gasp is all that comes out. A tear trickles down, even though he is still firing, firing, and I cannot breathe. It happens. He jerks backward, twisting sideways, red blossoms blooming on his chest and a wide blotch on his back, shapeless and spreading. He is gasping, now, cursing.

I scramble to kneel over him, but he pushes me aside, struggles impossibly to his feet.

"Hassan!" His name finally escapes my lips, but it is too late.

My brother digs in his pocket, coughing, bleeding, wheezing, stumbles out, pulls a dark round thing from his pocket, jerks at it, throws, falls.

I watch the black dot, the grenade, float lazily through the air, fall at the feet of an American soldier kneeling beside the body of a wounded comrade. The unwounded soldier shouts, throws himself over his friend's body and rolls away, clutching his friend. The explosion is deafening, shakes the whole earth, cracks the sky. Dust billows, fire flickers.

There are screams.

The dust clears, and I see a mess of blood and bodies and bleeding limbs where the grenade had been, and I vomit. The limbs wriggle and rise, and a red-bathed American in tan camouflage lurches to his feet, sways, drags his friend away by the hand. He presses a palm to his side, drags his friend with other hand. Blood stains the mud.

Something tugs at my heart, watching the scene unfold. Hassan lies motionless in the road. Gunfire rips apart the silence, an AK, and puffs of dirt mark where the bullets walk toward the Americans, both wounded.

Somehow, I am out in the road. I step over Hassan. Someone shouts in Arabic, "Get away, woman!" I don't know what I am doing. Something hot buzzes past my ear. The American collapses to his knees, picks up his rifle, holds it at his hip, and fires. A curse, a shout, silence, something thumps wetly in the distance. More gunfire. The American jerks again, falls back and to his side.

I am in another doorway, watching it all. Two bodies, but only one breathes, I think. Sporadic bursts of gunfire, moving away. An American soldier inches toward his friends, firing. A grenade explodes, throwing him to the side. He gets up, seemingly unhurt but dazed, and backs away. He shouts, shouts, but the two on the ground do not answer. The pain in his eyes as he leaves his friends is visible and awful. Bullets ricochet, ding, zing, buzz. He turns and runs, and then there is no one. The fight has moved on.

I leave my hiding place. *What am I doing?* The thought floats through my mind, but I have no answer. The one who still breathes is collapsed on top of his friend. I push him over so he flops to his back. He groans, cracks his eyelids to peer at me.

Vivid, arresting blue eyes stare at me, and suddenly I am thirteen again, watching another American die. I am just a girl again, helpless. Hassan is dead. I know this. Mother is dead, Father is dead, Aunt and Uncle are dead. Americans are dead. Iraqis are dead. Everyone is dead, I think. Except this man. He struggles for breath, whispers something to me in English, and his voice is a breathy gasp. He wrenches himself over, each motion obviously excruciating, and pokes his friend. He says something, his friend's name, I think. His voice breaks. A tear falls. He looks at me.

I can see the death on his friend. I lean over him anyway, touch his neck, feel no pulse. I shake my head, and the American sobs, collapses, saying the same thing over and over again.

I know no English, but it sounds like, "Derek, Derek." A name.

The American goes silent, and I know he has passed out from the pain, from the blood loss.

What do I do? I cannot let him die. There has been too much death.

I drag him to my home, several blocks away. I am exhausted by the time I get him there.

I cannot help wondering once more, *What am I doing?*

FOUR

Hunter

Operation Iraqi Freedom; Iraq, 2003

ROUTINE CP. Clearing houses, crouching in doorways, and following the APCs and Hummers. Rifle at the ready, ears tuned, eyes peeled. Derek is beside me, joking about something. A sex joke. I laugh, but I'm not hearing him.

I've got the jitters. My stomach is uneasy. This is my last patrol. I'm shipping home soon. My tour is done, and my four years are over. I'm not re-upping. I've seen too much death and blood for a lifetime. All I have to do is get through this patrol without anything going FUBAR, and I'm home free.

Of course, I don't have a home to go to, but I can figure that shit out when I get home. For now, I just have to focus on this house, this room, this street. Then the next one and so on through this sector, and then we ride the seven-ton back to the MEK and I'm back Stateside within a week.

And of course, I've got the jitters. My hands shake, my spine tingles. This is my gut telling me shit's about to go down, because of course, nothing is ever easy.

Derek acts oblivious, keeps joking. I want to tell him to shut the fuck up and pay attention, but I know better. He runs his mouth because he's nervous. He feels it, too. He chatters like a goddamn blue jay when he's scared. I can see his eyes scanning, see the tension in his shoulders, in the way his rifle is almost at his shoulder, ready to fire.

We round a corner, and my gut clenches. I slow, scan the rooftops. Derek is doing the same.

"Feel it?" I ask.

"Fuck yeah. Shit's about to hit the fan."

The others are piled up behind us. I see nothing, so I continue, even though my instincts are telling me to stop, go back, stay, get the fuck down. I creep forward a few more feet, and then my gut is screaming too loud to ignore. I shove Derek to the side and drop to the ground for no reason whatsoever. As I taste dirt, an AK barks from a rooftop. Bullets snap through the air where we had been.

Fucking knew it.

Someone behind us shoots back—Barrett, I'm pretty sure. Only Barrett fires like that, three-three, pause, three.

Then all hell breaks loose. AK fire erupts from all directions, and suddenly we're split, half our unit cut off from the other half. Derek has a bead on an insurgent on the roof opposite us, so I wait until a muzzle-burst gives away a location and pour fire at it. I see a head and shoulder pop up, black metal and tan wood and black-spot eyes. I squeeze the trigger, and a burst of pink mist tells me I dropped him.

There's a pause, and Derek and I lurch into a run, breaking for a better position. I hear boots pound behind us. We're nearly there when I hear a *hackhackhack* and then fire and pain gouts through me, centered on my left shoulder and thigh. I'm spun around, fall. I'm dragged by the hand through the dust, bleeding. The strain on my wounded shoulder as I'm pulled is agonizing. I see Derek beside me, firing at a doorway. I see a shape, a muzzle-burst, bullets peppering the dirt and the wall near us.

Derek hits his target. I watch, the world sideways, as the muzzle-burst goes silent mid-bark. Derek shifts, prepares to drag me farther into cover. Then a figure, thin and young, stumbles from the doorway, bleeding. He throws a grenade, and I try to move, but Derek is already on top of me, rolling away with me, and the seconds until detonation tick in my head like thundering drums, each one a heartbeat.

Heat and fire and pressure erupt, the sound so deafening it becomes silence, and we're thrown. I feel wetness spread, feel pins of pain stab me. The silence continues and I wonder if I've gone deaf, but then ringing fills my ears, and I know my hearing will return eventually.

Derek is too still. Too wet. I find my feet, bullet-pierced leg screaming, refusing to support me, but I don't care. Can't afford to care. Adrenaline powers me. I grip Derek's red-slick hand and pull him, needing him to be okay. Rifle fire is a distant roar, and I see puffs of dirt marking Death's walk toward me.

My side hurts, low, near the hip. Shrapnel, I think. I push my hand against it, trying vainly to dull the pain with pressure. I get Derek a few feet away, closer to the doorway that would provide some cover, but then I'm struck again in the shoulder. I fall to my knees, find my rifle, fire blindly. Find a target, fire. Dropped him. Another—*crackcrack*—dropped him.

Fuck, I hurt.

A slug of agony hits my thigh, right near the original wound. I can't stay upright any longer. I hear more rifles firing, M-16s, an AK, and then a detonation. Someone shouts my name, Derek's name. Barrett. I want to answer but have no breath in my lungs. It's been stolen by pain, by shrapnel and bullet holes.

I succumb to the pain, let it wash over me. I drift and float, and then I feel something push me. Pain breaks over me like a wave when I crash to my back, and I force my eyes open.

Goddamn, she's beautiful.

It's a stupid, random thought, out of place on this battlefield, but I can't shake it. She's kneeling above me, her head-scarf thing, a hidab, or...my pain-fogged brain won't spit out the right word. *Hijab*. That's the word. It's coming loose around her face, tendrils of bottle-blonde hair escaping to drift across her delicate-featured face. I want to touch her finely sculpted cheeks, but my hand won't work.

"What are you doing here?" I ask.

She looks at me in confusion. She doesn't understand.

I my head and see Derek. He's a fucking mess. Panicked horror is a thick, hot knot in my throat. *NO! Not Derek....*

We've been buddies forever. Second grade. He called me a sissy and I beat his ass and we've been buddies ever since. Joined up together, got lucky, and managed to get through Basic in the same unit, assigned to the same grunt squad. Impossible luck, to stay together like this for so long, through war, through death.

Now he's dead.

"Derek?" I claw toward him. Poke him; he hates being poked. "Derek?"

I look at the girl, bright brown eyes like sun-bathed earth fixed on me. She touches two fingers to Derek's neck, looks back at me, shakes her head. Her meaning is clear.

"DEREK!" I can't help the scream.

I know I'm crying, feel the salt burning down my cheek, but I can't stop it. I don't care if I'm crying in front of this gorgeous Iraqi girl like some kind of goddamn sissy. Derek is dead.

Dead.

Fuck.

Darkness swallows me.

I wake up in the darkness. Shadows have eaten me. Silence sits on my chest like a wet, heavy blanket. I look around me, see shapes in the shadows. A chair, a table. A mirror reflecting shards of starlight. A square of lighter black with a swatch of pinprick stars: a window. Hard earth beneath me.

I want to get up. Need to get up. Can't stay here. Gotta get back to the guys. I manage an inch upward before pure agony bolts through me and I cry out, a soft grunt, high-pitched and girly. Goddamn sissy whimpers. I grit my teeth to silence myself.

Scratching, motion, rustling cloth. Then a face appears above me, blocking my view of the stars. Blonde hair hangs loose in long waves around her bare shoulders. I'm struck again by how stunningly beautiful she is, even in the dark of midnight black.

She says something in Arabic and touches the center of my chest to push me down, a feather-light touch between bullet holes in each shoulder. I stare at her, unable to look away. I wish it was light so I could see her better.

She tugs a thin blanket farther up my body, and I realize I'm clad only in my skivvies. Clumsy bandages are held on by tape, not medical tape. Regular tape. I laugh, which hurts. The girl tilts her head in confusion.

I point at the bandage, the tape. "Did you do this?"

I know she can't answer me, or understand me, but I ask anyway. I don't know why. I just want to talk to her.

She says something back, her voice sharp. I think she caught on to my criticism.

I hold up my hands to stop the accusing sound of her voice. "Thank you." I know I've been told how to say it Arabic, but I have to think about it. "*Chokran*."

She nods once and turns away, lies down, facing away. Her shoulders look tense, and I can tell she doesn't trust herself to really sleep with me here, even wounded.

"You can sleep, you know," I say. "I couldn't hurt a fly right now."

She rolls over and looks at me, dusky skin starlit silver. She whispers something, shaking her head, shrugging.

"I know you don't understand me. It doesn't matter." I smile at her, but she stares at me, impassive. "Sleep."

I mime sleeping, hands folded under my face, an exaggerated snore, then point at her. I point at myself with a thumb. I try to move and a groan escapes. I look at her and shrug, then mime sleeping again. She frowns in thought, then gives me a tiny smile. She gets it. She closes her eyes slowly, her eyelids flutter, then close again. Her breathing slows, and then she's asleep. I watch her sleep.

Why did she bring me here? Why did she help me? I would have bled out, died. I'm a burden. I won't be able to do shit for myself for weeks. I'll need to eat. I'll need help shitting. How can she help me? This house is tiny. She can't have much. I'll need antibiotics, probably. I'd wish for morphine, but I know I won't get it. Probably won't even get aspirin.

Now that she's asleep, I let the pain wash over me and let it show. It hurts so goddamn bad it's hard to breathe.

I fall asleep again.

When I wake, bright sunlight streams through the square, uncovered window. I'm on the floor in a corner. There's another bed opposite me, a mattress on the dirt covered by neatly folded blankets. There's an old, battered stove in one corner, older than me. A single bare lightbulb dangling from the ceiling, a large hunk of mirror with taped edges leaning against the wall. The girl is nowhere to be seen.

I close my eyes again, and that's when I hear it: the unmistakable sounds of sex. Male grunts, female moans. The moans sound forced, too loud, too exuberant. It lasts for a moment, then stops. I hear boots scritching in the dirt and a male voice muttering under his breath in Arabic. Another moment, and then the girl appears in the doorway, smoothing her hair with her fingers. She doesn't glance at me, as if not seeing me. She goes into the tiny bathroom with the rusted stainless steel sink, slips out of her skirt, cleans herself with damp rag. I watch, embarrassed, but unable to look away.

She is lithe, slim, long-legged, with flawless dark skin. I make myself look away to give her privacy. I hear her say something, a curse if the tone of her voice is any indication. I look at her. She is staring at me, almost expectantly. She is still naked from the waist down. I avert my eyes, roll away, groaning in pain.

I hear clothing rustle and she's clothed again, standing over me. She has money in her hand, and that's when I put two and two together. Understanding must be visible on my face, because her features harden. Her fist clenches around the wad of bills.

"Hey, it's none of my business," I say.

She responds, but of course I don't understand what she's saying. She sounds angry. She gestures at herself, at the door, which I take to be a gesture at the world at large. She's explaining herself, I think. She touches her stomach, hunching over it, groaning.

"You don't owe me any explanations," I say, as if we're having a conversation.

Hunger. I realize what she was trying to say with her charade. She sold herself for food. Pity must have registered on my face, and she must have recognized it. Her eyes blaze with anger, and she tosses the money at me and stomps away, although she only goes to the other side of the little house, arms folded, back bowing out and shoulder heaving as she breathes through her emotions.

"I'm sorry," I say.

She turns to look at me over her shoulder and says something. My imagination fills in the gap: *I don't want your pity.* She turns away and opens a cabinet, finds a box, produces a pill, and dry-swallows it. Birth control, I imagine. I wonder if it's difficult to get a hold of, out here.

She brings me flat bread and a bottle of water, a packet of foil containing ground beef or lamb. I struggle to sit up, gritting my teeth against the pulsating pain. She motions at me to stay down, mimes feeding me. *Hell, no.* I ignore her and get my shoulder blades propped against the wall, panting and sweating. I think I have broken ribs. I hurt so bad I could cry, but I refuse to let myself.

She watches me, frowning, shakes her head and mutters something. *Stubborn ass*, I imagine she says. She sets the packet of foil on my stomach, which hurts from the effort of moving. I reach for it, but my arm is weak. I manage a few bites while she watches. She clearly wants to help, but doesn't. I'm glad. I refuse to be fed like a goddamn baby. It's exhausting and painful, but I manage to eat it all, and drink the water. I feel better.

She glances at me, then pulls the blanket off me. If I didn't know better, I'd think she was blushing. It's a ridiculous idea, though, given what she does for a living. She doesn't look at me as she gently peels at the tape around the bandage on my leg.

"Do it fast," I tell her. She looks at me quizzically. "Fast."

I show her, ripping the bandage off quickly. It hurts like a bitch, and I have to stifle a groan. She picks at the bandage on one of my shoulders, going slowly again.

"No, do it fast." I mime ripping quickly. She looks at me incredulously and says something. I shrug. "It's better to just get it over with."

She peels slowly. I curse, put my hand on hers, and rip it away, hissing through my teeth. She jerks her hand away and scrambles backward, chattering angrily, jabbing her finger at me.

She doesn't like to be touched, I guess. I lift my hands up. "I'm sorry. I won't do it again."

I put my hands on my lap, covering myself, fingers threaded. She moves toward me again and pulls the last bandage off, quickly this time. I nod and she shakes her head in disbelief.

Stupid ass, I imagine her saying again.

She takes a roll of gauze and rips a long, ragged piece off. I frown, wanting to show her how to do it right. I glance at the foot of my blankets and see my clothes, some of my gear. My combat knife. I tap her shoulder, point at the knife. She shakes her head, but I point again. She gives it to me and scrambles away, leaving the gauze near me. I pick it up, eyes locked on hers, and cut a neat square, show it to her, then a second and third. I sheathe the knife and toss it out of reach.

She creeps back toward me like a skittish kitten, takes the gauze squares from me and gingerly places them on one of the wounds. There's an aged bottle of peroxide on the counter and I point at it. The wounds need to stay clean. She frowns at me, but gets the bottle and hands it to me. I dump a small amount on my wound, and my teeth almost crack from the strain of containing my scream of pain.

Fuck, it hurts.

She takes it from me and does the same to the rest of my wounds, and by the end I pass out from the pain. I come to, and she's clumsily taping the gauze on, loose and off-center.

"No, no. Not like that," I say.

She starts and drops the tape. I rip off the bandage she did and re-tape it, centered and tight. She watches carefully, and then does the same. Her fingers on my skin are gentle, careful, feather brushes. She looks to me and I nod.

"Good job. Much better. Thanks. *Chokran.*"

She responds, and I shrug. She points at me, says "*Chokran*," and then points at herself and repeats what she'd said, which I understand to mean "You're welcome." I repeat it, and she corrects my pronunciation.

She touches my chest, and this time I lay back down, slowly moving to the floor, each inch agony. I lay panting, eyes squeezed shut against the pain. I open my eyes to see her watching me, her expression inscrutable.

I examine her in the light of day. She's the most beautiful girl I've ever seen. About my age, twenty-three or twenty-four, a narrow face with high cheekbones, small, delicate ears, full red lips framing a wide mouth. Her eyes are like chocolate, dark and liquid, watching me watch her. Her body is svelte. I remember that word from high school English class. Her waist is narrow, turning her slim hips into tantalizing curves, making her full breasts even more pronounced. I remember her mimed comment about hunger being the impetus for becoming a prostitute, and realize her thin figure is the result of true hunger rather than any desire to be thin for the sake of appearance.

She shrinks back under my gaze, realizing I'm looking at her appreciatively, like a man looks at a woman. Her eyes harden and her lip curls. Her fists clench.

I drop my gaze, but I feel her eyes on me a moment longer. She goes to the doorway, peers out, and ducks back in. Her face is shuttered closed, hard, ice-cold. She reapplies lipstick, retouches her blush, too much.

She has a trick, I realize. She's totally different, now. Her body is loose, her hips swaying as she moves to the door; before, each motion was tightly controlled, precise. Now, she's like liquid, exuding sultry confidence that I realize is totally faked. She glances at me once as she moves out of sight, and I see a flash of some inscrutable emotion, there and gone.

I hear a man's voice, hers answering, low and sweet. Fake. The air is still today, and I can hear everything. A jingle of a belt, faintly. Her voice, moaning, fake, too loud. His voice, grunting, porcine.

Vomit roils in my belly, anger pulses in my chest. Hate. Jealousy. Disgust.

Where is this coming from?

I don't know her. Don't even know her name. So why am I reacting this strongly? There's no answer, but each moment increases the tempo of my rage, beating with my frantic heartbeat. Each sound makes my gut clench. Her voice, so falsely enthusiastic, shreds my nerves.

I recognize the emotions now. All together, they form a single feeling: helplessness. I want to stop this, but I can't. Physically, I can't even move. It's her choice, her life, not mine. And I'm completely dependent on her.

Fuck.

After far too long, a span of maybe ten minutes, she reappears, repeating the process of cleaning herself in the tiny doorless bathroom. She fixes her hair and lipstick and blush and clothes. I don't watch this time.

She glances at me once she's done fixing herself. I try valiantly to keep my face neutral. I don't know what she sees, but she turns away from me and goes outside, leaning against the outside of her house near the window, just within view. I can see her back, a strip of skin visible between skirt and shirt.

I shouldn't want to touch that stripe of skin, but I do. The desire is overwhelming.

I lever myself up off the ground, holding my breath against the pain, and then let myself fall back down. Lightning bolts of excruciating pain shoot through me, blinding white, subsuming me until I pass out.

Darkness floats over me, welcome relief from desires I shouldn't have and don't understand.

FIVE

Rania

HE IS ASLEEP. So handsome. I do not understand what
is happening to me. From the first moment I saw him,
something in him called to my blood and made it sing.
Even now, my last client of the day gone as the sun sets,
my body thrums merely looking at him.

His jaw is square and strong, his hair as black as the
darkest hour of the night, making his shockingly blue
eyes even more vivid. Of course, he is sleeping right now,
so I cannot see his eyes, but they sear into me nonethe-
less, whether I am awake or asleep, working or at rest. His
eyes seem to see me, the real me.

His body...pale skin, smooth and hairless except
for a thin trail of hair from his navel down beneath the
band of his underwear. He is hugely muscled, each limb
sleek and thick and powerful. His chest is broad and

hard, bulging with muscle even slack in sleep. His belly is like a plowed field, squares of muscle delineated by deep grooves. His arms are like cords of braided rope, each bicep wider than my thigh, his hands large and rough and powerful. His legs are like the twisted trunks of old trees, nearly as wide as my waist

No man I have ever seen looks like him. Of course, the men I know, they merely jingle their belts and pull out their manhood and do their quick and dirty business on me. They never disrobe entirely. They are never naked. To do so would be allowing themselves to be vulnerable. To stay clothed demonstrates their power over me. I must be naked while they remain clothed and pay me money so they may violate me.

This man, this American. He is not naked. He has his underwear on, and I have not moved them, so I have not seen him naked. But, even so he seems more fully nude than any man I have ever seen. I want to look away from him, but I cannot, and when I look at him, strange things flutter through me, pulse in the secret places of my heart and soul and body. It is like hunger, but not.

I remember Malik, my first client. I remember all too well the way he looked at me, and I remember thinking he looked hungry then. Is that what this is? The thought douses me with coldness and disgust. Is this feeling in my belly and between my thighs the hunger for sex?

No. That is not meant for anything but work. Money. Men are pigs. I am not a woman, I am a thing. An object, a servant for their needs. Sex is a tool.

But…nonetheless, I cannot stop looking at him.

He must be in pain. He moans even as he sleeps, trying to roll over in his sleep, but the pain stops him. I remember his hand touching mine as he showed me how to rip the bandage off. My hand burned as if shocked by lightning, a single, innocent touch that set my entire being on fire. I could not help my angry response.

The touch of men sets my stomach to heaving, and all the while I am working I must contain my disgust and disguise it with pretended desire, pretended enjoyment. The louder and more fake the sounds I make, the more they like it.

His touch, this American…it did not set my belly to revolting, and that was the catalyst of my anger. I should hate him. He has killed my people. He may have killed my brother. But I do not hate him. I do not know why I did not leave him where he lay bleeding to death. I did not, though, and that is the fact. I brought him to my home. My *home*. He sleeps a few feet from my own bed.

He knows what it is I do. He does not like it, although I cannot say why. Perhaps I disgust him, although I doubt I disgust him enough to prevent him from prevailing on my services when he is capable.

I have seen him looking at me. He tries not to, which is strange. I am a whore. Why should he worry about my privacy? But he does. He looks away when I clean myself for the next client, when I change and reapply my makeup.

What does he think when he looks at me with those blue eyes? Does he hunger for me like all the other men? They hunger for me with the desire of the flesh. They see me as good for one thing. They barely know my name. And even that is not my name.

Maybe he sees me as a woman, a person.

No. Surely not. Why would he?

I blink, and he is awake, watching me watch him. I force myself to meet his eyes without looking away or flinching. I want to hide from him. I cannot shake the sense that he sees into me. That perhaps he can see my thoughts, my secret desires, despite the language barrier between us.

He speaks to me, says something soft in his low, rough voice like distant thunder. I watch his Adam's apple bob in his throat, watch his lips move. I wish I knew what he was saying. He asks me a question and waits for an answer as if I understood him.

He touches his chest with a palm, and says one word: "Hunter." Then he points at me and shrugs his shoulders. He wants to know my name.

I stare at him, considering. I have not told anyone my real name in a very long time. Not since Malik.

I touch my chest between my breasts. "Rania."

Why did I tell him my real name? It is not as if he would know the difference.

"Rania." He says my name slowly, as if tasting it on his tongue.

I know the answer when he speaks my true name: I do not want him to know Sabah, the prostitute. I want him to know Rania, the woman.

Why, though?

I do not know. But that is what I want.

I try his name: "Hunter."

He smiles when I say his name. I wish I could pretend to myself that his smile, even a small one like this, just a slight tipping up of his lips, did not make something flinch and flitter in my belly, clench in my secret heart. His smile is genuine. As if he does not want anything from me but to see me smile back.

I know better. I know what he wants.

So why am I smiling back? The corners of my mouth are lifting in a real smile, not a fake one like I give the clients. It is a smile that delves into my heart and pushes away at the heavy darkness. My smile is drawn from his, inspired by his, and it feels good on my face, in my soul.

Reality reasserts itself, and I get to my feet and move to the window. Why am I smiling at him? Why is he here? Why did I save him?

Another pair of blue eyes stare at me, these long dead, long since banished into the world of memory. Another American, dying by my hand. In the realm of remembering, my hands jerk, my shoulder twinges with the kick of pain, and there is a deafening roar. An American, young, handsome, blue-eyed and innocent-looking, dies. I watch him die. Watch him gasp for breath.

I had nightmares for a very long time about those sky-blue eyes staring through me, veiled by death. I would wake up alone in my blankets, Aunt Maida's scraping breath nearby, Hassan's louder snoring to the other side, and I would still see sky-blue eyes boring into me, seeing my soul with the blank stare of a ghost.

I still wake up some nights, seeing those dying eyes.

That long-dead blue-eyed man is why this American, Hunter, is in my home. Perhaps if I save him, I will not dream of dying blue eyes any longer. Perhaps I will see the living eyes, Hunter's eyes. Not merely sky blue, but the hot, sharp shade of lightning, of the ocean, which I saw once in a trip as a little girl with Mama and Papa to see someone in Beirut. The ocean was rippling and moving and endless and so, so blue, like a field of many sapphires. I see this same shade in Hunter's eyes, and it frightens me. It hurts when he looks at me. His eyes spike through my hard walls and see into the secret softness hiding deep within my soul.

I can feel his eyes on me as I stare out the window, and I wish I could ask him what he is thinking. I realize I can say whatever I want. He will not know what I am saying.

I turn and look at him over my shoulder and let words pour out, knowing my secrets are safe.

"What are you doing to me, American? It is as if you are crawling underneath my skin, somehow. I feel you in my heart, and I do not know you. Your eyes see into me. I hate it, and I love it. I do not want you to see me.

I am dirty. I am ugly inside. Men see my beauty, but not my ugliness. Or perhaps they do see it, and that is why everyone hates me, except when they want to pay me for sex, pay me for my beauty." I return to sit cross-legged on the pallet of blankets next to him. "I wonder what you see, when you look at me. Do you want me? Do you want to touch me? Do you want me to be the whore for you?" My voice is angry by the end, not yelling but rather intensely quiet.

I can see the confusion on his face as he hears me speak but understands nothing. He hears the anger, though, and feels it to be directed at him. I do not feel bad for his confusion, even though he has done nothing wrong to me yet. He will. He will expect me to be the whore for him, someday. He knows what I am, and that is all I can be now.

I am not Rania, the woman; I am Sabah, the whore. Now and always. For him and for every other man.

I turn away and prepare food for us both. I keep myself focused on the food when I hear him struggling to sit up. He hates showing pain. I know this about him already. He has to be strong all the time. No pain. No weakness.

I bring the food to him, and he eats it slowly, carefully. Each motion costs him pain. I wish I had some kind of medicine to alleviate the pain, but I do not. It is too much money, especially now that I am feeding two.

He thanks me when he is finished eating, using the only word of Arabic he knows. This time, when I say "you are welcome," which I taught him yesterday, he teaches me to say it in English. He says "thank you" in Arabic, and then repeats himself in English, his hand on his chest. Then he points to me and says "you are welcome" in Arabic, and repeats it in English.

We spend the morning exchanging words. I show him bread and teach him the word for it, and he teaches me the English equivalent. Objects are easy to learn, but abstract concepts like "please" are more difficult. I want to talk to him. I want to know how his thoughts flow into words.

My first client is scheduled for just after lunch. I find myself dreading it even more than usual. I hate the unreadable expression in Hunter's eyes as I dress in an absurdly short skirt and a top cut so low my breasts may as well be bare. I hate the disapproving look he gives me when I slather on the makeup.

I hate most of all the pain in his eyes when I leave the house to wait outside the mosque for my client.

This client is a repeat customer. He comes every week on this day, at this time. He is married, I know. I see the ring on his finger, or the shadow of it when he remembers to take it off. He tells me his name is Abdul, but he does not always remember to answer to it when I address him by that name, so I know it is not his real name. As if I care who is. Whether he is married or has children. I have no place to cast blame if he wishes to spend his money on me, if he needs to find sexual release with me rather than his wife.

If he would pay a whore for sex, he is a pig. If he can-not find what he wants or needs with a woman who does not demand money for it, then he is a pig.

Of course, I know nothing of such things, having never had sex with a man who has not paid me for it. Perhaps all sex is paid for in some way. I think this is true. A man who takes a woman to dinner first, takes her to drink, tells her she is beautiful, pays her father to arrange a marriage to her…this is paying for sex. It is cloaked in custom and tradition, but the result—sexual dominion of the man over the woman—is still prostitution.

I am not willing in this. I did not choose this life. I do what I must to survive. It is this, or starve.

These are the justifications I repeat to myself over and over again as Abdul approaches me, uniform straight and creased, medals polished, sidearm adjusted just so, boots shining.

I hate Abdul. His eyes are cruel. His fingers are hard and strong when they claw my top down, my skirt up. His breath stinks of garlic and his body of unwashed male sweat and flabby musk. His belly hangs over the zipper of his pants as he reveals himself, kneeling above me. His mouth is twisted in a cruel grin, as if he knows a secret that delights him.

There are different kinds of clients. There are those who hand me their money before they begin, eyes averted while I stash it under my blankets. There are those who dig it out of their pockets while they dress afterward and walk away without looking me in the eye. They are the ones who feel some shame for what they do with me.

Then there are men like Abdul. He wastes no time. He paws at my shirt, tugging my top down until my breasts bounce free, and then he paws at my skirt, pushing it up to bare my privates. He takes a moment to look at me, a hungry, evil grin on his thin lips, and then he shoves his short, fat member into me. He only takes a few moments, thankfully, and then he is done. He rises up to his feet, tugs his pants back into place, and buckles his belt. All the while, his greedy, leering dark eyes stare at me. And then, after a moment of triumphant silence, he digs into his pocket and pulls out a wad of money. He does not bother to count. He has made sure the correct amount is in that pocket beforehand, for the sole purpose of being able to toss the wad of filthy money onto my bare breasts.

He does this every time. He does it to show his power over me, to degrade me.

I play my own game. He expects me to scramble to count it, but I do not. I wait, motionless, while he leaves. I do not cover myself. I do not brush the greasy bills aside or stack them or count them. I leave them in place, and bear up under his gaze, let him look, let him feel powerful. When he is gone, I gather it together, stack it with the rest of my earnings, and go to clean up, stashing it in the cabinet.

Today, when Abdul tosses the money onto me, he waits. "Pick it up, whore," he growls.

I do not answer, make no move to comply.

"I gave you an instruction, whore. You must obey."

"You do not pay me to obey you. You pay me to let you have sex with me. You are finished. You may leave now."

His eyes narrow and grow angry. Fear gathers low in my gut, but I refuse to let it show.

"I pay you to do whatever the fuck I tell you. I told you to pick up the money. Count it. Now."

I lift my chin slightly. A refusal.

He snarls like a rabid animal, lunges for me, grabs my shirt in his hands and lifts me to my feet. He lifts me off the ground easily, holds me aloft. I refuse to show fear. Refuse to shake for him. He lowers me to my feet, takes a hand off my shirt, and slaps me across the face. It stings, but it was not a blow meant to cause damage, only to demonstrate power. Then he grins at me. The evil glaze of his eyes causes the first burst of real panic.

He grabs my nipple and pinches, twisting it. I scream through gritted teeth. He lets go, grinning in satisfaction, then rears back and slaps my breast so hard I collapse to my knees, breathless from agony.

"Pick up the money, whore." He stands over me, glaring down at me. "Count it."

I do as he says, rage burning in my chest tangled with the pain.

"Now you will remember," he says. "You will do as I say. You are a whore. You are paid to please me."

I remain on my knees, face to the floor, hiding my tears and my hate. He laughs and walks away. When his footsteps are gone, I adjust my clothing, but my breast hurts so badly from his blow that I cannot bear to have anything touching it. I take my money and leave the ruins of the mosque, stumbling the few feet back to my house.

Hunter is on his knees, his canvas uniform belt clenched between his teeth, struggling to get to his feet. He is growling, a long continuous sound of pain and determination.

"What are you doing?" I ask.

He stops, and the concern and the rage in his eyes startles me. "Rania?" He says something else I don't understand.

Are you okay? I imagine he is saying.

I shake my head at him. I mean, *don't worry about it*, but he takes it to mean I am not okay. He has made it to his feet, and the pain is etched into every line of his face. He puts a hand to the wall and shuffles toward me.

I point to the floor. "Lie back down. You'll start bleeding again," I say.

He shakes his head. Reaches for me. Concern, worry, anger. He heard me scream, heard the blows. He stands in front of me now, heaving, panting, sweating, groaning with every breath. I hold perfectly still, feeling oddly like prey caught by the gaze of a predator. Only, this predator seems worried for me.

Hunter's hand lifts slowly. I want to flinch away, but I do not, and I cannot figure out why. I should. I should be afraid of Hunter, for he is a man, same as Abdul. But... Hunter is nothing like Abdul. This is as clear to me as the difference between a sunny day and a thunderstorm.

Hunter's fingers brush my cheek, and I realize he thinks that is where I have been struck. He realizes my cheeks are unblemished, and his face shows his confusion. He says something, asking where I am hurt, probably. I shake my head, my only possible answer. He touches my chin, then, tilting my face up and away, to one side and then the other.

He gently nudges me backward, examining the rest of me. I cannot help but clutch my arms over my breasts in an instinctive move to protect myself.

Hunters' eyes narrow, move down to my breasts. I look down as well and see that my right breast is reddened where Abdul hit me. Hunter's eyes change, and I am frightened of him suddenly. He looks ready to kill. Hate emanates from him. He reaches out his hand to touch me, and I flinch away, cross my arms tighter. The contact is too much and I wince, drop my arms away, and cradle myself gently. I want to take my shirt off, but I dare not. Not with Hunter here. I do not trust my own desires.

He drops his hand, but the anger does not dissipate from his eyes. He says something, a short phrase, his intonation making it sound like a question. I shrug and turn away, facing the corner.

I need this shirt off. My breast stings. I peel my shirt off, and the muggy air feels cool on the hot, stinging flesh of my chest. I feel Hunter's eyes on my back, feel him still standing there. I hear him grunt, a shuffling hop of a footstep. I crane my neck over my shoulder to see him fighting for balance, standing on one leg, palm on the wall but not enough to keep him upright. His good leg is trembling, and I can see he is about to collapse.

I curse, then turn, clutching my shirt to my chest, wincing at the pain, and snug my shoulder under his. His weight on me is enormous, a huge, overbearing burden, and I can tell he is not even leaning on me. I straighten my legs, hear him hiss as this motion bumps his shoulder, which is injured as well. He does not move away. He just stands there, using me as a crutch, regaining his balance. His arm hangs down around mine, his fingers trailing on my hip. I try to ignore the touch, the tingle of it, the not-filthy, not-unwelcome feeling of it. He finally clutches my shoulder with his hand, hops toward the bed, and I move with him, slowly and gradually. He pauses above the bed of blankets, as if trying to figure out how he can lower himself down without hurting himself.

He lowers himself on one leg, an awkward maneuver, his wounded leg extended in front of himself. He reaches a near-sitting position, then sighs gently and lets himself fall, grunting as he lands. The bandage around his thigh seeps red.

He pretends not to notice. I shrug back into my shirt, and his eyes follow me, take in my body greedily before he turns away. I do not know what to feel about his gaze on me. I should be angry at him for ogling me. I am not. But then, I am a prostitute, and I should be used male eyes on me, and I am. But somehow Hunter is different.

He shouldn't be an exception, but he is.

I want him to look at me, and this makes me angry at myself.

I re-bandage his leg, trying not to touch him.

I ready myself for my next client, and Hunter's eyes grow dark with anger, with something else that I dare not identify.

SIX

Hunter

I HAVE NOTHING TO DO BUT THINK. Nothing but memory and pain.

Derek is dead. It just hit me. I was too involved in the pain and in the mystery of Rania, but now, alone while she "works," all I have to do is feel the pain. Derek is dead.

God. He was my best friend. My only real friend. My brother. I've killed for him. We've stood over each other's bleeding bodies.

He's gone, but the pain won't let me cry. I can't. I don't know how anymore. After my parents died I wept, alone in a bathroom. I haven't since. Not for anything.

I won't cry for Derek, either. He wouldn't want me to. He'd tell me to get drunk in his memory. Bang a hot chick for him. Of course, none of that will happen now.

The reality of my situation is hitting me. I'm wounded, surrounded by insurgents. There's no sign of my unit. They might eventually come back for me, or at least to find my body. Until then, I'm stuck here. Reliant on this girl, this slip of a thing, this prostitute.

Rania. Her name is music. Her eyes are veiled pools of expression. She hides behind anger, behind toughness. It's all an act. I see the pain. See the fear. See the need. She's lonely. She hates what she does.

I think I confuse her as much as she does me.

She's back, cleaning herself up. It's a familiar pattern now. She returns from the building next door, a half-destroyed mosque, I think it's called. The irony of a prostitute operating in a bombed-out church isn't lost on me. She goes into the bathroom, cleans herself, then sits with me, and we exchange language lessons. I'm picking up Arabic faster than she is English, I think. It's only been a couple of days, but I can understand a few words here and there, say a few of my own. I want to be fluent, so I can talk to her. So I can understand what she says. We both have a tendency to say what we're thinking as if the other can understand us. I told her about Derek earlier. How we met, how we've been friends our whole lives. How much I miss him. How he saved my life, and ended up dying for it. She heard the pain in my voice and let me talk, even if she didn't know what I was saying. It was cathartic, in a way. Like a confession, if I was Catholic. I can say the truest things in my heart without having to worry about feeling vulnerable. She can't tell anyone. Can't judge me. Can't level expectations at me.

Why do I feel so rotten when she goes out that door? Why do I care what she does? I've known plenty of sluts, men and women. People who sleep with anything that moves, anything with tits and a twat, anything with a cock and balls. In a way, that's worse. What Rania does, she does out of necessity. Those slutty people, it's totally different. They have no self-respect, no modesty, no morals. They fuck for the sake of fucking, as if it means nothing. Derek was like that. Total man-whore. Except he was honest about it. He plied them with drinks and took them home and fucked them, and that was it, and they both knew it going in.

Rania…the look in her eyes in the moment before she walks out the door, it's resignation. Disgust. Loathing. It's there, and then gone, hidden behind the careful façade of applied seductiveness. In private, with me, she's another person. Quiet, reserved. She hates getting close to me, hates touching me or being touched. As if she's afraid of what will happen if I touch her.

I think she expects me to try to sleep with her. To try to use her like…well, like a whore.

I won't deny the attraction. She's beautiful, and what I've seen of her body makes my mouth go dry and my cock hard. I've managed to keep her from noticing, but I have to keep my eyes off her when she forgets I'm here and changes in front of me, or cleans up in front of me. She's used to being alone. She forgets I'm here and then remembers, blushes, gets angry at my presence, at my eyes on her. I can't help looking at her. I try, but I can't. There's no privacy in this little house. No door on the bathroom, no curtain, nowhere to change. When she strips her shirt off to change it, I try not to watch her full breasts sway in the dim light. She peels her skirt off, and I try to stare at the wall or the floor, but my eyes are drawn to the dark triangle between her legs, the swell of her hips.

She's all woman, but she's...forbidden fruit. Her clients are enemy soldiers, officers, insurgents. We must be near a base of operations or something. I don't know.

All I know is I shouldn't want her. But I do.

She's sitting beside me, staring at me. Her brown eyes are narrowed and inscrutable. She's within reach. I could stretch out my hand and touch her knee, her slim thigh. My hand trembles beneath the blanket, straining against my self-control.

She saved my life. I owe her.

She doesn't want me. How could she? I'm an American, a man, a soldier...for all I know, I may have killed someone she loves.

My hand slips out from beneath the blanket to rest on my knee. Rania is watching me with a guarded expression, concealing her thoughts, her feelings. My hand moves toward her, and I sense her freeze. She was already stone-still, but now she's not even breathing.

I can't help it. My fingers touch her knee. Just her knee. No higher. Her eyes burn into me. Dare me to go farther, yet beg me not to. So conflicted, both of us. She wants, doesn't want. I want, don't want.

Her skin, so soft. So delicate.

Rania gazes at me, sighs gently, a sound of resignation, then grasps the bottom hem of her shirt and lifts it up, crossing her arms to draw it off. I'm the one frozen now. Her breasts, unhampered by a bra, are round and full, with small nipples surrounded by wide dark fields of areola.

My hands move faster than my lust, quicker than my desires. I want to keep looking. I want to touch her. I want her to keep stripping. Instead, I grab her wrists and pull them down. She fights me, trying to pull the shirt off. I'm weak right now, each motion causing excruciating pain, but I still overpower her easily, without hurting her. I force her hands away and pull her shirt down so her magnificent breasts are covered once again.

She stares at me in confusion. My hand has landed on her knee once more, and she looks at it pointedly. I withdraw my hand and she breathes a sigh, whether in relief or disappointment, I don't know.

Rania stands up and storms away, out the door and into the heat and brightness of the afternoon.

When she comes back, she won't so much as look at me. She's ignoring me.

I give her some time—there are no clocks here, so I have no way to measure the passage of time except the rise and fall of the sun—and then decide to break the ice.

"Rania," I say. She ignores me. "Rania. Please listen to me." This is in English.

Her shoulders flinch when I say her name, but that's the only recognition I get. I'll have to claim her attention, then. I learned how to say "I'm sorry" the other day. It took a lot of miming, but I think that's what she was getting at.

I lever myself to a sitting position. My broken ribs scream, send lightning bolts of agony through me, so blinding I have to stop and pant to keep the breath in my lungs. My shoulders hurt, too, but that's a dull, constant pain, not like the sharp spikes that pierce me when my ribs are jostled. I wait until my stomach is no longer about to revolt from the pain, and then I force myself to my one good knee. More panting, more gasping, sunbright lances of pain. Eventually I make it to my feet, or rather foot, and hop and hobble across the room to Rania's side. I'm without anything to balance me, as she's sitting cross-legged on the floor away from the walls, doing nothing. Just staring out the window at the cloudless blue sky.

I move so I'm standing in front of her. "Rania."

She ducks her head to stare at the floor. I growl in frustration, hopping in place to keep my balance. Eventually, I have to put my other foot down, but it collapses under me and I fall to the ground. Rania's expression is shuttered, and I can tell she wants to move to help me but isn't letting herself. I lie gasping, stunned, fighting the pain, and then work back upright onto my ass, game leg stretched out in front me.

She doesn't look at me, but now I know she's aware. Listening.

"I am sorry, Rania," I say in Arabic, and I know I've butchered it, by the way her lips twitch.

I'm not even sure what I did to piss her off besides touch her. I didn't let her strip. I think she meant to have sex with me, thinking that's what I expected. But why is she mad? I'd think that would be a relief, knowing I don't expect it from her.

She finally looks at me, brown eyes searching mine.

"I won't touch you again," I say in English.

Time for an Arabic lesson. I touch my knee and say "touch." I touch the floor, which she's told me the word for, and repeat myself. Touch various things within reach, repeating the word "touch."

Eventually she gets it and tells me the word in her language.

I know I'm going to butcher the grammar on this one, but I say it anyway. It's important that she trusts me. I don't know why, but it is.

"I not touch," I say, in halting Arabic.

She frowns. Shakes her head. Thinks.

She touches her chest, our symbol for "I," then produces a carefully folded bill from her pocket and holds it up, points to her crotch, then to me, then gestures with the money. Says a word.

Prostitute. Whore. She's telling me what she is. No. Not what she is. Not who she is. What she does. There's more to her than that.

I shrug, pause. Then point to her: "Rania."

I don't know what my point is. Maybe that I see her, not her job. It is a job for her, I realize. Not a profession. Not a lifestyle.

She stares at me in confusion. Says something, a long sentence in which I catch a reference to herself, the word she'd used before, which I take to mean "whore." And then points next door, where she entertains the johns, and says "Sabah." It's a name. I know that much. Then she gestures to the house around us, and says "Rania."

It takes a while to comprehend her meaning. I think she's saying she uses a different name for the johns. To them, she's Sabah.

I point at her. "You Rania," I say. "No Sabah."

Her face shutters closed. "No. Not Rania. I am Sabah. Only Sabah. Rania is—" and she says a word I don't recognize. She mimes being dead, eyes rolled back in her head, tongue lolling out, making a gagging, gasping sound.

Rania is dead. The sentiment makes my heart clench for her. She's only Sabah, the whore, to herself. Why is that so sad? This is all she has? All she knows? Has she ever known love? Has she ever known the beauty of sex, the joy in making love?

To her, it must be a dirty, shameful, ugly act. I doubt she ever gains any enjoyment from it. I wish I knew how to communicate with her. Show her. I wish there was a way I could give her joy. Give her even a moment of peace, or pleasure.

Her eyes burn into me, hunting for my reaction. I don't know enough of her language to express what I want to say.

"No. No dead." I use the word she did, hoping it means what I'm assuming it does. "Rania."

She shakes her head and looks away.

I start talking in English, needing to say it. "There's so much more to life. You're stuck here. Stuck in this shitty life. Stuck being a whore. You deserve more." I don't know why I feel that way about her. I've known her for a matter of days, and I can't even have a real conversation with her. "You're more than this, and I wish you could see it. I wish I could take you away. Give you something better. Except...I don't have anything to give you. I can't even walk on my own."

She speaks, slow and sad words. Eyes downcast. I catch references to herself, prostitution, the mime for hunger. She point out into the street, mimes shooting a rifle.

"Hassan is dead."

This Hassan must be the guy who threw the grenade and then died in the street. She knew him.

I point to her ring finger, then say his name, point at her. *Was he your husband?*

She looks confused for a split second, then understands. "No. Not—" and the word for husband, I assume. "Mama," she says, then mimes a pregnant belly, hand curving out over her belly, the points at herself and holds up one finger, then says his name, mimes pregnant again, and holds up a second finger.

I have to work at the meaning, but get it eventually. He was her younger brother. Derek killed her brother, and Hassan killed the closest thing to a brother I've ever had.

We both fall silent then, both reflecting on our lost brothers. Derek had family, a mom and dad and a sister. I wonder if they know he's dead. I wonder if what's-her-name, the girl he hooked up with over holiday leave—the Rack…Megan? Something like that. I wonder if she'll be sad for his death. If they were serious.

If I die, no one will care. Derek's family might, a little. I spent a lot of time with them growing up, especially after Mom and Dad died.

I look at Rania. "Your mama?"

She flinches, won't look at me. "Dead."

"I, too." I say it in my broken Arabic.

"Papa, too?" she asks. I'm guessing on that last word.

I nod. "Yes. Papa dead. Mama dead. Only I."

She looks outside, as if seeing the street where Hassan and Derek died. We should hate each other for our losses. Instead, I feel closer to her for it. She meets my eyes, and lets me see her pain.

Her hand is resting on her knee, and I, perhaps stupidly, rest my hand atop hers. She glances up at me sharply. I keep my eyes on hers, keep my hand on hers.

It's meant as a gesture of comfort, but I'm not sure she sees it that way. She leaves my hand on hers for a while. Perhaps she draws comfort from it, perhaps not. She doesn't seem mad this time.

She stands up, takes my hand in hers, and helps me to my feet, then to the nest of blankets that is my bed. When I'm finally lying down again, every fiber of my body is pulsating with pain and I can't breathe, and she's touching up her makeup. I hear an engine. Then it turns off, and there are footsteps.

Rania looks at me, and then as I watch she becomes Sabah. The pain is pushed away, the flash of disgust that crossed her face when she heard the vehicle is gone, replaced by a silky, seductive smile that doesn't reach her eyes.

My belly tightens, my heart rebels, my mind screams. No. No. I want to grab her and shove her back into the house. Go outside and beat the fuck out of the john waiting for her.

She's mine.

But she isn't. Where the hell did that thought come from?

I listen to the sounds of false enthusiasm and try to banish the whirling maelstrom of thoughts from my head. Her breasts flash into my mind. Her eyes on me. Her lips as she smiles, a real smile meant for me. Small and hesitant, as if she has to remember how to smile.

SEVEN

Rania

THE CLIENT, MAHMOUD, IS SLOW FINISHING. It is difficult to summon the strength needed to fake enjoyment.
He is thin, all hard angles and rough, clumsy hands.
Mahmoud is one of my few clients who is not a soldier.
He is an older man, widowed. Lonely. He pays me well,
is respectful, and does not hit me or try to extort more
from me than what he has paid for. But he is clumsy. So
slow. Unintentionally rough.

All I can think of is Hunter. His eyes on me as we
exchange halting conversation. His hand on mine,
a strange comfort. Just a touch. A hand on my hand.
But it tells me I am not alone. Not seeking to gain anything from the contact, but rather impart something,
give something. He, too, has lost his parents. I think he
was very close to the soldier who died. Derek. I saw him

grieving, when he thought I was not looking. He did not weep, and I do not think he can, any more than I.

Hassan chose to be a soldier, so his death was not a surprise, but it still hurts. My heart still mourns for him. I have always missed him, as I did not see him for many years. Now he is dead and truly gone. But I cannot weep for Hassan. I have cried all my tears, and now my sadness has no way to get out except through anger. I think Hunter is the same, except his anger is harder, deeper. Kept deep down in the bottom of his soul. I do not think he recognizes or understands his own anger. His loneliness.

Mahmoud leaves, handing over my money without looking directly at me.

When I go back home, Hunter is sleeping, or pretending to. I have felt his eyes on me when I clean myself, and I have sneaked glances at him and I have seen his discomfort. Mahmoud was my last client for the day, so I take a shower. It is quick and cold. I have no privacy, and I know Hunter is trying not to watch me. His determination to give me some semblance of privacy is difficult for me to accept or understand. I am a whore. Why should I care if he sees my nude body? But I do care. He knows it, and he does something about it.

When he touched my knee that first time, I was sure he meant to take it further. I was sure he meant to touch me, get me to touch him, and so I tried to give it to him. I thought it was what he expected, and I have learned the hard way that men will stop at nothing to get what they want from me. Hunter is wounded and weak now, but he can still hurt me. And when he heals, he could do worse. There is little worse than to have a man force himself on me. Even when they pay me afterward, they have still raped me.

Something in my heart tells me Hunter would not do that, but I cannot trust my heart.

Abdul comes today, which means it has been a week. Hunter has been in my house for over a week now.

Abdul is not the first to hit me, to force his will on me. I have no power to stop him, now that he has me. He could kill me and no one would know or care. He could beat me senseless, and no one would do anything. If Abdul finds out about Hunter, he would kill both of us.

I try to distract myself from my fear by talking with Hunter, learning each other's languages. Hunter learns quickly, more so than I. He can say many things, but not enough to allow us to really converse. Soon he will be able to, I think. He is making the leap from parroting words to stringing sentences together, making complete thoughts.

When he can, what will we talk about?

It is time. Abdul is coming soon. I wait for him in the mosque. I have a knife hidden in the blankets nearby. I do not know what I would do with it, but I feel better with it at hand. I refuse to let a man like Abdul be the end of me.

He is here. Swaggering, fat-bellied, beady-eyed. Like a giant hog. Bristly, greasy, violent, dangerous.

I do not stand when he swaggers in. I stare up at him, meeting his gaze. He stands over me, grins, then unbuckles his belt. Always before now, he has pushed me to my back and done his business. I can tell by the evil twist of his lips that he has something else in mind. He drops his pants, revealing his short, thick member, hard and sticking straight out.

He gestures at himself. "Suck, whore."

"It costs extra."

"I will pay you what I wish, bitch. Suck it."

"Pay first. One hundred extra."

I do not even see his hand move. I find myself lying on my side, cheek throbbing. Abdul is above me, a pistol barrel pressed to my forehead.

"Whore!" he yells. "Do what I tell you, or I will kill you. You are nothing but a filthy whore. I pay you because I am generous. Today, you will give me what I want, and you will not be paid. Your payment will be your life. Do you understand?"

I can only nod. He grabs my hair and drags me upright, thrusts my face against his crotch. His member bumps my closed lips. I consider biting him, but I know he'll kill me. The gunshot will alert Hunter, who will drag himself here to look for me. He will be killed, and then my work to save him will be wasted.

I do as I am told. He is unwashed. He tastes vile. He fists his hands into my hair, pulls me against his crotch, jabbing himself into my throat violently, choking me. I gag, nearly vomit, which is when he finishes, filling my throat with his seed. I cannot stop it then. I turn my head to the side and vomit on the cracked tile floor beside the blankets.

Abdul laughs. "Next time, do not argue." He leans down and puts his face next to mine as I heave. "If you argue with me again, I will kill you."

He swaggers away, buckling his belt. I remain there, kneeling on the hard floor, vomiting. Eventually I am able to stop, and I make my way back home, wiping my mouth. My cheek throbs, bruised.

I stumble into the bathroom and brush my teeth obsessively.

I cannot look at Hunter. He sees me, though, and exclaims angrily in English. Tries to get up.

"No. Sit," I say. "I am fine."

"Not," he says in Arabic.

He begins the long, torturous struggle to his feet, so I kneel beside him and let him look at me. He takes my chin between gentle fingers, turns my face to the side to examine my cheek. His brow furrows, and anger flashes in his blue eyes. He touches my cheek, his finger a feather-light brush along the swollen skin. The longer he touches me, the hotter the rage in his eyes grows.

He says something in English, a single growled question. I don't need to know the meaning of the word to know what he asked. *Who?*

I shake my head. "No." He understands that much. "I do not want you involved. He will kill you. He will kill both of us."

"Who?" He says it again in English.

"Abdul." I have to think hard about how to use gestures and our limited mutual understand to communicate who Abdul is. "Soldier, general."

He shakes his head, shrugs. I stand up, try to assume an "attention" position, heels together, back straight, and then I salute. Hunter laughs at my pantomime, but nods, understanding. I draw my fingers in a wide rectangle above my left breast, meaning the row of medals and other colorful things a high-ranking soldier wears there, then pat my shoulders, meaning the rank insignia. Hunter seems confused still. I sigh.

I hit on an idea. I put my forefinger on my upper lip, indicating a mustache, and say, "Saddam," and hold my hand above my head. Then I move my hand down a few inches, indicating a slightly lower rank, and say, "Abdul."

Hunter's eyes widen as he comprehends my meaning. Abdul is a high-ranking general not far beneath Saddam Hussein himself. Or, he was until Saddam was overthrown by the Americans. Abdul has been a regular client for many years, since before he achieved his current rank.

I sit down again, and Hunter touches my cheek once more. "No," he says. His voice is hard, angry, determined. "I dead him."

I laugh at his mangled Arabic and shake my head. "No. Say, 'I will kill him.'" I repeat it, pantomiming stabbing.

He nods and repeats what I said. "I will kill him."

There's no humor in my eyes or voice now. "*No!*" I say it in English and Arabic. "No."

He does not respond, doesn't argue, but I can see in his eyes that he hasn't changed his mind. He intends to kill Abdul for hitting me. I cannot make him understand. This is my life. This is my job. How I survive. If Abdul ends up dead, it could ruin my business, ten years' worth of establishing clients and a reputation as Sabah.

But something in my heart yearns to let Hunter do as he wishes. Something in me twinges and twitches, like an unused muscle coming to life. He wants to protect me. He sees me hurt, and there is pain in his eyes, anger for me.

He does not know me. He does not even truly speak my language, nor I his. We know nothing of each other. We are enemies. Our people are at war. He cannot protect me. Not from the likes of Abdul. Not from anyone.

Hunter's eyes are mere inches from mine. I suddenly realize how close I am to him. His thigh brushes mine. His body is near enough for me to feel the heat pouring from him. I can see the individual hairs of his beard growing on his chin and cheeks, thick and black. A bead of sweat slides down his temple, curves over his cheekbone to mingle with the stubble of beard. He wipes his cheek on his shoulder, smearing the sweat into a shiny patch of wetness.

His eyes pierce mine, so blue, hot and deep and quavering with a tangle of emotions. I wonder what he is thinking. He licks his lips, tongue tip sliding over his lower lip, a pink dart.

I do not realize what is happening at first. His face grows closer to mine, his eyes wide and locked on mine, so, so blue, so close. What is he doing? I cannot move. I am frozen by his nearness, trembling with fear and anticipation. This is it. Now he will take what he wants from me. He is still wracked with pain, I can see it in the way the corners of his eyes crinkle and the way his free hand clenches the blanket so tightly his knuckles turn white. But his other hand is still touching my chin, my jaw, the skin beneath my ear, his touch as gentle as a breeze. And now his lips are touching mine; why? What is this? He is kissing me? Clients do not kiss. They do not try, and I would not let them. It is sex, not love.

I remember my mother kissing my father once when she thought I was not looking. They loved each other, Mama and Papa. She put her lips to his, and their mouths moved together, as if they were eating each other's tongues. I did not understand it then, but now I do.

He tastes faintly of meat and garlic and something else unique and indefinable. Something distinctly male. I do not know what to do. I am afraid of this kiss, what it means, what it has begun, where it will lead, why it is happening. I am afraid of Hunter. He is confusing.

Strong, and huge, and hard, but gentle with me. Angry when I am hurt. I have seen wounded men before, and they were weak, barely able to move.

Once, a few years ago, a client hit me in the side because I would not do what he wanted. He broke my rib, and I could not work for many days. I nearly starved. I told Abdul what had happened, why I could not entertain him, and Abdul did something. Made sure the client never came back. Not for me, but so Abdul could continue to enjoy my services. Each motion was impossibly painful. Each breath hurt worse than the blow that broke the rib. I could not move for the pain. Hunter has at least one broken rib, and he continues to move. It hurts him, I can see, but he moves anyway.

He kisses me carefully, gently. Hesitantly. It is…soft and wet and hot. I do not stop. I want to stop, want to run away from him and his eyes that see me, his hands that touch me in a way I do not mind but should. His presence confuses me. I do not run away. I let him kiss me, and I know I should not, but I do.

He pulls away finally, palm flat on my cheek, eyes searching me for a reaction. I do not know how to react. How to feel. I am confused. So turned upside down by him and by the kiss that I cannot move, cannot breathe.

Something hot and salty stings my eyes. Am I bleeding? I touch my eyes and look at my finger. I am crying. Why? I do not know. Am I sad? What is this feeling in my heart, in my chest? It is a tightness, warm and thick, spreading through me. My skin tingles where he touches me. My thighs tremble, and between them...I feel a dampness, and a strange clenching heat, a tension like need.

His thumb brushes the tear from my cheek, then the other side. He is still close enough to feel his breath on my face.

My lips tingle and throb where his touched mine.

It is madness, I know, but I find myself kissing him. Pressing my lips to his, a slow falling forward into him. His lips part and his hand curls around the back of my neck, holds me at the nape and pulls me closer, kisses me back.

Something touches my teeth, my lips. His tongue. It is a bizarre sensation. Invasive and frightening. I pull away and look at him, and I can feel the confused expression on my face.

What in Allah's name am I doing, kissing this American soldier?

I flee, wondering why I suddenly called upon Allah, why I let Hunter kiss me, why I kissed him back, why his tongue in my mouth was not unpleasant.

I wonder, as my feet wend their way through streets and alleys, why do I feel a deep, coiling need in my belly to kiss him again?

What do I do? What is happening to me? What have I done?

EIGHT

Hunter

WHY THE FUCK DID I KISS HER? It wasn't a conscious thought or intent. It just...happened. She was there next to me, her leg brushing mine, that small point of contact burning through me with lightning awareness. Her cheek was bruised and purpling, sending white-hot lances of rage through me.

I heard the whole thing. I heard a male voice give an order, Rania's voice reply calmly, and then his again, angry. I heard a *smack*, fist on flesh. Heard her cry out. Then the jingling of a belt and an order. Gagging. Vomiting.

It's not hard to figure out what happened.

I swear to god I will kill the motherfucker. I will cut his goddamn throat and cut off his cock and shove it into his slit fucking neck.

I have to breathe deeply to calm the rage. My temper, a problem for me my whole life, is coming back with hurricane force. I've learned to control it, keep it contained, not lash out like I used to. I nearly didn't graduate high school because I spent so much time suspended for fighting. I nearly got expelled when a kid ended up in the hospital after a fight with me. Of course, he fucking started it. Jumped me in the parking lot after football practice. Beat my ass, too. Knocked me down, knocked a tooth loose, and broke my nose. He didn't expect me to get up, but I did, and I got mine. He spent a week in the hospital with a lot of broken shit.

Now this Abdul asshole is hitting Rania, and I can't see straight. Can't think straight. I shouldn't be reacting like this. She seems to be under the impression this Abdul character is some high-up general in the Iraqi army. I don't care. I'll still fucking kill him if he touches her again.

She ran after our kiss. After *she* kissed *me*. I didn't see that one coming. She was there next to me, lush and beautiful and hurting and needing comfort. Needing protection. No woman should ever be hit. No woman should ever be forced to do what she did. Something primal inside me reacted to her proximity and her pain. My lips touched hers before I knew what I was doing, and then I was lost in the soft sweetness of her lips.

Goddamn, but I'm screwed. She tasted like mint toothpaste. Felt like heaven. It was just a kiss, but it got me so hard I thought I was going to explode without even being touched. And then she pulled away, crying. I don't get why she was crying. She didn't seem to know how to kiss. She didn't respond, just let our lips touch, her whole body tensed and frozen. And then she was crying.

I think it was her first kiss. Seems impossible, but it feels true.

Then she kissed me, leaned in and took my lips with hers, and I think I did come in my pants a little. I'm still achingly hard. Painfully hard. She's gone now, running away from me, from our kiss. She's as confused as I am, if I'm any judge of her facial expressions.

I'm so hard, it hurts still. I need relief. I'd take care of it myself, but then I'd have no way to clean up. I slowly and painfully shift down to a lying position and focus on thinking of something else, anything else but Rania. I call up a memory of combat, but that only leads to remembering Rania's face above me when she first rescued me.

I owe her my life, and I refuse to let her be beaten.

My combat knife, the only part of my gear aside from my clothes that seemed to make it here with me, is lying in the corner near my feet. It takes several agonizing minutes to retrieve it. I have to keep stopping to catch my breath and let the bolts of pain lessen. It hurts so bad I could puke, but I grit my teeth and bull through it. I hide the knife under my blankets, near to hand. Next time I hear something like that happening, I'll stop it. I don't care how bad it fucking hurts. I don't care if I rip open my wounds and re-break my ribs. I won't let it happen again.

This animal fury inside me at the thought of Rania being hurt baffles me, confuses me. I don't know where it comes from, but I can't explain it away or ignore it. It's not just my temper, or my upbringing. My dad drilled into me all my life that women are to be protected. Never, ever struck. *Ever.* Women are to be cherished and taken care of. Dad held doors for Mom. He treated her like a queen. He was a difficult man, angry and disturbed and broken from his war experiences, but it never translated into violence against me or Mom.

My drive to protect Rania is something else. Something deeper, harder, fiercer. I don't dare look too closely at what it is, because that's impossible. Unworkable.

I'm exhausted from the pain now. I close my eyes and try not to picture Rania's face, try not to remember her lips. It doesn't work, though, and I pass out to an image of her bright brown eyes like melted chocolate, her red lips and her soft skin.

She kissed me.

Goddamn it.

I just need to heal enough to walk so I can sneak out of here and get back to the base. I can't deal with this. With her. With her lips on mine like a slice of sweet, hypnotic heaven, her breasts crushed against my chest, soft yet firm, her nipples pebbling. The smell of her arousal wafting up to my nose.

My cock is throbbing, rock-hard.

See? Shit. She's under my skin. She's in my head. What the *fuck* am I supposed to do? I can't kiss her again.

Can't let it happen. Certainly it can't go further. I'm not physically capable at the moment anyway, but…it wouldn't be right. It would be…a mistake. She's a prostitute. Iraqi. I'll get out of here at some point, and I'll never see her again.

Plus, she still has to work. Her tricks are putting food in my belly. Water. Bandages. Antibiotic ointment. Without her johns, I'll starve. If anyone finds out about me, I'm dead and she will be, too, or worse.

How could I sleep with her and then lie here and listen to her turn a trick? I couldn't. I would flip the hell out.

Fuck. Why am I even thinking of sleeping with her? I can't. I won't.

But goddamn, is she sexy. Tantalizing. That fine, thick, lustrous blonde hair draping across her face, her wide dark eyes blazing with so much emotion, so much I can't identify, can't fathom. Her lithe, lush body pushed close to me.

I groan and scrub my face with a sigh. My cock is tangled and bent painfully sideways. I push the blanket down past my hips and adjust myself inside my BDU pants. But then, dammit, touching myself was a mistake. I've got a mad case of blue balls going on. Kissing Rania, and then thinking about her…it's giving me a perpetual hard-on. I grasp my cock in my fist and consider again taking care of it myself.

As I'm touching myself, I get the sense of another presence. Rania stands in the doorway, watching me with a strange expression on her face.

"Shit," I say, tossing the blanket over myself quickly.

Embarrassment floods through me. I cast a hesitant glance at Rania, who is still in the doorway, staring at me. I expect her to look upset, or disgusted, or…I don't know. What I don't expect to see is her cheeks blushing, her gaze now darting around the room as if trying to forget what she saw but wanting to get another glimpse.

"I am sorry," I say in my halting, broken, poorly accented Arabic.

She shrugs, not looking at me. I want to explain, but I can't. Even if she was fluent in English, or I was in Arabic, I couldn't explain. I just wouldn't be able to get the words out. She finally shakes head as if banishing the vision and goes into the kitchen. She has a few bags of groceries in her hands, which I hadn't noticed. I want to get up take them from her, put them away for her, but I can't.

She doesn't look at me, and when her eyes do slide across the room to mine, I can't hold her gaze. I wonder if she knows it was she who gave me the hard-on?

It's subsided for now. God help me if she gets too close. It'll spring back fully erect if she so much as looks at me the wrong way. Or the right way, depending on how you look at it.

The worst part is, there will never be release. It can't happen. I have to be smart. It wouldn't be just sex, even if it did happen. I can tell. The way she gets under my skin, the way my heart hammers when she looks at me, touches me, the way I want so desperately for her to just sit and talk to me…it would be emotional, if anything happened. I'm smart enough to realize that much; now I just have to be smart enough to keep anything from happening.

I have to keep telling myself to think with my brain, not with my cock. Not with my heart.

And then she looks at me, curiosity ripe in her gaze, gaze eyes sliding down my bare chest to my crotch, covered with the blanket, and she blushes and looks hurriedly away, biting her lip.

Fuck. This is going to be difficult.

We're both extra cautious for the next few days. She doesn't sit close enough to touch, and I don't try. My hands stay on my lap, busy, fidgeting. She starts facing away from me when she has to change or clean up, and I make sure to look away.

I'm learning enough Arabic every day now that we are able to have halting conversations. They contain a lot of pantomiming and roundabout explanations of strange words, but they are conversations. We talk about neutral things. Usually words themselves, meanings and contexts and connotations. We don't know what else to talk about, I think.

Her false enthusiasm when working a john is quieter now. I hear her less. She seems to be having a harder and harder time summoning the ability to pretend. The loathing on her face takes longer to vanish.

We've started exchanging long, awkward glances. Yeah, that stage. Where I'm watching a bird on the roof

visible through the window, watching it peck and flutter, and then I feel her eyes on me and I turn to her,
and she's watching me, her expression at once hard and
curious and soft and tender and frightened. When our
gazes meet, she blushes and looks away, her expression
shuttering closed. Then I'll be watching her, wondering
what she's thinking, trying not to stare at her ass, trying
not to wish she would kneel beside me and kiss me again,
and then she'll catch me looking at her. I'll be the one to
shift my glance away, hoping my thoughts aren't visible
on my face.

Yeah, that stage.

Trouble comes later that week. She steps out for
something, leaves me with the door closed. I hear footsteps outside, think it's her, but they pass by, slow next
door where she works. A male voice calls out, then again
angrily.

My gut churns, and my instincts tell me get up, move,
hide. I grip my KA-BAR in my right fist and struggle to
my feet, gritting my teeth to keep from crying out at
the pain biting through my whole body. I can't breathe.
Fire burns in my chest, my lungs, my stomach, broken
ribs protesting my movements. A gasping, grating moan
scrapes out of my lips as I hobble and hop to the bathroom, the only place to hide in this house. I push myself
into a corner of the bathroom. Little cover, little protection, but the best I can do.

I hear the door open and footsteps in the house. The
creeping of my flesh, the prickling of my skin and the

shivers in my spine and rush of adrenaline tells me it isn't Rania in the house. I can't be found and reported. For my sake and Rania's. It's life and death.

The footsteps, stomping, dragging male boots, move around the tiny room. A smoke-roughened voice calls out, "Sabah? Are you here?"

I hold my breath. My knife is clenched in a white-knuckled fist, cutting edge up. The shivering in my belly tells me this won't end well.

The steps move closer to the bathroom, and I prepare myself. Hold my breath, hands spread, ready to pounce. Injuries are forgotten. Adrenaline masks the pain of being upright.

"Sabah?"

My first sight of him is a pair of scuffed military boots, then Iraqi military camo pants. He peers in, sees the empty shower, the toilet. My heart hammers and I want to vomit, but can't.

How can he not see me? Maybe I'll get out of this without having to kill him.

Nope. He sees me. I lunge, jab my hand in a stiff-fingered jab to his throat, silencing him. My knife flashes out and up into his stomach. Soft flesh parts easily, then bone stops the blade. He staggers back, gasping. I swipe the blade sideways across his throat, loosing a flood of blood down his front. Fuck. I'm making a mess of this. I stab out again, and this time I hit his heart, right between the ribs. Fucking lucky. That's harder to do than most people might think.

He staggers, stumbles, flops backward to the ground. I can't leave him bleeding out on the floor. Absurd panic hits me, and I wrench his body into the shower stall so he bleeds out down the drain. There's not too much blood on the floor; most of it is on him.

But what the fuck do I do with the body?

The adrenaline is wearing off, and agony is lancing through me, stealing my breath. Merely staying upright takes every ounce of stubbornness, toughness, and strength I have left. It won't last long.

"Hunter?" Rania's voice, worried, confused.

I stumble out of the bathroom, bloody knife held in a red-painted hand. Rania gasps.

"We have a problem," I say in Arabic. "A man came. Soldier. I kill him."

Rania curses softly and glances into the shower at the body. "Ahmed."

"What do we do with—" I can't think of the word for *body*, "…the dead man?"

Collapsing against the wall, Rania runs her fingers through her loose blonde hair, hissing through her teeth. "I do not know." She fixes me with a confused glare. "What was he doing here?"

I'm guessing at a lot of her meaning. I understand some words, and can infer the rest from context.

I shrug. "Looking for you. For Sabah. Went to other door first, then here. He sees me…I am dead. He sees me, bad for you. Bad for me. So…he dies."

I hate how I sound. I'm not a verbally eloquent man, but I hate knowing my words are bumbled and garbled. She has to think to understand a lot of what I say.

And that's all I have. I collapse forward, powerless to stop my fall. I have time to think as I topple, *This is gonna hurt*. It does, like a bitch. I hit the ground on my shoulder and my face. I know better than to try to catch myself on my hands or wrists, with the way my shoulders are. My shrapnel-wounded side takes the brunt of the fall, along with my already-broken ribs. I think they get re-fractured. Lances of agony shoot through me, and I can't breathe for the pain. Can't even gasp. I drag a long, stuttering breath in, face in the dirt, nostrils clogged with dirt, eyes stinging with dirt. The knife is still clutched in my fist, and I bear down with all my force, until the handle creaks. I cough, spewing dirt.

Rania is beside me, rolling me to my back, clearing my eyes first, my nose, my lips. Her fingers are tender and gentle, cleaning each individual speck with the pad of her index finger. Her eyes are huge, softly concerned as she cleans the dirt from my face. The sharp contours of her lovely face are brought into high relief by the afternoon sun blazing through the window, setting behind the roof of the building opposite.

I hate that my eyes stray to her breasts, swaying as she leans over me. I slide my eyes closed, try to focus on the pain rather than how gorgeous she is, how badly my fingers want to slip under her shirt to touch the silk of her skin. How badly I want to pull her down for another kiss.

Such awful timing. There's a dead man in the bathroom, and I'm trying not to kiss Rania.

What the fuck is wrong with you, Hunter?

When I open my eyes, she's sitting cross-legged next to me, watching me, her expression full of emotions I recognize within myself. Her hand rests on my stomach, at the exact midline between the intimacy of my chest and the erogenous zone lower down. Moments pass and our locked eyes search each other, wavering, flitting from side to side. We're each daring the other to make the first move, look away, move away, or do it. Move closer. Lean in.

A warm trickle alerts me that my thigh is bleeding. I don't care.

She smells like woman: sweat, arousal, deodorant. Her hand shakes on my stomach. She's breathing deeply, steadily, as if to prevent hyperventilation. Her nostrils flare with each breath, her full lips pursing and relaxing, trembling with emotions contained. Her breasts swell and shrink, drawing my gaze. Her skirt— she always wears a skirt, a little too short, marking her profession in this land of extreme modesty—has slipped up her thighs, her other hand casually covering herself. Her legs are endless, miles of shadows and skin pulling my hand toward them.

I'm trying hard as hell to resist her hypnotic sway over me. I'm Odysseus tied to the mast, drawn by the deadly song of the sirens. Except the bonds restraining me are weak and coming loose, intangible ropes that are only my own crumbling self-control. Logic is dead against the power of her beauty. Knowledge of right and wrong is meaningless in the memory of her lips scouring mine.

Fuck.

I kiss her. I move slowly, as if approaching a skittish wild animal, one hand stretching up to pull her down. Fear widens her already-round brown eyes. Her trembling spreads to her whole body, but she doesn't pull away.

My cracked, chapped lips meet her soft, warm, wet mouth, and heaven explodes through me. My eyes shut on their own, weighed down by the glory of her kiss. She is so hesitant, so careful and restrained. I don't dare touch her. Don't dare.

A kiss, a kiss, just a kiss. But god, so incredible. I'm electrified, wired, hardened by the taste of her, the feel of her. Intoxicated by her. I'm shaking all over from the effort to keep my hands to myself, to keep the kiss chaste. It's an impossible losing battle.

Then her hand leaves her lap and touches my face, palm against cheek, fingers curling in the hair around my ear. Something inside me swells to impossible proportions at the tenderness in that gesture, burgeoning until I could burst, break open, weep, or shout for joy. A simple, innocent touch, but so meaningful. This woman who sells touch, who must find men to be such nasty creatures, this woman who has seen the worst in the monsters that are men, she's kissing and touching me.

She shouldn't. I'm no better. I've killed. With gun, with knife. I've broken men with my bare hands. I've sundered families with my rifle. I've done such awful things. And I desire her, want her. I need her, carnally.

She needs Prince Charming to carry her away from this hell of dust and sin and war, and I'm not him.

But still her lips move on mine, her tongue sweeps my teeth and moves to tangle with mine, her hands clutch my face to draw me closer, to deepen the kiss. My control over my hands is shredded by the fervor of her kiss, and I find myself wrapping my hands around her waist, just her waist, above her hips and beneath her ribs. She's so small, so delicate, that my hands nearly span her waist. And now her hand descends from my face to my shoulder, inches from the wound.

I wince at the sting of pain, and she pulls away, breaking the magic. Her eyes search me, and I don't try to hide what I'm feeling. It's the only way I can communicate what I'm feeling, through my eyes. I can't help but wonder what she sees. I know what I'm feeling, but I don't know how that translates, how she interprets it.

Her palm still cups my cheek, no longer trembling. Her mouth opens as if to speak but then shuts again, and she's gone, suddenly gone, darting out the door, and I'm left gasping for breath, confused mentally and emotionally. I'm at once glad for her absence so I can think about what's going on, and missing her presence.

What the hell just happened?

Something shifted between Rania and me during that kiss, and I don't know what exactly it was, or what it means, but I know we can't go back.

NINE
Rania

AGAIN. I KISSED HIM AGAIN. He kissed me, and I returned it. Let him touch me. Touched him back. What is happening to me? What am I doing? Why did I save him? Why did I pluck the shards of metal from his body and bandage his wounds and feed him my food?

Why is he in my heart? His lips are soft and strong, his hands gentle but powerful. I have blood on my shirt from his hand. My lips tingle from his kiss. My body hums from his hands on my waist.

My heart aches, throbs, not from a hollowness this time or from pain, but with an odd, terrifying fullness. Oh, yes. I am beginning to feel him inside me, in my heart and my soul, and this is not good. This is the start of needing someone. Already I miss him, and I most definitely should not.

I push the trouble and the mystery of Hunter from my mind and attempt to focus on the more pressing problem: the corpse of Ahmed. Hunter was right to kill him. I know Ahmed well enough to know he would not have hesitated to kill Hunter without pausing to ask any questions. And then he would have gone straight to Abdul and told him I have an American in my house.

But what do I do with the body? I am not strong enough to dispose of it myself, and Hunter can barely stand up. I do not know how he even managed to do what he did. He should not have been able to, but he did. He defended my home. Me. Himself. Us.

I banish that notion. There is no us.

An idea strikes me. Masjid. He is one of my stranger and more frightening clients. He seldom speaks, shows up sporadically. I do not know what he does, but I know he is dangerous, not to be trifled with. I also know he has no love for the troubles of government and politics. He is a criminal of some sort, I think. A smuggler, maybe. It does not matter who or what he is. What matters is I believe with the right incentive he will dispose of the body without asking questions. The trick is to get the body to Masjid without him seeing Hunter.

When Masjid first came to me seeking time with me, he gave me a pager number where I can contact him to tell him I am available. I use a phone at a store not far from where I live, entering the code Masjid gave me, and then return home.

Hunter is waiting, stoic as always. I do not know how he tolerates the boredom. I have no time or inclination for entertainment. Survival is the only part of my day. I remind myself to find something for him to do while I'm gone, which is often.

I sit next to him and think about how to explain my plan.

"You must move," I say. "I have a plan, but you must not be seen."

"Where?" he asks. We're both speaking Arabic, as he speaks my language well enough to be understood by now.

I point at the wall, meaning the mosque next door. His gaze hardens, darkens.

I know why he is angry, and I can do nothing about it. "There is a room, separate," I say. "I will help you."

I rise and extend my hand to him. He watches me for several breaths, and then takes my hand in his, bracing himself against the wall with his back, powering upward with the strength of his good leg. He doesn't use my hand at all until he needs to acquire his balance. When he is ready, I put my shoulder under his and help him hobble to the doorway, and then I peer out. I see no one, so we move. Hunter grasps the danger and moves as quickly as he can, using his wounded leg more than he should. He is clenching his teeth so hard I can hear them grinding in his mouth. Sweat pours down his face and his entire body trembles, but he doesn't make a sound other than his harsh breathing.

The mosque is dark inside, lit by a sliver of light from the doorway, relatively cool compared to the oppressive heat outside. The interior is blackened, crumbling in spots. A lance of sunlight shines down on a corner, illuminating the thin, stained, blue-and-white striped mattress where I do my work. There are thick white candles arrayed along the wall and to either side, illumination for nighttime clients. There is a box of condoms, a jug of water, and nothing else. Hunter stops, staring down at the mattress. His face is shadowed, so I cannot see his expression, but I can feel the displeasure radiating from him.

He glances at me, then away, heaving a deep sigh. "Where?" he asks.

I point at a thin line of darker shadows marking the doorway to the other room. I never go there, for I have no reason to, but I know it is there. My parents did not often go to the mosque, except for holy days. The room where Hunter will hide is pitch black, smelling still of charred wood, smoke, and something else, darker, sickly sweet and hauntingly familiar that I cannot place.

Hunter stops in the entrance and sniffs. "Death," he says. "Death was here. I smell it."

Now I know what that scent is. I smelled it when Aunt Maida died. I have smelled it when I come across dead bodies after a bomb has gone off. It is the smell of death, as Hunter said. I am supposed to be supporting him, but somehow, he is comforting me. I see those who have died flashing before me like visible ghosts.

Hassan, staring at me from the middle of the road as he bleeds, bullets passing between us. Mama. Papa. Aunt Maida. Uncle Ahmed. So many others, nameless, faceless. All dead.

Hunter balances with one hand on the wall, curls his arm around my waist, and pulls me into his chest. He does not say anything. He does not need to. He, too, has seen death. Frequently enough to know it when he smells it.

Why does being held by this man give me such comfort? It should not. He should not. I should be afraid of him, run away from him. I should have left him to die. But here I am, hiding him. Holding him. Being held. Comforted. Protected.

I pull myself from his arms, mentally cursing myself for how empty I feel when I am not near him.

"You must sit," I say. "No matter what you might hear, do not make yourself known."

There is a long pause while he translates my words for himself. "If you are hurt, I will come," he says. I hear his back sliding down against the wall, and then his hand reaches out to curl around my ankle. "Be safe. Please."

I want to do nothing so much as crouch beside him and take his stubble-roughened face in my hands and kiss him until neither of us can breathe. I do not. I nod, then realize he cannot see the gesture.

"I will be safe," I say, then leave before my traitorous desires get the best of me.

Masjid will be here soon.

Masjid is tall and thin and dark. He reminds me of a knife. His posture is rigid, his face narrow, his prominent, hooked nose and pointed chin lending to the sharpness of his features. He has pockmarks in his skin around his forehead and on his right cheek. His eyes are small and nearly black, glittering with intelligence and malice. He does not wear a *keffiyeh*, normally. His beard is thick and shot through with gray. When he comes to me, he is reserved and business-like, not rough or violent, but not kind, either. I think for Masjid, sex is merely a tactic to help him focus, so he does not become distracted when working.

He is ghost-like, appearing seemingly at will, out of thin air. I am standing outside the mosque, waiting for him. I glance down the street in one direction, and when I look back the other way, he is there, a few feet away, hands in the pockets of his loose khaki pants.

"What is it, Sabah? I am busy." His voice is quiet and laced with latent threat.

One does not idly waste Masjid's time. I am not truly afraid of much, but I am terrified of Masjid. He has never shown anything but professional detachment, yet still, I somehow intrinsically understand that he could and would kill me without so much as blinking, if I were to anger him.

"I apologize, Masjid, but I have a problem, and I am hoping you will help me."

"I am not a djinn, Sabah, that you can summon me to solve your problems." His eyes narrow and his hand fidgets in his pocket.

I swallow my nerves and try not to let my fear show. "I know. I would not have called you if I had any other choice. I know you are busy."

He examines me with his hard, dark eyes. "Very well. I will see what I can do to help you. But this is business, yes? I will expect…payment."

"Of course." I allow myself three deep breaths to calm my hammering heart, and then move toward my home, gesturing for Masjid to follow.

I show him Ahmed's corpse, cooling and stiffening in the shower, still oozing thick, dark blood. Masjid examines the body with the ease of one used to such gruesome sights. He takes a pen from his pocket and probes the knife wounds at his throat, stomach, and chest.

He stands up and stares down at me. "You did not kill this man. Whoever did this knew his business." I say nothing, do nothing. I only wait. "Ahmed was a pig. No one will mourn his passing, although his absence will be noted."

"Yes," I say. "I need him gone. Please. I cannot afford the questions."

Masjid glances back at the body, then wipes the end of his pen on his shirt before pocketing it once again. "My gut tells me you are involved in something I do not want anything to do with. But I will help you." He pauses, eyeing me thoughtfully. "I will help you because you are a good girl. You were not meant to be a whore, Sabah. But you are, and a good one."

"Thank you, Masjid."

"I will expect—"

"I know," I interrupt. "I know what your payment will be."

He nods. "Good. I had better take care of this now. If your friend…Abdul—" the inflection in his voice tells me he knows exactly who Abdul really is, "—gets wind of this, it will not go well for you." He waves toward the door. "Go shopping or something. Come back in an hour."

When I come back, Masjid has removed the body and cleaned away any traces of blood. Now comes the payment. Masjid follows me to the mosque, pausing in the street to dump water from a bottle onto his hands, scrubbing them together. He produces a small bottle of clear, alcohol-smelling liquid, which he wipes on his hands, then gestures into the mosque.

He looks around carefully, even though he has been here a hundred times before. Can he know Hunter is mere feet away? I force emptiness onto my face, and then a seductive smile. I move toward Masjid, reaching for his belt. I have to distract him.

He bats my hand away. "Save the theatrics, Sabah. It is business. Just lie down."

I swallow, trying to wet my parched throat, then do what he says. His eyes search the shadows even as he moves above me. I stare at the ceiling over his shoulder, not bothering to pretend. He is done soon, and I lie in place, waiting for him to leave.

He pauses in the doorway of the mosque, backlit by the brilliant afternoon sun. "Be careful, Sabah. What you do is dangerous, and not just for you." And then he is gone.

I am left wondering how much he knows, and what he will do about it. The answers are not pleasant.

TEN

Hunter

THE DARKNESS OF THIS DANK LITTLE ROOM IS OPPRES-
SIVE. The stench of death is overpowering. Time ceases
to pass. I don't dare move from the corner, barely dare
to breathe. I don't know what Rania has planned, but I
can't do anything to help her. Merely breathing is excruciating. If I shift positions, searing pain spreads through
every inch of my body. I was starting to heal, starting to
have some semblance of mobility, and now it's gone. I'm
back to feeling as bad as the day I was first wounded.
Fucking sucks. But at least I know my presence is still a
secret.

And then, suddenly, I'm not alone. I smell him first.
Blood, harsh cleaner, sweat. I grip my KA-BAR in my
fist and tense. I have enough strength for one lunge,
and I have to get it right. I can't see anything, not even

shapes within shadows. I sense him nearby, gather my legs beneath me, snake-slow motions.

His voice is a low rasp. "I would not do that, my friend." Thickly accented English. "Why are you here?"

I don't know what to say. "Sabah, she—"

"You killed Ahmed?"

"Yes."

"Why?"

I hesitate, knowing my answer holds my life or death. "To protect myself. To protect Sabah." I'm careful to use her assumed name.

"Can you protect her from you?" His voice is casual, but I can sense the threat.

"I'm trying."

"Try harder." A shuffled footstep, done on purpose so I know he's leaving. "Abdul, he will kill her soon. He is evil. A devil in man's flesh. He hungers for things that no man should. She will refuse, and he will kill her. I let you live so you can stop him."

"I will."

"Yes, you will. Or I will make your death slow." I don't even feel him move, but suddenly there's a sharp point digging into my chest. My knife meets flesh, a return threat so he knows I'm not completely helpless; he doesn't flinch, and neither do I. "She is not for you, American. Don't get any ideas."

And then he's really gone. I don't sense or smell him anymore. An unknowable amount of time later, I hear footsteps and voices. Hers and his. He says something I don't catch, and then something about it being business, tells her to lie down. My stomach clenches, and my fist trembles around my knife. I know what's about to happen, and I want to fucking die so I don't have to listen.

I focus on breathing, slow, shallow breaths, each one a wealth of agony. I hear cloth rustling, the slap of flesh against flesh, male grunts, and then an extended groan of release. I nearly vomit. I have to clench my teeth against the bitter bile. Hate burns in my chest. I could kill everyone in this moment. Every fucking person in the world except Sabah. I even hate her for a brief moment, for letting this happen. For being a whore. For getting inside my walls and into my heart, where I have to care about her. I don't want to care. I don't want to feel this burning hell of jealousy and hatred.

He leaves, saying something about danger. I'm too upset to be able to translate.

I feel her, smell her. "Are you okay, Hunter?" she asks.

"No."

Her hands touch my shoulder, search me by feel. "Are you hurt?"

"No." I push her hands away. "Ahmed is gone?"

"Yes." She takes my hands in hers and tugs.

I let her help me to my feet, hissing in pain. We laboriously move back to her house, and again I have to hobble quickly to minimize my exposure in the street. When I'm lying down again, I'm sweating profusely, gasping for breath, fists clenched as pain throbs through me. She sits a few feet away, out of reach, watching me.

I wave a hand toward the mosque. "Him, *that*, was to pay?"

She nods, eyes downcast. A thousand different things flit through my head, but I can't say any of them. I don't think she wants to hear them, anyway.

I close my eyes, trying to make it clear I have nothing to say. I hear her move, and then her hand touches my chest.

"What you are thinking?" she asks, in halting English. "I feel your words. Speak them."

She feels my words. Strangely, I know what she means. I shake my head. "Too much. No good," I speak in Arabic. The more I use it, the better I speak it.

"Say." She touches my chin, rubbing her thumb along my jaw. The gesture makes something in my heart twinge, balloon, and burst.

"Fuck," I mutter in English. Then, in Arabic, "I hate…" I gesture at the mosque, "…*that*. What you do."

She takes her hand back, examines her fingernails. "I do, too." She shrugs. "No choice. That, or starve. You, too."

"I know." I scrape a series of lines in the dirt with my finger. "I will go soon."

I look down at what my finger drew in the dirt: *RANIA*. I wipe it away roughly.

She glances up sharply at my words. "No. You die." She switches to Arabic. "If you leave me now, you will die. You are not well enough to leave. You cannot even walk on your own."

"If not for me, you wouldn't have had to do that," I say in English, knowing she won't catch it all and not caring. "If not for me…" There are too many ways I could finish that statement, and I say none of them.

"If not for you, I would be alone." She speaks slowly in Arabic, so I can translate. "I was alone for so long. Now, you are here, and I'm not alone. I like not being alone."

She looks down, as if ashamed of her admission.

"We are different," I say in Arabic. "Too different."

"I am an Iraqi whore. You are an American soldier. I know. But…still. Should be…is…they are different things."

Ain't that the fucking truth. *Should be* and *is* are completely different things.

I can't help it. I can't help kissing her. I know what just happened next door and disgust rifles through me, but it's subsumed beneath the tsunami of need for her. There is so much pain in her eyes, raw and potent, and I just want to erase it. Fuck, she tastes good. She feels good. She's like a drug whirling through my system, banishing intentions and logic. All that's left is desire. My hands hunger for her skin, her silken flesh. My palm finds the hem of her shirt and brushes it up to cup her waist near her back. My fingers skim up her spine, trace the knobs and ridges to the bumps of her shoulder blades, protruding as she kneels above me, her hands on either side of my face, knees next to my chest. Her hair drifts to fall around us, a golden waterfall shimmering in the early evening light.

She tenses at my touch at first, then relaxes and· lets my hand roam her back. When our kiss breaks, she leans back to sit with her legs folded beneath her.

"I know what you want," she says, sounding resigned. "I will give it to you. Just be still."

She unbuttons the first two buttons of my fly before I have the courage to stop her. "No, Rania. You don't know what I want."

She struggles against my grip on her wrists. "Yes, I do. You are man. I am woman. I know." Her English is fractured by emotion, but clear.

"It's not like that." I don't let go of her wrists. "Do you kiss them?" I ask, gesturing at the mosque.

She flinches at my words. "No. *Never.*"

"Do they kiss you?"

"No." She looks confused. "Why are you—"

"I'm not them. I'm not one of them. I don't want you like they do."

Her eyes search mine, brown shining with tears. "Then what are you want with me?" She shakes her head, realizing her grammatical gaffe, and switches to Arabic again. "What do you want with me? I do not...I do not know anything else. This is what I know."

I've loosed my grip, and she breaks free to undo the third button. I'm hard at the thought of her touching me, but I can't allow myself let her. I take her wrists in my hands again and tug her down to me. She resists, then complies. I arrange her so she's laying her head on my chest, one arm around her shoulders, the other keeping her hands pinioned. Her weight on my chest fucking hurts like hell, but I ignore it. She feels natural, cradled here in my arms. She's tense but slowly relaxing.

"There's more, Rania," I say in Arabic. "More than just sex."

"Not for me."

"There is caring. There is…" I search for the right words in her language, "…there is wanting, but with the heart and also the body."

"Wanting with the heart? Is this not love?" she says in English.

We go back and forth like this in each other's language, trying out the words we know, running out and switching to our own.

"It can be. It doesn't have to be."

A long silence, full of unspoken thoughts.

"Is it, for you?" she asks. "Is it love? Your wanting with the heart? For me?"

This is a terrifying, dangerous conversation. We've been avoiding this for days. I've lost track of how long I've been here with her. Days run together, nights run together. Has it been weeks? Most likely.

We shouldn't be talking like this. How can we be speaking of sex and love like it could ever be anything, go anywhere? This is a morbid fantasy. If I survive, I'll end up leaving her to go back to Camp Fallujah or Ramadi, or wherever the hell, and then home. The States. I'll go back to jumping out of seven-tons and tossing candy bars to the locals. IEDs and car bombs and ambushes in the wavering, suffocating heat.

She'll keep turning tricks to feed herself. All this will be a dream. Good dream, bad dream. Just a dream.

If I let anything happen, it'll be heartbreak. I'm already broken from Lani's betrayal. Love is a joke. I loved Lani, and she fucked around on me. Fucked me over. How can I even pretend anything could happen between Rania and me? It's complete horseshit. I don't love her. She's a sexy-as-hell local girl. Off-limits. Not for me. I'm a danger to her, and she to me.

And she's right: All I want is to sleep with her. Fuck her. That's what it would be, right? Just fucking?

Yeah, right. I can't fool myself. It would be more. She saved my life. She's gone through hell keeping me fed and bandaged and infection-free.

I've kissed her. I'm fucking cuddling with her right now. Lani never wanted me to hold her like this. She'd leave the bed to clean up and then lie down away from me. She never just lay in my arms like this.

I know I'm upset by how much the word "fuck" is going through my head. Lani always claimed her barometer for my mood was how often I dropped the F-bomb.

"Hunter? Is it?"

I realize I never answered her. She cranes her neck to look at me. Her wide brown eyes are vulnerable, soft, pleading. I don't know if she's pleading with me to say yes or no. She deserves the truth, though.

"I don't know, Rania. Maybe. Yes."

"Maybe? Maybe yes? Or yes? Which is it?"

I can't look at her anymore. Her eyes pull too much from me, incite too many emotions I don't know how to deal with. "I don't know, Rania." I find myself stroking her hair, smoothing the long white-gold locks beneath my fingers. "If I did, what of it? What does it mean for you?" I'm talking in English.

She doesn't answer for a long time. "I do not know. I want you to say yes, but also to say no." Her hands are free now and resting on me, one tracing the gap between ribs, the other on my stomach. "I have never known anything but that," she says, gesturing at the mosque.

"Never?"

She shakes her head. "I was…fourteen, I think. When I first sold myself. It wasn't for money then. It was for food. I was starving. So near to dying of hunger."

I can't fathom what she's telling me. She's twenty-three or twenty-four, which would mean she's been a prostitute more than ten years, at least. More like eleven or twelve. Insanity. I can't make it make sense in my head. How has she avoided pregnancy and disease all this time? Maybe she hasn't.

"I'm sorry," I say.

She shrinks away from me. "Why? What have you done?"

"No. For…what you have been through."

"Oh." She shrugs. "I have survived. It is enough."

"Have you ever been happy?" I ask.

She looks at me as if I've sprouted horns. Like I've suggested an irrelevant and foreign concept. "Happy? I don't know. Maybe when I was a girl. Before the war. Before Mama and Papa were killed. Before the other American."

"The other American?"

She doesn't answer for a long time. When she does, it's in quiet, slow Arabic. "When I was a girl, during the first war with the Americans and the other soldiers, my brother and I were hiding. An American came. Hassan had a gun. He was only protecting me, but the American, he wasn't a soldier. He was a picture-taker. But he had a gun, a pistol." She's going back and forth between English and Arabic as she tells the story. "Hassan shot him, and missed. He shot back and hit my brother. I…picked up the gun and killed him. The American. Hassan ran away to be a soldier, and then my aunt died, so I had no one. I managed for a while to live. And then there was no food, no money, no work. I begged a soldier for food, and he gave it to me. And then he made me have sex with him."

"He raped you?" I ask this in English.

"No. Not…not really. He told me he would only give me the food unless I agreed to let him have sex with me. I had not eaten in days. I was so hungry…"

She trails off, and I feel wetness seeping through the thin fabric of my wife-beater tank top. It's a non-reg piece of gear, and I was busted several times for wearing it. She's crying into my shirt.

Crying for her lost childhood.

"Shitty choice," I say in English.

She doesn't answer, and I just hold her. Let her cry for a long, long time. Eventually she stands up and goes to the bathroom, readies herself. I look away. Watching her get ready has turned into a ritual. I watch her put on the uniform, the makeup, the blank face, the hard eyes, the seductive smile. I hate it. She becomes Sabah, and Rania, the kind, vulnerable girl I know is gone.

"Don't go," I say.

She stares down at me, all Sabah now. "I must. Abdul is coming."

I'm confused. I thought he came during the afternoon. It's nearly dark outside now.

She sees my confusion. "He sent word. He is coming now, not tomorrow."

I'm never sure how she arranges her appointments. It's clear she has a client list that comes to her. She doesn't work the streets. She has a number of regular johns who visit her, and they seem to always just show up, but she knows when to expect them. She doesn't have a phone that I've seen, or a computer, or anything. But still she knows. It's a mystery to me.

"He hurts you," I say.

"He can. He is powerful." She shrugs, seeming fearless. I see the fear lurking behind her eyes, though.

She leaves then, and my gut churns. My instincts are telling me something bad is about to happen.

I prepare myself for pain.

I prepare myself to kill.

ELEVEN

Rania

Terror hounds my every heartbeat as I wait for Abdul. He will hurt me again. Make me do something awful. I sit on the mattress and wait. I will not welcome him. Will not pretend or play games with him. He is a monster, and all I can do is try to survive him.

He comes. As he swaggers through the door belly first, his hard beady pig eyes rake over me, going first to my breasts.

"What, no kiss for your lover?" he asks, laughing as if he has told an uproarious joke.

I do not answer. Just wait, staring at him. He licks his lips, then draws off his belt with the gun holster, pulls the gun out of the leather and holds it at his side. His demeanor changes, and I know it has begun.

"On your knees, whore."

I move to my knees, facing him, hands resting on my thighs.

"Take your clothes off. All of them."

I strip, and then kneel naked in front of him. My legs shake, and my skin is clammy, cold, and sweating all at once. My heart is a mad drum in my chest, and I could vomit, if I did not know it would anger Abdul. This is about survival, I remind myself. Not about pride.

"On your knees, whore."

"I am," I say, not arguing, but calmly pointing out facts.

"No! Like a dog. Like the bitch dog you are. Face away from me."

I swallow hard and move to comply, shaking so badly I can barely move. I have done many vile things as a prostitute. I have faced fear. I have been beaten, threatened, injured. Forced abortions. Raped.

But this, what Abdul is doing to me…this is different. Little causes me true terror anymore. But now, my knees digging through the thin mattress into the hard ground, elbows and arms barely able to support my weight for the trembling, now I know terror as never before.

I know he will push me to a certain place, and then I will refuse, and he will kill me. And then it will be over.

I hear him behind him. I hear the signal, the jangling belt, and my mouth goes dry. I hang my head, arch my shoulders and my back, preparing for his brutal entrance. Instead, he slaps my backside so hard I cannot help but yelp in pain.

Again and again, he slaps my backside, until I scramble away.

"Get on your knees, whore!" he screams. "I'm not done with you."

I force myself back into position, fighting tears of pain. And now he slaps the other side of my bottom, again and again, until my backside is stinging, burning as if on fire.

He laughs. "Look at you, whore. Your little ass is red. You are ready." He caresses my backside, absurdly gentle after his abuse. "I am going to fuck you in the ass, whore. You are going to like it. Do you understand?"

I feel the cold metal barrel of his pistol against the back of my head. I cannot move. I know this is it. That is my one hard line. I would not let any man do that to me. I have been beaten for it before, but I have always refused. And I will refuse now.

It takes several tries to swallow enough saliva that I can speak. "No." It is a small, fierce whisper.

"What did you say?" Abdul's voice is low and deadly.

"I said no." My voice is louder now. I am ready for death. "You will not do that. I will let you do whatever else you want. I will let you fuck me. I will suck you off. I will not fight you. But you will not touch me there."

I am still on my hands and knees, I realize, and I move to turn and face him. He is too quick. He grabs my hair by the root and jerks it, hard. I scream. He jabs the top of my head with the butt of his pistol, brutally hard. I see stars, and a knife of pain shoots through my head. Something hot and wet trickles down my scalp and across my forehead.

"Let go!" I scream. I am committed to fighting him now.

He jerks my hair again, and I am lifted off the ground. His knee gouges into my spine, and I am left breathless. His pistol butt jabs into my side, my kidney, and now I cannot even stay upright for the blinding agony, cannot even breathe to cry.

He forces me down to all fours, his hand still fisted in my hair. His knees shove my legs apart, and now I feel his manhood at the crease of my backside. Panic flares through me, spurring me to writhe and flop against his grip, shrieking, screaming. I kick backward, and my bare foot meets soft flesh. He roars and his grip on my hair loosens, but not enough to let me get free. He jabs his fist into my kidney again, and the pain stills me against my will. Something hard and hot pokes at my backside, but does not penetrate, stuttering and stabbing, nearly ripping the delicate flesh there. I am screaming as best I can despite the pain stealing my breath, fighting. Fighting.

I wish, fleetingly, that Hunter could save me, but he cannot.

Then Abdul is gone, and he is yelling, roaring. I flop to my back, and through the haze of tears see Abdul backing away, clutching his hand. I scramble backward away from Abdul, see something wet and red sluicing between his fingers. Sticky hot blood drenches my back and my hair. There are pink things on the ground at his feet. Fingers, dismembered. Abdul is screaming. His pants are around his ankles, and he is struggling to get free of them so he can move to fight.

Hunter stands lit by the dim candle flames. His face is a mask of rage, blood-spattered. His knife is held in one fist, low near his waist. Blood drips from the blade onto the tile floor with a slow *pit-pit-pit* sound. Except for that, silence reigns, now that Abdul has stopped screaming.

The men face off. It is almost comical, Abdul being naked from the waist down, but it is not. The gun lies on the floor, out of reach. I cannot move, frozen by the violence. There is no warning. Hunter is standing, and then he impacts with Abdul, swifter than a striking snake. I hear the crunch of bodies colliding, and Abdul stumbles backward, bleeding from the stomach.

I want to be sick, but even that reflex is frozen.

Hunter is not trying to make this quick. Abdul is upright, clutching his stomach with his fingerless right hand. He bleeds, bleeds. He is mortally wounded, I think, but Hunter is not done. He has not said a word.

Hunter lunges again, and I see the telltale wince flash across his face that tells me he is still feeling the pain, but he is refusing to let it stop him or slow him. The knife flashes across Abdul's chest, and the general stumbles backward farther yet. Hunter's lip curls in disgust and contempt.

He crosses the intervening space and knocks Abdul to the ground with a brutally hard blow. Hunter stands over him, staring down with a grin of victory, but then he sways, blanching, pale and dizzy, hobbles backward to retain his balance. He does not see Abdul's hand stretching, reaching, grasping the pistol. I scream a warning, but it is too late. The pistol cracks with a flash of fire, and Hunter grunts, spins aside, and falls.

Someone is screaming…me, I think. Abdul rolls away, grabs his pants and stumbles away, dripping blood.

He will not die, but he is very badly hurt and will not be back soon, I think. It is not an end to my troubles with Abdul, but it is a reprieve, for now. I let him go and scramble to Hunter's side. The bullet hit him in the side, and I know enough to realize this is more serious than all his other wounds. An organ may have been hit, or something. I do not know. I only know it is a serious wound.

I am crying, pressing my hand to the crimson-seeping hole. Hunter reaches with his hand and tugs weakly at my shirt, which lies near his hand, tries to press it to his wound, but then faints. I am bawling, crushing the shirt to his side.

I do not know what to do.

I shake him, shake him. He wakes up.

"What do I do, Hunter?" I beg him.

"Need…a doctor. Surgeon. Someone." I understand his English, thank Allah.

There I go again, calling on Allah, in whom I have not believed since I was girl.

I pull on my skirt, dart next door for a shirt to cover myself, then run for the clinic where I get my birth control and disease checkups. It is several blocks away, but I make it in record time. I have blood on my hands.

The doctor whom I know best, a man named Hussein, is on duty. "Sabah! What happened to you? Are you hurt?"

I shake my head. "No, not me. A—a friend. Please, come with me. He needs help."

Hussein eyes me warily. "What are you involving me in?"

"Doctor, please. You know me. I have been coming to you for years. Please help my friend. Please."

Hussein's expression changes, and I know this will not be free. I usually pay Hussein with money, but I know by the lecherous gleam in his eye that he will claim more than *dinar*, this time. He will claim me.

"You will get what you want, Doctor Hussein. But please, come."

He nods, once. "Very well, Sabah. Let me get my bag."

I lead him to the mosque, but stop him before we go in. "Doctor, before you see my friend, I must ask…please, just keep this between you and me. It is important."

Hussein's eyes narrow. "Something tells me I will not like this. But I am here, and I took the Hippocratic oath."

"The what?"

He shook his head. "An oath to help those who need help. But I will not endanger myself or my family, Sabah." I nod and lead Hussein into the mosque. He halts in his tracks when he sees Hunter. "An American? Are you mad, Sabah?"

I cannot answer, except for a whispered, "Please."

Hussein searches my face. "Allah help me, Sabah. You *are* mad. You love him."

I shake my head, but I am not sure if I am denying what he is saying, or refusing to answer. Hussein only blows a gentle sigh between thick, fleshy lips, scratches his thick beard, and then kneels next to Hunter. He pushes Hunter's shirt up past the wound, examining it before doing anything. He probes the wound with his finger, then pulls Hunter up to look at his back.

"Well, it went straight through, so there is no bullet to extract. Without any equipment, I cannot say if the bullet hit anything important, but judging by the placement, I would say your...friend, should be okay, eventually. Of course, he has lost a lot of blood already, and he has a number of other wounds." He glances at me. "Your American is very resilient."

He examines Hunter's other wounds, cleans and re-bandages them as well as the new one, then digs in his bag. "These wounds on his leg are growing infected. He will need antibiotics."

"Do you have them?" I ask.

Hussein glances at me, a smirk touching his lips. "Yes, but they are expensive."

I sigh. "I understand."

Hunter, whom I thought was unconscious, grabs Hussein's wrist. Hussein pales and tries to pull away, but I know well the power in Hunter's grip, even weakened.

"No," Hunter says in Arabic. "Not that. Leave me to be sick, but do not ask that of her."

"Hunter, please," I say in English, "you will die without the medication."

Hunter glares at me. "No. No more. Not because of me."

Hussein stands up and gestures for me to follow him outside. "This is madness, Sabah," he says. "If that infection is not stopped now, he could die. Or lose the leg."

"I know," I say. "He…does not like what I do."

"What are you going to do?"

"Your price has not changed?"

Hussein shakes his head. "You know it has not."

"Fine. I will not just let him die. Come." I gesture at the door to my house.

Hunter will be angry with me, I know this. My stomach turns at what I am about to do, but it must be done.

Hussein demands much of me before he considers the debt paid.

He helps me carry Hunter back next door to my home.

Hunter pretends to be unconscious until Hussein leaves, and then he levels a glare at me that makes me shrink in fear.

"You did it anyway." It is not question.

"Yes," I answer. "I did it for you."

Hunter is quiet for a long time, staring at me. I hand him the bottle of pills Hussein gave me before he left.

"Take them," I say. "It is done. Not taking them would be stupid."

He takes one with a swallow of water. I look down at my hands, still covered in blood.

"Hunter, I...thank you. For saving me from Abdul."

"I had to stop it. I heard him hit you. I heard you scream. I had to..." He shakes his head and trails off, rage contorting his face. "Are you okay? Did he—did he hurt you?"

He is worried about me? After getting shot, he is concerned for me? I shake my head. "No. A few slaps. I am fine."

Hunter reaches out to wipe away something from the side of my face. "You're bleeding."

I wipe the blood away. "Nothing. It is nothing. Stop worrying about me."

He does not look at me when he speaks next. "I can't stop worrying about you."

I have no answer for that.

I turn away and take a long, frigid shower, scrub my body and my hair furiously until my skin stings from the soap, until every inch of me is cleansed, purified. I am shivering from the icy water when I am done.

Night falls. I lie down in my bed, turn on my side. Hunter's eyes meet mine, his face silver in the dim starlight. We do not speak. I remember the warm comfort of lying in Hunter's arms and wish I could feel it again. I am so cold. So afraid.

I should not tempt myself.

I watch Hunter sleep for too long, trying keep myself in my own bed by force of will.

It is not working.

TWELVE

Hunter

Something soft gently nestles against my unin-jured side, rousing me from a light sleep. I breathe in, smell clean hair, soap, woman scent. Rania. My arm curls around her. God, she's in my bed. She's tempting me so badly, but she doesn't realize it, I don't think.

The last thing I care about right now is the pain shoot-ing through me. All I want is to roll over and pin Rania to the floor and kiss her until she can't breathe, explore her luscious body with my fingers and my mouth.

I can't. Not after what she just went through. I try to content myself with just holding her. She's warm and soft. She makes a sound in her sleep, a low contented sound in the back of her throat, and then moves closer to me, burrowing in as if she can't get close enough. My eyes open and I'm watching her sleep, watching the moon-light shed a silver glow across her skin.

Her shirt is bunched up just beneath her breasts, and her habitual miniskirt is rucked up by her hips. So much skin on display. I draw as deep a breath as my healing ribs will allow, summoning my self-control.

Fuck.

My hand betrays me, steals from her shoulder down her back to skim across the exposed flesh above her skirt. It's a fairly innocent stolen touch, just her back, but it has me hard, needing more. Needing flesh, warmth, touch.

She moves again, one long leg sliding up and over to cover one of mine. Goddammit. Now her skirt is so bunched out of place that her ass is fully exposed. I squeeze my eyes shut, working at self-control. Self-control. *Hands to yourself, asshole.*

I'm weak. I just can't help myself. She's so fucking gorgeous and—despite her profession—oddly innocent. It's clear she's never known love, never known affection. She's never had a lover, never had a boyfriend. I doubt she's ever had an orgasm.

Why the fuck am I thinking about Rania orgasming? Not helping. Not helping. Dammit. Now that image is stuck in my head: Rania above me, hair like a golden halo, brown eyes bright, gleaming with pleasure, sweat beading between her glorious breasts, hands braced on her thighs as she rides me, head thrown back now and moaning, true helpless moans of pure pleasure.

I squeeze my eyes shut and open them, fix them on her hair to banish the image.

My hand is cupping her thigh just above the knee, on the back of her leg. Upward, now. Her skin is like satin, pure warmth, pure softness. She moans sweetly and wiggles into me as I touch her leg, move farther up her leg to the crease just beneath the swelling bubble of her ass.

Oh, lord. Oh, god. Why am I torturing myself like this? I'm such an asshole, fondling this girl in her sleep.

I close my eyes, hunting for the will to act the gentleman rather than the lecherous bastard.

I'm suddenly aware of her breathing. It's not the soft soughing in and out, rhythmic and deep. I glance down warily, and sure enough, her eyes are open, bright in the moonlight.

She doesn't say anything. She doesn't move away or shrink from my touch. She's frozen, staring up at me, barely breathing. Like any second she might bolt.

I'm reminded of nothing so much as being in the woods on a cold, still January morning just after dawn, a fresh blanket of snow silencing everything, a huge doe stepping gracefully into the clearing and looking right at me, wide eyes assessing, watching. Rania's gaze on me is that moment, when the deer's nostrils twitch and her ears flick, and then she's gone, bounding off into the forest.

My hand is still on her thigh, just beneath her ass. I can see the gears turning in her head. I don't know what to do. Should I move my hand? Is she mad at me? Does she like it? Should I kiss her?

Time stalls, and moments pass in taffy-slow stretching spans, her chest swelling against my side as she sucks in a shuddering breath, her eyes locked on mine, her skin hot under my hand. She seems to come to some decision, for the fright in her eyes, the wariness, evaporates. Changes. Now her fear is different. She's not afraid of me. I know that much. She's afraid of what's happening. Perhaps, what's about to happen.

Am I afraid of this, too?

Hell, yes.

I know there's no going back now. This moment, our locked gazes and her soft, delicate, strong body cradled in my arms...this moment is printed indelibly on my heart. If nothing else happens, I'll always remember this.

Rania slips her hand up from between our bodies to touch my cheek. I slide my palm down her thigh, stop at her knee, and then begin the hesitant drift back up. As my hand nears her ass, her eyes widen and her breathing grows shallow. I stop where I had before, just beneath the curve. She lifts her chin, never taking her eyes off me; it's a dare, a defiant, permitting gesture. *Go ahead*, the chin lift says, *touch me. I dare you.*

She's daring herself, not me.

I take a deep breath, gathering my courage, and skim my palm oh so slowly up the taut swell of her ass, cupping the cheek. I can feel her heart pounding furiously in her chest. She's terrified.

"Rania, I—"

She cuts me off by pressing her fingers to my lips. Her fingers trail down my chin, my throat, my chest, my stomach, halting at the fly of my BDU pants. I realize once again she's trying to go about this how she thinks I expect it. It can't go that way. This should be about her. I take her fingers in mine and move them away, place her palm on my cheek. Her brow wrinkles in confusion.

I want her to feel pleasure. To experience a moment of happiness that she hasn't paid for through sacrifice. She opens her mouth to speak, and I cover her lips with mine, a quick, innocent kiss to quiet her. She whimpers in her throat when our lips meet. She moves to kiss me again and I lean away with a grin, shaking my head. Now her expression is openly baffled. I laugh, a silent shaking of my shoulders, and then move back in to kiss her. She moans softly and writhes closer to me.

I deepen the kiss, taste her tongue with mine, and feel the tightly closed bloom that is my hurt and broken heart open a little at the eagerness with which she returns my kiss. She's discovering this for the first time, the upwelling joy of a kiss, the way your heart expands and swells at the touch of lips to lips, the strange tang of tongues tangling.

I begin to slowly explore her skin now. She's lost in the kiss. She makes a noise in the back of her throat when my palm skims across her ass, cupping one firm globe and then arcing across to the other. Her hips press her ass back into my hand, a subtle, almost imperceptible motion, but enough of an encouragement. She likes my touch. I slip my hand up her back, underneath the shirt, circling her back, her shoulders, tracing her spine, and then back down to her ass. Her body is tensed, taut with nerves. We kiss languorously, and I make a circuit of her body, soothing and exciting her all at once. She grows used to my touch and her tension ebbs.

I break the kiss, cup her face with my hand, brushing her cheekbone with my thumb. I kiss her again, but this time I put all my nascent emotions into it, all my fear, my desire, my need, my...how much I care about her. That's as far as I'll let myself go, even in my own thoughts.

She felt it all in the kiss. When I pull away, her eyes are wet, her chin quivering.

"What are you doing to me, Hunter?" Her voice cracks, whispered Arabic that I barely hear, have to work to understand.

I only smile at her. My heart is beating furiously, anticipating what I'm about to do.

"Trust me?" I ask in Arabic.

She hesitates, searches my eyes with hers, then nods.

I push her gently so she's lying on her back, and then I lift up on an elbow. It's painful, but it doesn't matter. I can take it. This is about her.

I kiss her, and when she relaxes and leans up to deepen the kiss, I rest my hand on her knee, hesitate, and then slide slowly upward along the impossibly silky skin of her thigh, inching nearer and nearer to her core.

She pulls away from the kiss, eyes probing me. Fear is rampant in her gaze. I've stopped, waiting for her to decide what she wants.

Rania

This is a new kind of terror. It is fused with excitement, anticipation. His hand on my flesh is frightening, but glorious. He touches me so gently, so carefully. He waits until I am sure I want him to continue, and then, when he touches me in a new way, he opens my eyes to a new world of sensation.

I did not know my body or my soul could feel these things. My heart is at once afraid and ready. I feel it opening, like an unused muscle stretching.

Why will he not allow me to touch him? I thought that is what men like. That is what he expects, yes? Now I do not know. Every time I think he is going to have sex with me, he stops it. He does not let me touch him. We kiss, and I can sense he wants me. He looks at me. He likes the way my body looks. But he has not touched me sexually until now.

I have never, ever been touched this way. My clients...they grope me. They pay me to let them touch me. They do not ask permission. They are not gentle. They touch to possess my body.

Hunter, he is touching to make me feel something. He does nothing unless he is sure I allow him to.

I could not help myself from getting in bed with him. I was nearly asleep, but unable to fall over the edge. His arm was flung out to the side, as if inviting me to nestle into the hollow. I crawled across the square of silver moonlight and curled into his arm. Instinctively, his arm tightened around me, pulled me closer. For those brief, blessed moments, I felt safe. I knew he would protect me. He suffered pain and injury to protect me. He took a bullet for me. In his arms, I knew I was safe.

I fell asleep and knew nothing, no dreams, no memories. Only Hunter's arms and his smell and his strength.

I woke up gradually. I knew from the coolness of the air and the silence that it was still night. I felt something rough yet gentle sliding along my back. Hunter, touching me. It was a comforting touch, not a sexual touch. As if he merely wanted to know what I felt like. I wondered sleepily if he wanted me closer the way I want to be ever nearer to him. I want his touch.

My fear is not that he will hurt me. I know by this point that he will not. My fear is that once I let him touch me, once I let him do what he wants, that he will not want me any longer. He will go away, and leave me alone again. He will expect me to be the whore for him, to be Sabah for him, rather than Rania.

I am afraid of how much I want him to keep touching me. It is a strange, unnaturally powerful desire. I do not want things. I have what I need to stay alive, and that is all. The only thing I have ever wanted is to not have to sell my body anymore.

Hunter cannot give me this. No one can. I will be a whore until I am too old and too ugly for men to want me, and then I will starve to death as I should have so many years ago.

I am frozen, unable to respond, unable to stop his exploring hands.

My leg is draped over his, casually intimate. I want to draw it back to myself, gather my feet beneath me and run into the night, away from this desire burning through my body and soul like fire consuming paper.

Soon, my will to resist will be ash in the wind.

Allah help me, he is caressing my leg now. Just above the knee, still innocent enough, but growing more daring and familiar with every centimeter his palm glides higher.

I have to fight myself to retain the lie of being asleep. *Breathe in; breathe out; slow and steady, deep breaths.* Perhaps I will be able to merely lie here and let him touch me. I do not have to return his affection. I can resist. My desire does not have to dictate my actions.

Oh, I am a fool to think thus. Now his hand is resting frightfully, tantalizingly close to my backside. The edge of his hand is brushing the underside of my left buttock, and Allah, Allah, I want him to move it higher. I want him to touch me intimately, sexually. I do. I must admit the truth to myself, if only to myself.

I must also admit that I am afraid, for so many, many reasons.

I should not let him. I should not let myself. But I am going to, am I not?

There is no point in pretending any longer, is there?

No, indeed not.

I squeeze my eyes shut tighter, cursing myself for being a thousand times a fool. Then I open them and look up at him. His profile is so handsome, so strong. His hair is thick, black as deepest shadows, and getting a bit long, curling around his neck and sweeping across his brow. He is not looking at me; his eyes are closed, squeezed tight, as mine were. He, too, is struggling for control, I think.

We are both fighting this, battling ourselves. He looks down now, meets my eyes, and I know I have lost my battle to resist this American warrior. His eyes are shining in the moonlight, the blue washed into silvery orbs, his tanned skin like marble.

I have not prayed in years. I have called on Allah, blasphemously perhaps, in moments of pain or fear. But not since I was a girl did I speak to Allah as an entity or god who might care, or hear. I do now.

Allah, the all-merciful and all-compassionate, hear me now. Protect me from myself. Protect Hunter from the foolishness of what I am about to do. You see that I am weak, Allah. You see, and if you care, be here now.

I feel childish, foolish, for praying in this moment. I am helpless to stop myself now, for I feel the decision in my body, in my heart. My mind, my reason and logic, they tell me I am a fool, a weak little girl to be lying in this man's arms, to be letting him touch me so with such familiarity Even more so to be considering the intent that is swirling in the fire of my blood.

All this time, Hunter's eyes are fixed on me, watching me. I know if I were to make clear I did not want his hand on me, he would respect that wish. I nearly ask him to stop touching me, simply to test my theory, but in the end I do not need to. I know.

I have not been breathing, and my lungs protest. The decision to throw myself off the edge into the abyss of desire flows through me like flood waters through a wadi, and I suck in a stuttering breath, searing my burning lungs with cooling air.

I snake my hand out from between our bodies and up to touch his stubbly cheek. His hand slides down my leg, the wrong direction, and then back up, and I feel my breathing grow shallow, panicked panting. He stops at the outward bell of my buttocks again, once more waiting for me to demur. I lift my chin slightly, a silent gesture of permission. Or perhaps daring him to touch me.

No, that is not it. I am daring myself. *Let him touch me*, the lift says. He does. My heart hammers madly as his hand burns a hot trail over my bottom, cupping and caressing. I could weep from the pressure of pleasure his touch causes.

"Rania, I—" he begins.

I touch my fingers to his lips, silencing him. I do not want words, in any language. I want the language of touch. He would argue, he would discuss, he would try to convince me why, convince himself why not. I care for none of that any longer. I know what he wants, and I know what I want.

I run my fingers down the front of his body to the buttons of his camouflage pants. I am afraid of this moment. So much fear of so many things. It is nothing

I have not done a thousand, thousand times since I first allowed Malik to have his way with me in exchange for food. But...this is different. I want Hunter's comfort, I want his touch, and this is the only way I know to make sure he does not push me away. I must give him what he wants.

I steel my resolve, feeling the hardness forming in my stomach. It is the hardness of doing what I must. Yes, this is different, this is to get something I want rather than something I need, but...

Enough.

I move to undo the first button, but my fingers are imprisoned by Hunter's. His eyes are probing me, looking into me. His fingers tangle with mine and move them away from his privates, back up his body, placing my hand on his cheek once more.

I do not understand. I thought this was what he wanted? To be touched? To achieve release?

I said I did not want words, but I feel my mouth opening to ask him what he wants from me. Instead, he kisses me. I want to cry, but I cannot. This pleasure is pain. His lips on mine are hot and wet and hungry, devouring my mouth as if he were starving. His hand cups my bottom and explores it. I cannot help the moan that slips up from my throat. It is a sound of desperation.

How does he know what I want? Can he read my mind? My fear is gone, evaporated by the heat of his kiss. All I know is his body hard against mine, his mouth searching mine, his hand on my flesh, inciting such fiery desire that I will be soon consumed by it.

He pulls back to look at me, but that is not what I want. More kisses. More. I need him. Allah, help me, I need him. I do not know what to do, what is happening. All I know is his mouth on mine is more happiness than I have ever known, and I do not want it to ever, ever stop.

I move to kiss him, but he pulls away, teasing me. What is this new game? I dislike it. I want his lips. He laughs at me, amused by something I cannot understand. Then he kisses me again, to quiet the questions he must see bubbling up.

I drown in his kisses. It is like nothing so much as falling, surrounded by him. Enveloped by him. I moan again, and I feel his body respond. He wants me. I know what the desire of a man feels like. He does nothing to alleviate his desire. He only touches me, slips up my back, down my leg, caresses my bottom, one side and then the other, so tenderly. His touch calms my worry, buries my panic beneath the fires of lust and something else, something softer and more potent than mere desire.

We pull apart again, and his eyes, oh, Allah, they contain so much. I cannot put names to the emotions I see in his eyes. I dare not. That would be to invite even further heartbreak. He is playing a game with me. He will get what he wants, and that will be it. He is a man. Men are all the same. It will come down to sex. Perhaps he will not pay me, but expect it for free. Which makes me all the more the fool, does it not? I cannot resist the magnetic pull he has over me, the magic he is using to control my desires, my actions.

His kiss, this meeting of lips, it contains all that I saw in his eyes. It is…too much. A sun bursts in my heart, lighting my body on fire, burning away the high walls erected to protect my heart.

I weep now, for my heart, which will be broken. I am lying to myself. I know better. I cry because I have never felt such vulnerable tenderness directed toward me in all my life as Hunter expressed in that one kiss. First he is hungry for me, lusting as a man for a woman, then he is kissing me as if he…as if he feels—

No. I cannot allow such errant foolishness any place in my heart.

But I cry, because I know what I felt from him, even if I cannot and dare not allow it to be named.

"What are you doing to me, Hunter?" My whispered words are meant for myself, but he hears them, comprehends them.

He gazes at me, and then I see resolution firming in his eyes. Yes. Now it will come.

But his words stop me.

"Trust me?" His accent is awful, his pronunciation butchering the simple syllables, but I understand his meaning.

Do I? Should I?

I do not know what he is going to do. Nothing about this man is what I expect. I am nodding my assent even though I am unsure of anything, everything.

Fear again blazes through me, and he is not kissing me to lessen its burn. He pushes my shoulder so I am lying on my back. His eyes betray nothing but hesitant tenderness, quiet desire. My heart is beating swiftly as he levers himself up onto his side, supporting himself on one arm. I do not know how he is able to lay like he is, leaning on an elbow, but he is. I can see the strain at the corners of his eyes, but he seems to simply push away the pain and focus on me.

I am a statue, motionless on my back, only my eyes moving to search his bright blue eyes.

Now he kisses me, and the boiling fear transmutes into need. His hand is on my knee. My bottom is against the ground, so I know he cannot mean to resume touching me there. Where will his hand move to next? Upward his palm slides, and I know his intent then. My throat goes dry, and the beating of my heart intensifies. Can he really mean to do what I think?

My clients, they pay for one thing: release. A willing female who does not expect anything in return. A pair of legs to open but which will not turn out children for them to support. Men do not touch me there. They have no reason to want to.

My breathing is shallow, approaching panic, and even his kiss cannot quiet me. I pull away and watch Hunter's eyes. He stops his upward glide at mid-thigh and waits, eyes wide.

He is asking my permission to touch me in my most private place. Why am I so afraid? Men push their manhood into me there. It is not a sacred, private thing, my womanhood. But...yes, it is.

His fingers, *there*? Allah, I am terrified of the idea. Hands are the medium of expression, as eyes are windows to the soul. What does he want? Why does he want to touch me there? He would not let me touch him, but he will kiss me. He will touch me, explore my skin. He asks permission before pushing the boundaries.

I am confused and frightened, but my desires are sweeping me away.

I *want* him to touch me. Everywhere. His hand on my buttocks felt wonderful. It was exciting, thrilling. There? My womanhood? I cannot use the vulgar terms. I do not know why. It makes me uncomfortable, as if to use the vulgar slang terms for body parts would make me even more dirty, even more the whore. I do what I must to survive, but in my most secret heart, I am still a little girl, innocent and pure. I am not, in reality, but I want to be. I wish I could be. My actions reflect a primal, blood-deep need to survive, but in my soul, in my dreams, I am a good girl, a woman who does not give in to lust. If not for war, I would have been married, and birthed children. I would have gone to mosque to worship, instead of working in one...instead of—of *fucking* in one. The curse word floats through my mind like a spreading stain.

He is still waiting. Watching me patiently. He must see the war within me written on my face. If he can read my trepidation and my doubts, then he can read the book of my features well. To read a person's expressions on their face is to know their soul.

I can read him, too. He wants me to want this, but he will not rush me, or force me, or do anything unless I want it. I move my leg so it presses against his, and I feel his arousal, thick and hard behind his pants.

I think I understand his game. He will let me touch him because he thinks, correctly, that I am doing what I believe he wants, expects. So instead he shows me what I want. He knows what I want, even though I do not. How strange.

His hand is on my thigh, his eyes search mine, and my heart pounds drum-loud. I put my hand on his and, without taking my eyes from his, inch our fingers slowly, slowly upward, closer to my privates.

I swallow hard and breathe deeply. His eyebrows lift and his hand slows. He knows I am afraid. I shake my head and close my eyes. My thighs are pressed tightly together, instinctual protection. I cannot speak, cannot form words, so I tell him to continue by forcing my legs to relax.

His fingers are tracing circles on the top of my leg, skating up my thigh muscle to my hip bone, to the bunched fabric of my skirt. Now he slides his flattened palm over the hollow where hip meets core, and I tremble, with both anticipation and fear. What will his hand on me feel like? *In* me? I cannot begin to guess.

Down to the inside of my leg now, my thighs still touching each other, pressed close, and his fingers slide between them to move down. I need to touch him. Perhaps that will provide me with the courage to let him go further. I put my hand on his back, feeling the broad, hard muscle ridged beneath my palm. More contact, more heat. I slide my hand under his shirt so I'm touching hot skin, bare flesh.

His lips meet mine, and now need shoots through me. More. Yes.

I arch my back and lift my face to deepen the kiss, and now my tongue darts into his mouth to taste him, explore him. His hand drifts down to my knee and applies gentle pressure outward. I move my leg aside an inch, and then two. His lips close on the kiss, and he pulls back slightly to watch my face as he moves his hand up the crevice between my legs, rough calluses brushing soft skin. He does not stop this time, and his index finger makes first contact with my privates. I flinch, and he pauses, the side of his finger against my core. My thighs are crushed together, and I force them apart again, drawing in courage with a deep breath.

My thighs are far enough apart now that he is able to turn his hand so his palm cups the mound of sensitive flesh. My breath is coming in short, panicked gasps. Heat is billowing through my body, centered on my core. He moves so slowly, like a creeping sand dune. His middle finger traces up the crease of my womanhood, not parting the lips, only touching. I lick my lips and grip his shoulder, turn my face to press against the column of his arm.

I feel shame rising in my throat like gorge. How can I be letting this happen? I should not. I should stop this. But I do not want to. His touch feels good. His middle finger tracing the crease once more sends lightning shooting through me. I slide my legs farther apart, nod my head against his arm.

He hesitates, though. He nudges my forehead with his lips, pushing my face away from his arm so I am forced to look at him.

"Do not feel shameful," he says in mangled Arabic. "You want this? I will make you feel nicely, if you want me."

His words are confused, but I know what he means.

I kiss his lips, summon my courage, and meet his eyes. "Touch me," I say in his language. "I fear, but I also want." I am aware that I mangle his language as he does mine, but I do not care, as long as he understands what I intend to say.

He kisses me, gently at first, sweetly, chastely, then with intensifying heat. I give in to the desire, stop fighting it and kiss him back with all the need I feel raging inside me. I kiss him hard, curl my hand around the back of his neck so he cannot break the kiss, crush him closer, taste his tongue and his teeth. My legs fall open wide, my heels drawn slightly in so my knees lie flat on the ground.

He takes this as the invitation it is, and his finger slices up the line of my privates and back down, pushing in ever so slightly with each motion up and down. I feel at once hot and wet down there, as if wanting him has set loose a flood inside me. I worry that he will feel the wetness inside me and think it is gross, and almost clamp my legs closed, but do not.

His finger slides into me, and I hear his breath catch. I force my eyes open so I can watch for the disgust on his face, but instead I see only desire, pleasure, a smile of delight, but concern touches his eyes.

Then something wild and magical and terrifying happens. He curls his finger upwards and brushes the small nub of sensitive flesh near the top of my privates, and when the tip of his finger touches me there, my universe explodes. I hear a moan, loud and shamefully wanton, escape from me.

I thought I was awash with heat and damp desire before, but in the instant of his finger's contact with my clitoris, a flood of fire and liquid shoots through me, drenching me. My cheeks burn with shame. I can smell myself, my desire, and I know he does, too. Surely that scent will turn his desire to ashes, cause his face to wrinkle in displeasure. Surely. I watch his face, but all I see is his blue gaze burning into mine, and there is nothing in his eyes but concern for me, and a need so intense my breath catches.

He *likes* this. His nostrils flare and he draws in a deep breath, pulling in my scent. His head falls onto my chest between my breasts, and his chest heaves. His finger curls against my clitoris once more, as slowly as the shifting of desert sands. My throat betrays my pleasure with a long, high-pitched whimper, and my body arches clear off the ground as lightning strikes my core.

What is he doing to me? I cannot take this. It is too intense. Too much. My heels scrape the dirt as the wave of ecstasy rolls over me. He waits until my back returns to earth, and then he does it once more. This time, however, he circles the little button of flesh with his finger, slowly still, but without stopping. My breath scrapes past my throat, and a moan hits my teeth and forces my mouth open wide. I can feel my face contorting, my eyes clenching shut, my face lifting to the ceiling as sensations I never knew were possible shoot through me. Such intense pleasure it is nearly painful bolts through me, lightning at my core. Quivers of ecstasy lance through me as his finger swirls around my clitoris.

Now he moves away from my button and his fingers, two of them, descend and thrust gently into my womanhood…my vagina. I know there are other words; I have heard them all before, but I do not want them in my head. I am fighting enough shame as it is. The sounds I am making are wanton, loud and shameless, even though my mind keeps trying to tell me to be quiet. I cannot. I have no control over my body now. I am a puppet, and Hunter's fingers within me are controlling me.

I crack my eyes open and glance down to watch him, seeing his hand, his middle and ring fingers pushing into my privates. He is inside me to the knuckle now. Watch it happen. Let it happen. Enjoy it. His palm faces my body, and now his fingers curl upward, explore my inner walls. My breath is coming short stutters, gasps, whimpers. His curling fingers brush me in a certain spot, high on the inside, and the lightning bolts shiver hotter than ever, send me into a writhing, helpless spasm, and he does not relent, but presses his thumb to my clitoris and moves it in swift circles, barely brushing me.

Pressure wells up inside me, and my hips are moving on their own, rocking up into his hand as he moves his thumb against me and his fingers inside me. The pressure is rising, rising, turning into fire, into earthquakes within me. I do not know what is happening. Fear is a cold wave in my heart, threatening to douse the fires raging in me.

I feel like a tea kettle about to boil over. His every touch makes me writhe and whimper. His head rests on my chest, on my shirt, and his breath washes hot against my neck. He, too, seems overwhelmed, barely holding on to his sanity or his control.

I touch his chin so he looks at me. The vulnerability I see in his eyes is what does me in. I am on a ledge, about to fall over into madness. I want to see his eyes, so I may retain some semblance of my self through it all.

Hunter

My god, she's so beautiful. She's barely holding on. I can see how afraid she is of what lies beyond that edge. She's so close, about to come, but she won't let herself. She's gazing at me, fear in her eyes, desire in her eyes, confusion, need, worry, shame.

Shame. She's ashamed of this. I saw her blush when I first touched her. She is so wet, her desire a pungent aroma that has me so hard I could come if she'd only brush her thigh against my cock. Just the smell of her pussy is enough to make me lose control. I can't take her eyes on me any longer. I let my head thump down against her chest. The thin cotton of her shirt is strained by the swell of her breasts, each mound pulled aside by gravity. Her nipples are beads poking the cotton, tempting my tongue.

Not yet. She's not ready for that yet.

My fingers slide inside her channel, and her body is writhing against me. I touch her clit with my thumb and I feel her nearly lose it right then, but she doesn't. She's afraid. How do I make her forget her fear?

I kiss her. God, she tastes so good. Her lips drive me crazy, the way she nibbles at my lower lip, the way her tongue traces my teeth…I want to kiss her forever, but I can't. Her clit is a hard little bump, intensely sensitive. If I so much as brush her clit, she whimpers. Her G-spot is a roughened, ribbed patch of skin, and she moans when I rub it with my fingers, her hips bucking against my hand.

I'm so hard, so fucking hard. I'm about to come in my pants just touching her, just hearing her moan for me. Thank fuck she isn't trying to touch me, because I wouldn't have enough self-control to stop her. I desperately want to feel her slim little fingers wrap around my cock, stroke me and touch me.

No. No. This is about her, not me.

She moves beneath me, sliding down so her knees rise up, her heels bumping against her ass, thighs spread wide as I drive her wild with my fingers. Sliding down made her shirt bunch up even more, and now the bottom swell of one breast is visible.

Fucking goddamn it. I can't take it, can't help it. I've wanted to kiss her breasts from the very first moment she accidentally flashed me while changing. I've seen them again since, but I've always forced my gaze away. To look was to want. Now I have my fingers in her pussy and her juices slathered on my hand, and all I want is to touch her breasts. Need to.

Fuck.

I give in, nudge the hem up with my nose so her breast is bared completely. My god...so perfect. A taut, round globe of silky sweet skin with wide, dark areolas and tall, rigid nipples begging for my mouth.

I swallow hard, working my tongue to produce saliva. My mouth is dry, my throat clenched up. I'm nervous, oddly. It's not as if I've never done this. Not by a long shot. But this, with Rania...it's different, somehow.

I glance at her eyes, and she's watching me again through hooded lids. I slow my fingers inside her, and her hips lessen the wildness of their bucking. Her mouth is open, and her eyes betray her weltering emotions.

"Please," she whispers.

I don't know what she's asking. Stop? More? Make her come? I don't know. I don't want to hurt her or scare her. I want her to experience this. The fear in her eyes tells me she's never felt this before, and I'm not surprised. Sex for her must be an impersonal thing, a transaction. I can't image anyone has ever taken the time or expended the effort to give her pleasure. This must be confusing and frightening for her, especially if she thinks I'm going to use her like she's accustomed to being used. I can't tell her I won't. I don't have the words, and I do want to. I want to be inside her. She's so close to coming, and I want—*need*, so fucking bad—to move over her and push into her and feel her tight around me.

She is tight, too. I didn't expect that, considering. Guilt and shame at the thought burn into me, but it's true. I didn't expect her to be tight, but she is.

"Please," she whispers again, and touches my face so I look at her.

She arches her back and rocks her hips. She wants more.

She stares into my eyes, and then peels her shirt off so she's naked from the waist up, glorious breasts bare to my touch, bare to my mouth. I let myself look this time, take in the expanse of skin and mounds of flesh.

Her breath is coming in shallow pants, and I can feel the tension in her muscles. Baring herself like this is taking effort, courage. I want to touch her breasts. I wish I could kneel above her so I have both hands free to touch her all over, but my wounds won't let me, and I don't think she'd react well to having me above her like that.

I take my fingers out of her, and she moans in protest. Her cheeks flame with shame as I lift my fingers to my nose to inhale her aromatic scent. I think she's ashamed of the musk of desire from her juices. I put my fingers to my mouth and taste her essence, meeting her eyes all the while. Her eyes widen in pure shock and disbelief, perhaps even something like disgust. I can't help a little laugh from escaping at the expression on her face. I swipe into her slit again, gather essence on my fingers, and lick it off again, just to prove the point. Her brow wrinkles, and she shakes her head.

I slide my palm across her ribs, and her expression smoothes out into pleasure as I cup the heavy weight of one breast in my hand. She watches me as I lower my face to her skin, kiss her flesh between her breasts, kneading it. I rub my palm across her nipple, and she gasps. When I roll it between my fingers, she bites her lip to keep from moaning out loud. I wish I could tell her how much I love the noises she makes for me. I can't, don't try. Words would fail me. Her beauty has captured me, imprisoned my capacity for language. All I can do is pay homage to the temple of her body.

I pinch her nipple again, delighting at the gasp that tears from her, and then I take her nipple into my mouth and suckle, and I feel joy rocket through me when she moans so loud it's almost a scream.

I find myself wondering how mad with ecstasy I could make her if I went down on her. God, she would respond so beautifully. I can almost feel her thighs clenching my face as she writhes against my mouth. I can almost feel her fingers tugging my hair and hear her voice raised in pleasure.

I don't know if she's ready for that.

I lick her skin, flick her nipples, each one in turn, with my tongue, and I return my fingers to her pussy, slide them against her clit slowly, circling gently, mindful of her sensitivity.

She gasps and moans and whimpers, all control over her vocal responses shot to hell now. I love it.

Fuck, I have to stop thinking that word. That word isn't possible.

She feels so fucking good. Her skin is flaming hot against me, her breasts softer than the softest silk, her hips rocking and writhing against my fingers. I have to fight myself to stay up here, to keep myself from startling her too much. She's still skittish. But, dammit, I want to taste her. I know she would like it, once she got past the shock.

I really shouldn't. It would freak her out.

But I want to make her come, want to taste her as she comes apart around me.

Rania

Allah, I am so lost in the wilderness of ecstasy Hunter gives me that I have no control over anything I do. I hear my mouth making such shocking sounds, not faked now, but real. My knees are sticking up in the air, my heels against my backside, my hips moving as if they're alive as Hunter moves his fingers against me.

His mouth is on my breasts, moving from one to the other frantically, nibbling, kissing, licking. Every once in a while he bites my nipple, just hard enough to make me insane, to send jets of pleasure whirling inside me.

I feel him moving, but I cannot fathom what he might be doing. I cannot think, cannot form coherent ideas. All I know is his fingers inside me, his mouth on my breasts. His fingers never cease their movement, and I am about to explode, but cannot. Not yet. I do not know why, but I cannot fall over the edge. I am afraid of what lies beyond, what that will feel like, but I also want it, more than I have ever wanted anything.

I feel him moving slowly, adjusting his position, but my eyes are glued shut as the lightning from his fingers, moving slow and then fast and then slow, fills me. I feel his shoulders brush my knees, and I know he is going to mount me now, and I am not even afraid, especially if it means relief from this boiling pressure within me.

But he does not mount me. His lips touch my breasts, his shirt-clad chest brushing my stomach. Then, impossibly, terrifyingly, he moves downward. Toward my privates. No. No. I tense, freeze, but his fingers on my clitoris take over for me and I move once again, yet my fear does not abate.

When he licked the fingers that had been inside me, I nearly died of shame. The smell is embarrassing enough, but when he licked the wetness off, the moisture that I could see glinting on his fingers, that was mortifying. And now…and now he is moving as if to put his *mouth* on my vagina. I have heard of this, of course. Soldiers are vulgar beasts, and they tell vulgar jokes, suggest vulgar things. They suggest this very thing, but when they visit me with their greasy, folded *dinars*, they do not follow through. Not that I would have let them. I have to retain some sense of power if I am to survive. I dictate what they may do, and to let a man do what Hunter is about to do, that would be giving up the little vestige of power I actually have. That would be vulnerability.

Except I am letting it happen. His mouth leaves my breast and I feel his breath on my stomach, and now it is hot on my privates, burning me. I know I am panicking, truly panicking now. My breath is ragged gasps, and my heart is thundering like the hooves of a thousand horses. His fingers continue to move, and the diversion of pleasure centered powerfully on my core is enough distraction that I do not go completely mad.

And then his tongue laps at my core, and I am undone.

Hunter

My god, she tastes so good. Her strong soft thighs rest on my shoulders, trembling like a leaf in the wind, and I can't believe she would let me do this, but she is. Her whole body is shaking, quivering. Her breathing is panicked, each inbreath a whimper, each outbreath a moan.

This position, on my stomach, is excruciating. It's too much weight on my healing ribs, and I can barely breathe for the agony, but nothing—*nothing*—matters except Rania in this moment.

She's closer now. I swipe my tongue up her slit and she groans low in her throat, shaking her head, denying I don't know what, and her hips lift, fall. I lap my tongue against her clit, an upward thrust with the tip of my tongue, and she gasps a shriek. I do it again and again, and each time she makes a sound so impossibly erotic that my cock jerks and I nearly lose it again. I have to clamp down with every muscle in my body to keep from exploding right there, as if I was fourteen and a virgin again.

I lick her clit in a rhythm, and now her hips go wild, and yes, god, yes, her fingers clutch my hair. She doesn't seem to know whether to push me against her pussy or push me away. She settles for just tangling her fingers in my hair tightly enough that it hurts, but that pain is a mere drop in the bucket compared to the fire in my ribs, the burning in my lungs. I mean, *fuck* it hurts. I don't stop, though. I'll stop when she comes. She's close, so close.

I want to feel her shatter around me. Her legs are clenched so hard I'm almost worried she'll pop my head like a grape, but then she remembers on her own and lessens the pressure.

I slip my fingers beneath my chin into her pussy, focusing my tongue on her clit in ever-faster circles, and I rub her G-spot with my fingers to match the rhythm. I take her clit into my mouth and suck on it, flicking it with my tongue like La—*no*, not going there, not even thinking her name—*she* liked it like this.

Rania screams past gritted teeth, her body arched off the ground, fingers tangled in my hair.

Yes, now…

Rania

Oh, God, oh, Allah, oh, sweet Heaven…

I call on the Christian god, on my parent's god. Words are ripped from my lips, actual screams. I am past feeling shame at the noises I am making. His mouth does things to my body that I cannot fathom, cannot understand, cannot bear. It is too much, too intense.

I want to shove his face away from my privates, but I cannot make myself do it, because it is too much to stop. His tongue flicks my clitoris and I nearly sob, but gasp instead. His fingers slide into me just as I begin to think it cannot feel any more impossibly intense, and I could die from the storm of fire in my belly.

How can this keep going? How can he do this? I can hear the grunt in his chest, the stubborn refusal to capitulate to the pain, and I cannot believe he is able to move at all, let alone give me such incredible pleasure.

This is a gift, I realize. I will treasure this all my life, whatever may happen once this is over.

My body is writhing like a serpent, my back undulating, my hips lifting and falling. My hands are on his head, my fingers in his hair. I am still torn between conflicting instincts to push him away and pull him closer.

When his fingers go inside me again and find that spot unerringly, I lose the fight. I clutch him, pull him wantonly, selfishly against my womanhood. Then his mouth forms a suction around my button and I scream.

The fires in my belly, the pressure, the storm, it is about to break.

He slows, just at that moment, and I moan in protest.

"Hunter..." His name comes out of my mouth, torn from me.

I tighten my fingers in his hair until I know it must hurt him, but I am past the ability to care about anything. I pull him against me, push his face deeper into me, my legs around his shoulders. It takes all my power to not crush him with my legs.

And then...

And then it happens.

"*HUNTER!*" I scream his name as I explode, coming apart at the seams.

Every fiber of my body is on fire and I am helpless, caught by the lightning, every muscle clenching and releasing, lights bursting behind my eyes, my hips thrusting against his mouth crazily as he sucks and licks and flicks with his tongue, driving the detonation inside me into ever more furious waves of orgasm.

I cannot sustain this and go limp, unable to move, wrung into exhaustion. Hunter stops then, when I collapse. He rests his face against my hip, and I can feel the sweat smearing on his forehead. His body trembles.

I lean forward and pull at his arms. He crawls slowly back up next to me and then crashes to his back. He is gasping; sweat is pouring from his face, and his eyes are shut tight. His hands are fisted into the blankets.

I touch his chest. "Hunter? Are you okay?"

He nods. "Fine. Just…need a minute," he answers in English.

I can barely breathe, and I feel my eyes burning. I am still trembling, and even as I lie worrying about Hunter, an aftershock hits me, a mini-explosion rocking through me, and I curl against Hunter's side until it abates. His arm wraps around me, pulling against him. We shake and tremble together for long minutes.

My gaze roams his body, his thick muscles slack as the pain recedes, his stomach no longer heaving with every breath. My eyes catch on his groin. I can see his manhood outlined behind the buttons of his pants. He is huge and hard. He adjusts himself with his hand, pushing at his manhood through his pants, shoving it aside, one way and then the other, as if seeking comfort that will not come.

It is time to repay him. I touch his stomach, let my hand drift down, but he catches my wrist yet again. I meet his gaze.

"Why?" I ask, in English.

He responds in Arabic. "Not for me. Not this night. Another. Maybe." He kisses me softly. "This was for you. Only you."

His eyes betray the fact that he is still in agony, the lines of his forehead deep, the corners of his eyes wrinkled in focus. He twines our fingers together on his stomach, as if to assure himself that I will not try to touch him.

This really was a gift to me. He expects nothing in return. He put himself through unimaginable pain to give me pleasure, the greatest pleasure I have ever known, and will not let me do anything for him in return.

I cannot stop the sobs then. He is too much for me to bear. What will I do when he is gone?

Another thought strikes me, and this one is worrisome, making me sob uncontrollably: How will I work now? I have tasted heaven, and I cannot forget it. I have known the pleasure that is possible. It will be difficult.

No, it will be impossible.

I glance at Hunter. He is asleep, his handsome features relaxed. His forehead is still wrinkled with pain. I cannot stop my hand from touching his brow, smoothing the lines. I touch his cheek and marvel that one man can contain such fury as I saw when he fought Abdul, along with the tenderness with which he kisses me, the strength and stubbornness to refuse pain its paralytic hold over him. So many contradictions. I know he wants me. I see the way he looks at me. I sensed it when he touched me, when he kissed my breasts, when he moved over me to begin his journey downward. He denied himself pleasure, taking instead pain.

I let myself cry, pressing my cheek to his chest, away from the tender area where he was wounded, and eventually fall asleep, held close by Hunter's arms, contented, confused, awash with physical pleasure and emotional pain.

One last thought pierces the fog of impending sleep:

Is this love?

THIRTEEN

Hunter

I'M WOKEN BY A MALE VOICE SHOUTING RANIA'S NAME. Rania, not Sabah. Before we can move, a familiar-looking young man appears in the doorway, heaving and sweating from extreme exertion.

Rania gasps, and I look at her. She's pale and visibly shaken.

"Hassan?"

Shit. That's her brother, whom we both thought was dead. Rania is still naked except for her miniskirt, and she's sitting up, bare nipples peaking in the cold air. Her brother halts in the door, stopped short by what he sees: his sister in the arms of an American soldier.

He starts jabbering in Arabic too swift for me to follow. Rania listens, clutching the sheet to her chest.

My heart is pounding, and I can feel adrenaline begin to rush through my system. My skin is prickling, and my spine is shivering. I'm sweating, even though I'm cold in the early dawn.

Battle.

Rania tells me her brother is claiming that Abdul is coming to kill us. That evil fucking camel cunt who tried to rape Rania. He thinks he's gonna get revenge.

Fury boils through me.

There are nearly fifty men coming for us, Hassan says.

I turn to Rania, who has put a shirt and shoes on. "Hide. Don't come out for anything. No matter what you hear, stay hidden. I'll come for you."

She shakes her head. "Hunter, you cannot do this." Her English is nearly unintelligible. "You are badly hurted. Please. Come with me. We run."

I snatch the rifle from Hassan's hands, check the clip, and then limp out the door. My leg blazes with every hitched step, but I have no time for pain. "I'm not running, Rania. I'm a fucking Marine. Marines don't run."

Hassan follows me, jabbering in rapid, angry Arabic. I don't catch any of it, but I'm guessing he's pissed I stole his rifle. I swing around and face him. "Protect your sister. Hide her. Protect her."

"Give me my gun, American." Slowly-enunciated Arabic.

I hand him my knife. "Use this."

"Wait," Rania says. She comes out dragging a bundle wrapped in a sheet. "It is your weapons, Hunter. I did not know what to do with them, so I hid them."

I open the bundle to see my M16, spare clips, and body armor, which is battered and rust-red stained with my blood.

"Fuck yeah," I say to myself. "Real gear."

I toss Hassan his rifle back and strap the armor on over my wife-beater. My M16 could use some love, but there's no time for that. I can feel shit coming. My blood runs hot, ready for battle. I'm gonna fucking finish that bastard Abdul. He's dead—he just doesn't know it yet.

I feel a small hand on my arm, and Rania's breath on my neck. I wrap her close with one arm. "Hide, Rania. I'll be fine. This is what I do."

She gazes up at me, brown eyes liquid now, hot chocolate framed by loose blonde tendrils. "Please, Hunter. Come with me. Come away. There are too many. You are only one man. I…please." She presses her warm, soft lips to mine. Her next words are whispered. "I need you."

I'm rocked down to the core of my soul by her admission. She needs me?

I'm tempted. It would be easy to run.

But, tactically, I know better. They'll catch us. I can't run. I can ambush them, fight them door to door. Go down swinging. Give Rania a chance. I don't expect to make it through this, but I'll damn well give it a try. Ooh-rah.

I don't know what to say to her. I'm in battle mode. Shut down. Hard. I'm not Hunter anymore. I'm Lance Corporal Lee, USMC. Semper Fi, bitches.

I look down at her, brush a stray wisp of hair behind her ear with my forefinger. "It'll be fine. I promise."

She frowns and backs away from me. "Go, then." She seems angry. "Stupid men. Always wanting to fight."

She turns and runs, vanishes around the side of the mosque.

Hassan laughs. "She is afraid for you, American. She is angry at me for becoming a soldier." His eyes are hard and challenging. "I have killed many of your kind."

I blink. "Just keep her safe."

He spits. "For once in my life, I will." And then he's gone, chasing after her.

Finally, I'm alone. I spin in place, looking for the best spot. There, a burned-out wreck of a car nudging into a wall on an angle, not far from an alley. Cover, and a retreat. I limp to it, hide in an agonizing crouch. I can see the road in both directions, and the alley behind me isn't a dead end. All I have to do is wait.

There, a dark face below the red and white of a *keffi-yeh*. Wait for it. My finger twitches on the trigger, seeing the rifle in his hands, but I wait. Spring the ambush after they're committed. Two, three…six…ten. All in a line. I've got no grenades, nothing but my rifle and three clips. They're stopping, now, crowding around the mosque. I see Abdul, striding in the middle of a cluster of heavily armed thugs.

Now.

Crackcrackcrack. I drop two, wet spray, pink mist, red blooms on chests. I don't get Abdul, who ducks and runs as soon as the gunfire echoes.

Crackcrack…crackcrack…crackcrack. More drop, spreading red life into the dust. They can't see where I'm shooting from yet, so I keep firing. My bad leg is beneath me, screaming, my good leg supporting my weight, tensed, ready to propel me into flight when they catch sight of my muzzle burst.

They're dropping like flies. I don't miss. There are too many of them clustered in the street. They were expecting to ambush, not be ambushed. Thank fuck for Hassan's warning.

Then they see me. Or rather, they see the flash of fire from my M16. I duck behind the rusted hulk of the car, listening to the metallic thunk and ping of bullets hitting the vehicle, the snap-buzz of rounds hissing past my ear. I shuffle sideways laboriously, shifting positions. My chest burns, still-healing muscles not ready to wield a rifle but given no other choice.

Hackhackhackhack…hackhackhack. A few rounds hit too damned close for comfort, plugging through the weakened, rusted, blackened metal. Time to move. I lurch to my feet and throw myself backward, firing into the mass. They're spreading out now, seeking windows and doors. I move down the alley, duck through a random door, and crawl out the window, ignore the huddled mother and children and aged grandmother in the corner. I flop to the ground roughly, cursing as I try to catch my breath. I roll to my stomach, gasping, panicked as my lungs struggle to release. I hear the muffled sound of a round going past my face, roll again and again, lift the rifle and find the muzzle-burst, fire. Hit, wounding but not killing.

Then I hear a sound more welcome than anything I've ever heard in all my life: the answering *crackcrack* of M16s in the distance. Marines. I fire again, pinking an elbow sticking out from behind a wall.

Crackcrackcrack.

There, from the east. Now AK fire chatters up, individual rifle voices blending into a cacophony. I think I hear four rifles. One fireteam. There, there's the SAW, short coughing buzz-saw bursts. I could cry I'm so relieved. I make it to my feet, then duck again as bullets whine past my ear, reminding me I'm out in the open. I feel a stinging burn cut along my bare arm, a bullet scratching a red line. I run awkwardly, dragging my stiff leg behind me. I need to tie in with that fireteam.

I round a corner and have to scramble back. There's a cluster of rag-heads—I feel a twinge of guilt at the racial slur, thinking of Rania—*insurgents* gathered with Abdul in the center. They're surrounding a door, and there's a lot of shouting, rifles pointing, but no one is shooting.

I have to drag a hasty translation from my whirling head: *Give her up, Hassan—No! You're a devil, Abdul!— One last warning, boy...*

They've got Rania and Hassan cornered. Fucking shitfuck. What do I do? I slip a fresh clip home, peer around the corner, count. Seven, plus Abdul.

M16s bark a few hundred yards away, answered by AKs and interrupted by the SAW, and then there's the glorious sound of an M203 coughing up a grenade, followed by the dull thunder of the explosion. An

RPG, *whistle-whoosh, boom.* Not far away, moving this direction.

I have to fix this. Can't let that turd-sucker Abdul get his filthy hands on Rania.

I lick my lips, drag a burning breath, knead the howling muscle of my injured thigh, wish this was over, wish I was still holding Rania's sweet soft naked body against mine in the gray dark of dawn.

No time for that, dickhead.

Roll around the corner, open fire, swing the barrel horizontally, spraying recklessly, against all training. Hose the fuckers down. Get them looking this way.

Bullet pluck at the stone wall and whizz and hiss-snap; that got their attention, I'm thinking. Wait... wait...drop to a knee, pivot, fire. Blood blossoms, Abdul is yelling, screaming orders. Need him to fucking die. *Fucking die, asshat.*

Yells in Arabic, curses, and insults are directed at me, and I realize I shouted that last out loud.

There's three left, plus Abdul. They're coming this way, crouching, firing, sneaking. Abdul has an AK held in one hand, the stock held across his forearm of the fingerless, bandaged hand. Be damned if he's not fairly accurate that way, too. I back away, knowing I can't win a four-on-one showdown in the open.

They round the corner just as I duck into a doorway, pressing my shoulder tight against the splintering wood. Hesitate, suck up my fear, push down the pain, teeth grinding so hard my jaw aches, sweat running down my face along with trickles of blood from where shards of bullet-sprayed stone peppered me.

Deep breath, roll out and fire, drop back. One down. They scramble back under cover. Roll out, suppressing fire, wait…glimpse a body as he peeks out, plug him with ugly holes, drop back behind cover.

New clip, last one.

My breath comes in grunting gasps. The pain is winning.

Cannot fucking give in. I grind my teeth and suppress a groan of agony.

I see Hassan peek out the doorway, rifle barrel first. He creeps out into the road in a passable tactical crouch, rifle against his shoulder but not tucked up, waiting for a target. I roll out, he sees me, I point at the dead-end alley where Abdul and the last one are waiting. He nods. I hold up two fingers, pat my shoulder to indicate rank, although I'm not sure if Hassan will understand that. It was the gesture Rania first used. Hassan shrugs, holds up two fingers. I mime cutting at my fingers with the knife edge of one hand, then make a fist, and Hassan nods, comprehending.

I creep toward Hassan and the alley mouth, muttering fuck under my breath with every step. Throbbing pain gouts through me with every motion, every breath, every step, every eye blink. I'm running on stubbornness now.

Abdul has to die before I'm allowed to collapse.

We rush the alley at once, together. Abdul is waiting for us, his last man standing next to him, holding Rania captive. The goon has his arm around her neck, one hand groping her breast greedily, the other pointing a pistol at her, near her, not pressed directly at her head.

It's a standoff. Hassan has his rifle aimed at Abdul and I'm kneeling, my bead drawn on the other one.

Tense silence.

Hassan shifts his feet, drawing the gaze of the man holding Rania. It's all the distraction I need.

Crack.

Rania bolts the instant she feels his grip loosen. A black hole blooms red in the center of his forehead. Rania is behind me now, Hassan beside me.

Abdul doesn't even flinch. His rifle shifts between Hassan and me, as if he can't decide who he's going to shoot first.

A real Mexican standoff.

Seconds stretch like taffy.

A shot blasts, deafening in the confined alley.

Rania

I see it happening. I see Abdul's finger tightening on the trigger. I do not know who he is aiming at, because Hunter and Hassan and I are all close together now.

Hassan moves like a serpent striking. He jumps in front of Hunter as the rifle goes off, and I see him jerk, jerk, jerk. Abdul is shooting wildly. I am on the ground, unhurt, watching helplessly. Hassan is on the ground, too, but he is bleeding out into the dust. Again.

Hunter is moving, knife in hand, crashing into Abdul. The black blade flashes and Abdul screams. Screams. Hunter growls like a feral animal, rabid and snarling, his blade is a claw and Abdul is dead and gurgling but Hunter does not stop, stabs, stabs, ripping, slashing, killing the killed.

I pull him away, and he almost slashes me before he recognizes me. His face abruptly shifts from one of malice and rage and bloodlust into one of relief, love. Love. That look says so much. His eyes are soft. Where before he was a killer, now he is the lover. He is before me, mere inches away, reaching up to touch me, to kiss me.

Something within me melts. I hear shouting, a vehicle's engine roaring, tires skidding. Gunfire echoes behind us, answered and silenced by American rifles. I see none of this. Only Hunter's handsome face. His sky-bright blue eyes on me, taking me in as water to a man dying of desert-thirst.

He shifts forward, and I think he is moving to kiss me, so I wrap my arms around his neck and press my lips to his, but instead of kissing me back his strong mouth is slack and his weight presses upon me.

"Hunter?" At first I am only confused. I pull back to look at him. "Hunter? Speak to me. Please."

He does not. His eyes are rolling into his head, and he is falling down onto me.

I try to catch him, but he is too huge, too much man for a frail girl like me to hold up. He falls hard, crashing to the ground. This rouses him enough to peer at me through heavy-lidded eyes.

"Rania?" His voice is faint. There is blood on him. Too much. So much. His, Abdul's. "I'm done for, Rania."

I shake my head. "No. No. Your friends is here. They will make you okay." I am having trouble with his language, but I know he is too hurt, too tired to speak mine. "Please. Do not go from me."

I turn and see Americans in camouflage approaching us. Hunter's eyes glance behind me and widen in shock.

"Derek?" Hunter's voice cracks.

"Yeah, man, it's me. I'm here. Time to go home, buddy." Derek's voice is a raspy drawl.

Hunter looks at me with pleading eyes. "Come with me, Rania. I'll make them bring you. I'll make you mine." The last sentence was in garbled Arabic.

"Go with you?" He is still struggling, still fighting to rise, to move; I touch his chest to still him. "I will go with you. Anywhere." I kiss him gently. "I will go anywhere with you. I love you. I love you." I repeat it in English and Arabic.

His eyes widen at the words, and I still feel, even now, panic that he will not want me if I profess to love him.

But instead he lifts his arm, straining to move even his own appendage as if it were a great weight, touches my face. "I love you."

He faints, and I am torn away from him by rough hands, gloved hands and American arms. Pushed away. Dismissed. Ignored.

He is watching me, whispering, pleading. They do not hear him, or are not listening. He is wrestled into the American vehicle, one of those things like a car made into a tank, and at the last his eyes are on me before he faints.

I hear screaming, and realize it is me. My words are unintelligible, even to me. I hear myself as a stranger. *Do not take him from me, please, take me with you, please, I love him*—but they are heedless, and Hunter is gone and I am alone.

Hassan bleeds into the dirt, and I can hear him gasping.

I kneel beside him. "Brother." I do not know what else to say; I cannot lie to him now, at the last. "You saved him. You saved me."

"You are…my sister." It is all the explanation he has strength for. It is enough.

My hands are on his chest, gloved by his blood, and I am weeping. For him, yes. But for me, for Hunter. For my broken heart. They took him, although he loved me, and would have made me his. I wanted to be his. Someone's.

Anyone's.

Hassan dies quietly, watching me until his eyes take on the far-seeing blankness of death, and I know he has gone to be with Allah, if Allah exists.

I kneel in the dirt and the blood-mud, bending over the cooling corpse of my brother, my last connection to anything, and weep.

He was dead, and then he was miraculously alive again, protecting me. And now he is dead again. Truly dead. I smell it on him, the stench of death.

And then I hear them behind me. Angry, wounded, bloody men. Iraqis. I harbored an American.

They want my blood in payment for theirs.

They can have it.

FOURTEEN

Hunter

I WAKE TO PAIN, and a sudden, intense need to remember something I'm missing, or something I've forgotten.

Fuck if I can remember. Hot lances of raw agony stab through me, arms, legs, chest, lungs, head…my heart. Not my physical heart, but my emotional heart. My core.

Where Rania lives.

I bolt upright, clunking into someone's chin, causing a curse. "Where is she?" I demand.

Derek is next to me, clutching a bleeding bicep. "Who? And yeah, you're welcome for rescuing your sorry ass, motherfucker. Good to see you, too. Yeah, don't worry about me, I'm fine."

"*Where is she?*" I'm looking around me, feeling the familiar rumble of the Humvee beneath me.

I see Dusty, driving, turning to glance at me, blood running down his cheek from a deep gash on his forehead, deep enough to show white bone peeking beneath the grooved, flapping flesh. Chink is there, riding shotgun, staring at me, unspeaking, grimacing, dirty, in pain but unbloodied that I can see. Benny, arm creased and seeping blood. Derek, confused, angry at my lack of gratitude.

Fuck gratitude.

"Who the fuck are you talking about, Hunt?" Derek is annoyed and in pain.

"The girl. The blonde girl. Rania. Where is Rania?"

"Oh, her?" Derek waves a dismissive hand. "We left her back there, bro. She was just a native hooker, man. You're on the way home."

"*Turn around.*" I glare at Derek, and he sees the seriousness in my eyes.

"What? Are you fucking nuts?" He leans forward. "No way, man. Uh-uh. That place'll be swarming with rag-heads."

"Don't call 'em that, D. And turn the fuck around. I'm not asking."

"You can barely move," Derek says. "It ain't happenin'."

I dig deep for strength and swing my fist, knock him back against the seat. Then I lean up and snatch Benny's pistol from its holster on his hip before he can react. Tension fills the Humvee as I press the barrel to Derek's forehead.

"Turn. Around." The words are low, grated, filled with whispering death. "I swear to fucking Christ I will kill you if you don't."

Derek pales. "Fuck, man, okay. Okay. Turn around, Dusty. We're going back."

No one says a word as Dusty slews the vehicle into a skidding, fishtailing U-turn. He drives recklessly fast now. The men grip weapons, slam fresh clips home.

"She's important to you, huh, bud?" Derek says, after I lower the pistol.

"You have no idea." She's alone. Her brother is dead by now. The other locals will be scared and angry. She'll be an easy target.

"She was pretty fine, wasn't she?" Derek is trying to cajole me into a better mood. "Did you tap that ass, Hunt?"

I snarl at him, a feral sound. "Shut your goddamn mouth about her, Derek. You have no fucking idea about her. None. So shut the fuck up."

Derek slumps back, confused; I've never acted like this before. "Jesus, dude. Take a pill. It was a joke. We'll get her back, bro. We're almost there. We'll get her. Stay in the fuckin' truck."

I hear shouts in Arabic, and then the Hummer slides to a stop and the boys pile out. I'm out with them somehow, moving on pure panicked rage and protective instinct. The pistol is gripped in my fist. I see red. A crowd is gathered in a semicircle, and now that the battle seems to be over, they don't pay us much mind. I shove through them.

A knot of Iraqi men are clustered around a prone figure. Kicks fly. I see skin, blood, ripped cloth, a flash of blonde.

I fire, unthinking. A head bursts pink and a body thumps. The men turn from Rania, but I'm too enraged. I fire again, and then the pistol is stripped from me and arms wrap around me, but I fling them off and I'm attacking hand and foot. I feel no pain. Punch, kick, head butt, knee. Bodies scatter, curses in Arabic and English boil loud around me. The crowd is angry, restless, but the guys are holding them back, playing the familiar role of crowd control.

I slump to my knees next to Rania, who has split lips, puffy, bruising eyes, blood running from her mouth. Her clothes are ripped, and I can see bruises on her skin.

I scoop her up into my arms. Tears prick my eyes, and I blink them away. And then she rolls her head to look at me, and she smiles.

"You came." Arabic, but simple enough that I understand, even through my adrenaline and rage and pain and panic and fear. And love.

"I came. I'm here." I think some of that was Arabic, some was English. Don't know, don't care.

"Come on, man, move it." Chink, bumping into me from behind, his back to mine. "These folks are pissed. Go."

I stumble, move with Rania's precious form to the Humvee. My legs betray me, and I falter, shuffle. Derek is there, catches me, takes Rania from me, cradling her carefully, and climbs into the truck.

I'm empty now, past empty. Agony washes white over my vision, and I vomit into the dust, collapsing.

Hands haul me into the Humvee, and I can't see anything, but I smell Rania, sense her, hear her. I'm sitting and I feel her move, collapse on top of my legs. I nearly pass out again, but manage to hang on.

The rest climb in, and we're moving, Dusty driving insanely fast, skidding around corners. Shots ring out, ping off the sides, spider-web the glass, and then we're out of range there's only the rumble of tires and silence and breathing.

Rania's head is on my lap, her soft brown eyes looking up at me. Her head sways with the bumping of the road, and darkness encroaches on me, numbness spreading through me. I've pushed myself past the limit, but she's safe now, okay now.

I can stop.

The last thing I see before blackness takes me is Rania's sweet smile, blonde hair stuck to her lips and forehead and chin and splayed across her finely sculpted cheeks.

Rania

Hunter sleeps for a long time, healing. He took another bullet, I am told. His friend, Derek, says that the American doctors are amazed that he is alive at all. He should not have been able to do the things he did. Derek speaks to me through the translator, who is a Kurd named Suran, a short, squat man with a thin and wispy black beard, gap-toothed, intelligent enough to speak his native Kurdish, plus Arabic, Urdu, English, and several other dialects.

My Hunter is strong. I feel pride for him. He endured much, and still came back for me. I get to know Derek in the days of Hunter's long sleep. Suran spends many hours translating for us. Derek wants to know about me, about how I saved Hunter, and why, what happened.

I tell him, strangely. I did not expect to like him at first, this friend of Hunter's. But I do. He has kindness, but it is buried deep. He risked his life, and that of three other men, to save his friend. He is courageous. And so I tell him. The words pour out, and Suran translates it all faithfully. It is easier to say it all in Arabic and let Suran translate. I speak enough English to know he tells it true. I speak of the photographer, the man I killed so long ago. Hassan becoming a soldier as a boy of only twelve. Starvation. Desperation. I tell him, haltingly, of Malik. The strange sort of not-quite kindness he showed me in giving me food, making me pay for it with my body, and in the process showing me a way to survive when I would have surely starved otherwise. I hate being a whore, but it kept me alive. Malik saved me, but at a high cost. I am not sure if I would thank him, if I saw him again.

Then I look down at Hunter's slack face, handsome in repose, and I know I would. I survived so I might know Hunter, and he saved me.

One day, past noon, Hunter wakes up. I am next to him, as I always am, unless eating or sleeping.

"Rania?" He looks around, finds me. "Are you okay?"

I nod. "I am well." I move my chair closer and brush a strand of hair from his face. "How do you feel?"

"Better. It'll be a while before I'm back at a hundred percent, but I'll live."

I have to guess at much of that, as it is in quick English. I cannot help but lean down and kiss him, and at first it is gentle, tender, but then it turns hungry, desperate.

I think of that night in my house, lying in the dim gray dark with his hands on me and the incredible ecstasy he showed me, the gift of pleasure he gave me, all without taking anything for himself.

I want him. I need him. I want to kiss him until I am breathless, until I melt into him. Now, I have felt desire, and I have known what my body can feel under the tutelage of his hand and his lips, and I want it. I am not afraid. I want to know his love, his touch. I want…

I want to be bare to him. My skin layered over his, moving against his, my body whispering above his. I want this, this thing, this act.

For once in my life, I want to have sex. To make love. I need it with Hunter. It would bind us, bring our odd journey to completion.

Hunter pulls away when Derek clears his throat behind us.

"Sorry to break it up, you two, but we gotta talk." I catch most of this from Derek.

Hunter struggles to sit up, takes my hand. He has an expression on his face which I take to mean he knows what is coming, although I do not.

Suran appears from nowhere, sidling up next to me. He reeks of cigarettes. He whispers a translation into my ear.

Derek pulls a chair up next me on the other side of Suran, facing it away so he straddles it. "She can't stay here indefinitely, Hunt. You know that."

Hunter nods. Fear hits me. He will send me away now. "Yeah. Sarge told you that?"

"No. Comes straight from the Colonel. Our little… escapade didn't go unnoticed, you know. People are pissed. She's a local, but she's not connected to anything here. She's just…here. Now that you're awake, they want her gone, or something done."

Hunter pinches the thin sheet between his fingers, rolls it. "I'm not letting her go, D. I'm not."

"I know, bro. I talked to her while you were asleep. She told me her story, and man, she's been through hell. And she loves you. You love her. It's plain as day." Derek glances at me, knowing I'm understanding and that Suran is translating. "There's really only one solution."

Hunter nods. "Yeah. I know. Go get the chaplain and some witnesses. Your team. Dusty and the boys."

Derek nods. "You got it." He rises, glances at me again, and then at Hunter. "You sure about this?"

Hunter just nods, staring at the blanket. "Sure as shit, D. Give us a minute." The last part was aimed at Suran, who bobs his head and vanishes.

Hunter takes my hand in his, rubs a knuckle with his thumb. "Do you know what's happening?"

I shrug. "I think yes. I cannot stay. I am not American, not worker, not translator. So I go."

Hunter frowns, brow wrinkling. "No, Rania. I mean, yes. You can't stay since you're not...well, they want you go back to...to go back. But there's a way you can stay."

I glance up at him. Hope hits me like pain. I do not want to hope, but it is hard not to. "What way is this? You will not send me away?"

He pulls me down to perch on the edge of the bed, wraps his arm around my waist. "No, Rania. No. You can stay if you marry me. Come back to the States with me."

Shock rocks me. "Marry?" I am not sure I heard him right. I switch to Arabic. "Be your wife?"

He nods. "I...don't have a ring," he says in English. "But...I'll give you one, as soon as I can. It's not just a way for you to stay, though. It's what—I want you to be mine."

I shake my head, disbelieving. "You...you want me, always? I have nothing. No one. If you take me to America and then do not love me, where will I go? Back to whoring?"

Hunter touches my cheek, kisses my chin. "I will always love you. You saved me, Rania."

I shake my head. "No, you have saved me."

"We saved each other, then," he says.

I smile my agreement.

"So you'll marry me?" he asks.

"Yes," I say, shedding a tear. "Yes. I will."

Derek returns with the other soldiers I recognize from Hunter's rescue, and another man, older, with the soft, gentle face of a religious person, not a killer's eyes, but peaceful ones. He is a priest, or an *imam*. Something. A holy man, but I do not know the English word. I think, make myself remember. *Chaplain*, Hunter said. That is the word. The chaplain holds a thick black book, a religious book. Not the *Q'uran*, but the Christian book. The Bible.

Hunter struggles to his feet, stands facing me, takes my hands in his, with the chaplain in front of us. We are in the hospital in the American base. Camp Fallujah, I think it is called. They referred to it as something else, three letters. M-E-K, or something like that. My knowledge of the English letters is next to nothing, and it does not matter. Hunter's eyes are soft on mine, blue as the ocean in the photographs I have seen in the magazines and stores, blue as the sky on a hot day. He is smiling, calm and confident and reassuring me.

Fears pulse through me. Marriage is for always. To marry is to belong to that man. I have never belonged to anyone. I have never wanted to belong to anyone. I am my own. I survive. And now this American whom I have known for only a few weeks has swept me away from the only life I know, and I am marrying him. It seems mad, foolish, rash. But...it is right. It is what I want. I want to belong to him. He will not hit me, as I know many husbands do their wives. He will not make me take the hijab, I do not think. He will not make me continue to be a whore. He will not *let* me continue to be a whore, I think is more true. He wants me all for himself. I do not know why, but he does.

I swallow hard, my throat thick and tight and dry.

The chaplain speaks, and Suran translates.

"We are gathered to witness the marriage of this man, Hunter Lee, to this woman, Rania…" He pauses and glances at me, then Hunter, and I realize he wants my last name.

I hesitate. I have not thought of my family name in a very long time. In the end, it does not matter.

"Only Rania," I say.

"To this woman, Rania," the chaplain continues, "in the bonds of holy matrimony…"

He says many other things, regarding the sanctity of marriage and the bride of Christ—which I do not understand, since Hunter is Hunter, not Christ—and then he asks Hunter to repeat after him, and there is an embarrassing moment in which the chaplain is made to understand there are no rings, but I do not care for such things. I have never owned jewelry, and have never expected to. And then the chaplain asks me to repeat after him.

"I, Rania, take you, Hunter Lee, to be my lawfully wedded husband, to have and to hold, for richer or for poorer, in sickness and in health, till death do us part."

I repeat the words, and I mean them with all my soul. I will be all I can for Hunter for as long he will have me, through anything.

And then we have both said "I do," and Hunter kisses me, a short but passionate kiss, and something clicks inside me. My fear abates, my fear that Hunter will not want me, my fear that this is all some kind of game, or trick.

I find myself weeping again, quiet tears, soft tears. Hunter brushes them away with his finger.

"You okay?" he asks.

I nod. "It is just…much. So fast. Is it real?" I am whispering for some reason. The other men have left, and Hunter and I are alone, but my fears must be voiced, but not too loud lest they come true. "I am afraid this is not real. I am afraid that you will not love me until death parts us. I do not know what to do. I do not know what will happen to me."

"It's real," Hunter says, pulling me down onto the narrow hospital cot with him. I lie next to him, cuddled into his arms. "I promise it's real. It's fast for me, too, but…I can't let you go. I can't…I *won't* let you go back there, go back to being a whore. I love you. You belong with me."

"I belong to you."

Hunter frowns. "I hope you understand something, Rania. You are your own person. When you come home with me, you'll be…free. You can do anything you want. You can learn. You're smart. You don't belong to me, like a dog or a car. I don't own you, and I won't try to control you."

I nod. "But I am only yours. You will not…share me."

Hunter's eyes blaze. "*Never*! You're *mine*." He takes my face in his hands. "You're not a whore anymore, Rania. Never again."

"Then…what will I do, for food?"

Hunter frowns as if confused. "I will take care of you."

"But…then…" I do not know how to say what I am thinking. I start over. "Nothing is free, Hunter. If I am not a whore, and you feed me and clothe me and give a home, then I must work to earn it. I cannot do nothing. You will be simply paying me in food, rather than with money."

"Paying? Paying for what?"

"Sex."

Hunter drags his hand through his hair. "Rania, listen. I don't expect anything in that way. I'll never demand or expect anything from you. I'll take care of you, feed you and give you clothes and share my bed with you—or give you your own, if that's what you want—because I love you. I'll take care of you, and I will never ask you anything in return. You don't owe me sex. You don't have to obey me. You don't…" He trails off, staring out the window at a big truck with soldiers in the back as it rumbles by. He seems to be searching for words to make me understand something. "Some things *are* free, Rania. My love for you is free. All you have to do is take it. Accept it. If you want to work, I'll help you find a job. But not because you have to earn your keep. You're my wife. What's mine is yours now."

I shake my head. "I have never…I do not—" I stand up and pace away, turn back and stand in front of him. He wraps his arms around my waist, gazing up at me. I try again, this time in Arabic, slowly so he can follow. "This is a new way to think. I have survived by doing what I must to earn food. I have never known anything else. I am a whore because it is the way I could get money for food. You say you will take care of me. I will have to learn how to let you do this. I do not know how. No one has ever taken care of me. I take care of me."

Hunter's gaze hardens. "You are not a whore anymore, Rania." He pulls me closer and rests his head on my body just beneath my breasts. I cannot help my fingers from tangling in his hair, and realize that now, I do not have to help it. "Everything is going to change for you now, Rania."

I whisper my next words, because I am not sure if they are meant for him or for myself. "That is what I am afraid of."

Hunter

I can't sleep. I'm feeling better, but the docs tell me I'm stuck in the hospital for observation for another few days. I just want to go home. I want to get Rania alone. I'm fucking married to her, but I can't get a single hour of privacy with her, damn doctors coming and going all the time.

I'm not even sure if she wants me like that. She's skittish still. Hesitant to touch me, like she's not sure she's allowed to. I'm basically alone in this part of the hospital, so she's been bunking in the bed next to mine, the curtain between us drawn back. Not a lot of privacy, but then, we haven't needed it.

It's odd being back here, back among Americans, in the base. Rania is clearly unsure of herself here. She used the Sabah mask to get by, I think, but deep down, she's still a scared little girl. Now, without Sabah's fake confidence, she doesn't know who to be. She's been so alone for so long, and she doesn't know anything different. She doesn't even know what happiness is, I think.

I'll have to teach her.

She's asleep, curled on top of the blankets, wearing a pair of BDU pants and a T-shirt drawn from supply. Her feet are bare, the socks and boots I got for her set neatly at the foot of the bed. The hospital lights are dimmed, moonlight filtering in through the window. It's air-conditioned in here, cold. I can see her skin prickling with goose bumps.

"Fuck it," I whisper to myself.

I slip out of bed, dragging my blanket with me, and lie on the edge of the bed behind Rania. She rustles in her sleep but doesn't move. I drape the blanket over both of us and wrap my arm over her waist, intimate but not sexual. I want to touch her, want to kiss her and slip my hand underneath her shirt.

Damn it.

That one night was such a fucking tease. I can't get her voice out of my head, the insanely erotic way she writhed and moaned as she came, the hot silk of her skin...I'm teasing myself thinking about it. I'm getting hard, and I can't help it. I should be sleeping. I should've stayed in my bed because this is just going to make things more difficult on me.

She twists in the bed, making a little noise in her throat as she does so. She's facing me now, and her hands are clasped up between our chests, almost as if she's praying in her sleep. I let my hand rest on her waist, and I just can't help but let it slide down to her hip.

Then her eyes are fluttering open and she's looking into me. Not at me, but into me.

So beautiful, soft and lovely.

One of her hands uncurls, flattens against my chest. I blink hard, desperately, pathetically hoping she'll touch me. I feel like a teenager again, working so hard for a first kiss, awkwardly groping in the dark back seat of my car, hoping she'll touch me anywhere, hoping she wants me like I want her.

This is crazy. I'm married to her, but our relationship is so odd, so hesitant, so careful and exploratory.

Minutes pass, my hand on her hip, hers on my chest, neither of us moving, barely breathing. I wonder if I should try to make a move, kiss her, or touch her, or let her set the pace.

My gut tells me to stay still and see what she does, and I've learned to trust my gut.

Her eyes widen slightly and waver as her gaze shifts on mine. She runs her hand over my shoulder and down

my arm, just her fingertips along the bicep. And then
she's sliding her palm down my chest again, twisting her
hand so her fingers face sideways, cupping my waist and
my side. I stay frozen, letting her touch me. She scoots
sideways along the edge of the bed, pulls me toward her,
and then pushes me to lie on my back, adjusting her own
position again so she's lying half on me, my arm now
cradling her head.

"Okay?" she whispers. "Not hurting you, am I?"

I shake my head. My fingers are twisting in her hair,
smoothing it, toying with strands. I just watch her, examine her lovely features, memorizing, admiring.

She places her hand on the center of my chest, staring
at my body now rather than my eyes. Her fingers move
down the fabric of my shirt, a proper regulation green
BDU T-shirt now. She slips her fingers under the bottom
edge of the shirt and explores upward, pushing the cotton as she goes. I lift my back slightly so the shirt is free
to bunch under my shoulders. It's a bit uncomfortable, so
I tug the shirt off with one hand and toss it on the floor
next to the bed.

I don't know what the doctors are monitoring, since
I'm not hooked up to any machines; a random, aimless,
displaced thought.

Her hand rests on my right pectoral muscle, and she
traces around my nipple, rubs her thumb across the tip
of it, then traces the arc of my pectoral with one finger.
Now the stomach, her palm sliding across my taut belly,

tracing the grooves between my abs, like she did that one night in her house. I resist the urge to flex for her.

She runs up the other side of my body, then back down. Farther, closer and closer to my waistband. She's working up the courage to go farther. I won't stop her this time. I think she's just exploring, for herself. Exploring her own sense of desire.

She takes a breath, slow and deep, lets it out as she snakes her palm down my torso to the fly of my pants. I unconsciously suck in my belly a little, then force myself to relax it. She glances up at me, unsure. I tuck a wayward hair behind her ear, run the side of my thumb over her cheekbone, then kiss her, as slow and soft and sweet as I can manage.

This seems to give her courage.

She twists the first button free, then the second. She stops, looks up at me. I quirk one side of my mouth up in a tiny smile and keep playing with her hair. She glances away, smiling shyly. So innocent, approaching this almost like a virgin.

I lick my lips and focus on breathing evenly as she unbuttons my fly the rest of the way. She puts her fingers in the waistband of my underwear, then hesitates, shakes her head.

"Hey," I say. "It's okay. This is whatever you want. No rush, okay? Just…just relax."

"I am not so much afraid," she says. "I am only nervous. Unsure of what I want, or what I am doing."

"Just do whatever you want. If you're not sure, just ask."

She bites her lip and looks at me, long and hard. "I want…I want to see you," she says.

"See me?"

She nods, not looking at me now, embarrassed. "Just see what you look like, first, as a man."

"Oh. You mean you want me to take my pants off?"

She nods her head against my chest again. "Is it okay?"

I laugh into her hair. "Of course. Everything's okay. Listen, only do what you want, okay? I told you, I don't expect—"

"I want to," she interrupts. "I just am not so sure of what to want, or how to want it. You know? I have never wanted a man before."

"And you want me?"

She nods. "It is frightening, a little, how much I want to touch you. To be touched." I can feel her heart beating hard in her chest. "What you did, before, to me. To make me…" she makes an exploding gesture with her fingers, "…that was…I liked it. Very much."

I chuckle. "Me, too."

She tilts her head to look at me, nose wrinkled in confusion. "But you…I did nothing for you."

"It's not just about that. I enjoyed that as much as you did, but in a different way. Watching you…making you feel those things…I loved it. I'll do it again, if you want me to."

She shakes her head. "Not yet. First, this. I am afraid to touch you, but yet I want to. I cannot be only afraid. I must know in my heart that it is okay to want. To touch."

I think I sense what she's saying. "This is different for you. Different from…being with someone as Sabah."

She flinches and goes tense. "That is not 'being with.' It is… 'doing to.' You see the difference? Sabah…she is one who allows men to feel what they want, do what they want. Sabah? She does not feel. She is cold. So cold that she cannot feel."

"Numb."

"Numb?"

"That's the word for when you're so cold you can't feel anything."

"Oh. Then yes. Sabah is numb. She pretends." A long silence. "I am not Sabah. I am Rania. And I feel."

"Good. No more Sabah. Only Rania."

She nods. "But you are right. This is very different. Maybe you think because I was a whore for many years, I should know much about sex, about men." She shakes her head. "No. They do. I…do nothing. Only let them and make the noises they like."

"Not anymore," I say.

She shrugs, a tiny movement. "Perhaps. If you say so." She's drifting away.

I've fucked it up. She's distant now, cooled off. Thinking about then. About Sabah.

"I'm sorry I brought it up."

She shrugs. "You need to know these things. I know nothing of sex. Of men. Of what to do, or how. What you might want. What I should want, or like to feel. It is all strange to me. I liked what you did. I did not know I could feel that way."

I roll slightly and kiss her. She freezes at first, as she always does when I kiss her, but she softens into it quickly, opens her mouth to mine, and nudges closer, gives in to the kiss. Her hand slips back onto my ribs, drifts around to my back, and explores it as we kiss, break for breath, and kiss again.

When we stop, she touches my chest again, drifting back down to my open fly. She glances at me, and the look is the request. I lift my hips and wiggle out of my pants, taking the underwear with them, and then I'm naked beneath blanket. I feel oddly nervous, even though I'm usually comfortable with my nudity.

She pushes the blanket past my hips slowly. Her breathing is shallow as she gazes at me. I'm hardening under her gaze. The scrutiny is almost embarrassing, nerve-wracking. I'm perfectly still, except for my chest rising and falling with my breath, and my slowly unfurling cock.

Her hand rests on my stomach, over my belly button. Again, some bizarre instinct causes me to suck in my belly when she begins to slowly, so slowly move her hand downward. I'm fully erect now, thickening, hardening. She glances up at me, then back down.

She extends a single finger and traces my length from the tip to the base, just the pad of her finger sliding along the bumps and ridges of the skin. Now her palm, down the length and back up. It's been a long time, and I'm full of raging desire, burning, aching with need, but I have to contain it. Keep it in, keep it back. Let her touch, and that's it. Let her explore.

I focus on her hair, toying with the cool strands between my fingers.

I heave in a deep breath when she takes me in her hand, lifts me away from my body, from side to side. God, her hands on my cock feel so good. So goddamned amazing. Her tiny little hands, long fingers, slim and strong and warm, grasping me, sliding along me. I'm clenched with all my muscles.

She has no idea what she's doing to me.

I'm so close.

What the fuck do I do?

I wrestle with myself, trembling, trying so hard to hold back as she fondles me, examines me. She traces my length, grips me, lets go, cups my balls in one hand, touches them and explores them, then returns to my cock.

I'm leaking. I'm about to come, and I have to hold it in. Have to. She's just exploring. This isn't sex.

I can't wait much longer.

Rania

His whole body is shaking, as if he is flexing every muscle. His back is stiff, his eyes closed, his fingers tangled in my hair.

His manhood is a thing of contradictions, so soft yet so hard. It is long and straight and thick, lying flat against his belly. It seems so big, and I am a little frightened of when we will have sex, even though I know it will be okay. I push those thoughts away. That is not for now.

I let myself touch him. It is okay to touch him. I like touching him. I like the way it feels in my hand, filling my fist. He is making little noises in his throat, although I do not think he is aware of it. His other hand is clenching into a fist in the sheet of the bed. I glance down at his feet, peeking out from beneath the blanket, and his toes are curled. His arms are flexed, his stomach muscles are flexed.

He is tensed, and every time I touch his manhood, he flinches, moves his hips slightly into the touch.

"Why are you making muscles?" I ask. I have been trying to use only English with him, and he tries to answer in only Arabic.

This time, he answers in English. I do not think he is capable of Arabic right now. "I'm…holding back."

I do not understand at first, but then awareness dawns on me. He is about to release, but is holding back.

"Why hold back?" I ask, gripping him more firmly now and sliding my hand on him.

He laughs once. "Because this isn't…about…me." He is moving his hips to the rhythm of my hand on his manhood. "It's about you. Doing what you want. Learning to want. Also, because it'll be messy."

I know what I should do. I am not quite ready, but it is the best way. I start unbuttoning my pants. Hunter stops me.

"No, not like this. I want it to be special. Just…stop touching me for a minute and I'll…I'll be okay."

"You do not want to have sex with me?"

"No," he says, and my heart shrivels, hurt. But he continues, "I want to make love to you. It's different."

My hand is still on him, but not moving.

"Oh," I say. "But not now?"

He shakes his head and takes my wrist in his hand, tries to pull me away. "No, not now. When we have all the time in the world. When we have a big bed and privacy."

I do not want to stop touching him. I want to see him release. I do not care about a mess, or privacy. I like touching him. I understand a little now what he said about enjoying making me feel good.

"Do you like how I am touching you? Does it feel good?" I ask.

He gasps and releases my hand. I move my fist around his manhood, and I feel more confident in it now. His face gives me my answer, but he nods anyway.

"Yes," he says. "God, yes. It feels so good. I love it. I don't want you to stop. But…I can't hold back much longer."

I continue to move my hand on him, and now his hips are starting to jerk. Leaning close to his ear, I whisper to him, "I want you to feel good. I am enjoying this. I do not want to stop. I do not want you to hold back. You can release."

I know something I could do. Before I have a chance to think about it, I move my head down toward his manhood. He stops me.

"No, Rania. Not that." Something in his voice tells me he is serious, so I return to leaning on his arm.

I can hear beneath his voice what he may be think-ing of, and I think of it, too, but push it away. I am glad he did not let me. It would have given me memories of other things, bad things.

I kiss his jaw and taste his sweat, his stubble, his skin. I had slowed my hand on him when I began to move down, so now I speed up. My fist is loose around him, skin barely brushing skin. Now I hold him more tightly, move slowly, from the top of him to the bottom. He is jerking, shifting up and falling down. He gasps, tilts his head back.

"Oh…oh, god…I'm about to…" He grates the words past his teeth, and then falls silent and arches his back.

Now.

He goes still at the apex of his arch, and his manhood jerks in my hand. A thick stream of viscous white seed spurts from him, shooting hard across his torso, in his belly button. I keep moving my hand on him, and his hips swivel his manhood into my fist. Another stream overlays the first, not as much now, nor does it shoot quite as far, and then a third jet, even less, and his body flops down against the bed. He is gasping, writhing his hips.

"God…goddamn." He is breathless, amazed, flushed.

I feel a thrill of something powerful inside me, hot and swelling through every inch of me. It is a pleasant-ness, happiness. He liked it, and so did I. I made him feel good, and I felt a joy in return for having given it to him. I feel content.

He laughs, a low rumble in his chest. "Shit, now I'm a mess."

I look at him, at the thick river of white seed on his belly. "I will clean it."

I go to the bathroom not far away, wet some paper towels, and return to the bed.

"I can do it," Hunter says, reaching for the towels.

"No," I say. "Let me. Please."

He drops his hand and watches me as I scrub the seed from his flesh, folding the towels and wiping until he is clean, the fine curly hairs low on his belly damp and sticking to his skin. I throw the paper towels away and lie down next to him again. He drapes the blanket over us and pulls me across him.

"Rania, that was—"

I kiss him, and he goes quiet as we kiss. "It is a beginning," I say.

FIFTEEN

Hunter

ALL THE PAPERWORK HAS BEEN SIGNED. She's officially
Rania Lee now. Goddamn. I'm a married man. Crazy.

I'm officially honorably discharged and we're on the
way home. Well, back to the States. I haven't mentioned
to her that I don't have an actual home yet. If it was just
me, I'd probably bunk out on Derek's parents' couch, but
that's not an option. Too many questions.

Derek. Fucking Derek re-upped. Says he wants to
make sergeant. I could kick his ass for splitting us up
like this, but it's his choice, I guess. It just sucks. This
will be the first time since goddamned second grade that
Derek and I won't be doing the same thing together. I'm
going home to make a life with my wife, and he's staying
behind to do another tour in the clusterfuck that is OIF
2—maybe Afghanistan next, if the scuttlebutt is true.

We're on a plane headed west. Rania is in the seat next to me, clutching my hand so hard I think she might actually be bruising bones. I don't blame her. We're in the middle of an awful goddamn thunderstorm and the plane is bucking like a roped steer. Poor girl's first plane ride, and it's the roughest one I've ever been on.

I need to distract her.

"Hey, Rania." She turns to look at me, teeth clenched, eyes wide. "So when we get to Des Moines, we're gonna look at houses. That'll be fun, right?"

She just looks confused. "Look at houses? What does this mean?"

"It means we're going to pick out a home."

"I thought you said we *were* going home."

I shrug. "I just meant the city, Des Moines, where I grew up. I don't have a place of my own. I joined the Marines out of high school, so I never had a place."

"So we are alone together with no home?"

"Yeah, baby. It's just you and me. We'll find a nice place together."

"Baby? I am not a baby." She wrinkles her nose.

I laugh. "No, I know. It's…a term of endearment." She gives me a blank look. "It's like 'honey' or 'sweetie.'"

She still doesn't seem to know what I mean.

I laugh and shake my head. "It just means I love you."

"If you say so," she says. "But it is strange, to call the woman you love as a baby. But then, Americans are strange."

"It is kind of weird," I agree. "I never thought about it before. I guess it's a cultural thing. We call each other pet names. It's a way of…showing affection, I guess."

She nods. "Ah, now this I understand. Like to call a son or a little brother '*habibi*,' even if he is no longer a little boy."

I nod. "Yeah, basically."

She changes the subject. "So we will choose a home together? Do they not cost much money in your country?"

"Yeah, but we're not going to buy it outright. I have a good bit of money saved up, and I know the loan officer at a bank in town, so we'll get a good deal. We'll have a nice place."

"If you say so." The plane hits a rough patch of turbulence, and she shuts down, clenching my hand again.

I let her crush my fingers and try to imagine having a home of my own, with Rania. It's a nice image.

I lease a furnished condo in the downtown area on a month-by-month basis until we find somewhere permanent. Rania has no clothes, nothing of her own, so the first thing I do is take her shopping. At first she just wanders between the racks at Macy's, looking puzzled.

Eventually she stops and turns to me. "What am I supposed to do? There are too many things here."

I laugh. "Pick what you like. Pick a bunch of stuff that you like and try it on. Keep the stuff that fits you good and looks good, and leave the rest."

She takes a skirt off the rack, then puts it back. She does this a dozen times. "I do not know what I like."

In the end, I ask one of the Macy's associates to help her, and she ends up with a bunch of nice outfits. She's wearing one of them now, a skirt fitting tight around her hips and thighs and loose at the ankles. The top is a button-down blouse that accentuates her frame without being too revealing. I was careful to make sure none of the clothes even remotely resembled her old outfits, all miniskirts and low-cut tank tops. Everything is tasteful and modest, skirts down to her knees, at least, tops that don't show too much cleavage. I get her bras and panties, makeup, pajamas, shoes, sandals, shampoo, conditioner, all the stuff I know girls like.

Rania seems overwhelmed. "Why do I need all these things? I have never had any of this. A little makeup, some clothes to wear. All this…it is so much."

I laugh. "You don't *need* it. But I want you to have it. It's just stuff."

"More *stuff* than I have ever owned in all my life. You should not waste so much money on me."

I lean across the cab and kiss her. "It's not wasted, Rania."

"If you say so."

I growl. That's her fall-back phrase when she disagrees but won't say anything else. "Rania. Seriously. Disagree with me sometimes. Don't just accept whatever I say. I want you to tell me your opinion and stick with it. If you don't like what I'm saying, tell me. If you think I'm wrong, tell me."

"You are my husband. It is my duty to support you."

"Bullshit. You're my wife, and it's your duty to tell me when I'm being a stubborn jackass. Don't just roll over and accept everything."

She stares out the window without answering for a long time. "I have never had the luxury of opinions," she says in Arabic. "Like so much, I will have to learn."

"You will learn. I will help you," I tell her in Arabic. "I want to you become the person you want to be. Who is Rania? What does she want? What does she like? What are her dreams?"

The cab pulls up and lets us out, and I carry the bags into our condo. Rania crosses the room to stand at the window, arms akimbo under her breasts.

"I do not know the answers to those questions. They are the questions of someone who is living, not only just surviving. I do not know how to live. How to be…a person."

I stand behind her and wrap my arms around her waist. "I'm not sure what you mean, 'how to be a person.' You *are* a person."

She shakes her head, her hair tickling my nose. "No. Well, perhaps now I am becoming one. Before, I was only a whore. A whore is a thing. Like a refrigerator, or a cow used for milk. I was meant for use. A whore does not have dreams or desires for the future. There is only the next client."

"That's not who you are anymore. You're a person, now. A wonderful person."

She spins in my arms to face me. "You think I am a wonderful person?"

I smile and kiss her lips. "Yes."

She lays her head on my chest. "Then that is who I am. Your wonderful person."

The first night we were back, we were so tired from travel that we could only fall asleep, collapsed side by side but not touching. Tonight, I hope for different.

And then I realize that her whole life has changed, her entire reason for existence has been stripped away, and she's faced with the task of reinventing herself in a new country, married to a man she's known for maybe a month.

Maybe I should just give her space. Let her adjust rather than pushing her into things.

I want her so fucking bad, but again…I can't rush her.

I show her the shower when we finish eating our dinner. I ordered pizza, and Rania was in awe of it. She only ate a little, which was probably smart. I ate most of it myself. Pizza is one of the things I always miss the most in the desert.

She strips unselfconsciously, stands at the open door of the shower, one arm across her breasts, the other hand beneath the spray, testing the temperature. Her shower in Iraq was almost always cold. She sets the water hot, scalding hot. I can't help but watch her, long legs flashing in the steam, wet skin glistening, tempting, tantalizing. Her long blonde hair drapes wet across her back, hanging down between her shoulder blades.

I want so badly to strip and step in there with her.

I see her glance at me out of the corner of her eye, and I wonder if she's expecting me to go in with her. If she wants me to.

I'm afraid of pushing her too fast. Of making her think I expect it. I want her to want me on her terms, in her time. I want her to want me in her own way. It will take time. I might explode before that happens, but I don't see much choice.

I turn away, and as I do so I see a flash of something almost like disappointment in her eyes, but she doesn't call me back. I undress to my boxers and lie on the bed, waiting. She comes out in a towel, stops, facing me on the bed. Her eyes are wide.

My throat is dry, my pulse pounding. I can feel myself hardening.

I watch a bead of water run down her neck and between her breasts, beneath the towel.

We're both breathing deep, neither of us speaking. I make a vow to always let her make the first move, to wait for her.

It's testing my control right now. She's wet and clean and sexy as hell, and all I want to do is crawl across the bed, rip the towel off her, and kiss every inch of her lithe, lush body.

I don't dare, and I have to fist my hands into the sheet to stop myself.

Rania

He does nothing, just watches me. I know him well enough now that I see the desire raging in his eyes. His manhood is hard, and his hands are bunching into the sheets. But he does nothing.

Does he not want me? I am clean, and the shower was glorious. So hot. No end to the hot water, soaking me, warming me. Cleaning me. I feel cleaner than I have ever been. But he does not move. Just watches me. I do not know what he waits for.

I want him. I want to feel his arms around me, holding me. I am still nervous at the idea of true sex with him, but still I want it, and even the desire itself is a strange, foreign feeling.

Everything about my life now is strange and foreign. I am in this huge, fast, busy, wealthy place. He bought me so much, more than I need or thought existed. Makeup I do not know how to use. Things for my hair, six different kinds of shoes. Enough clothes that I could go for a month and never wear the same thing twice. The amount of money he spent, the number I saw on the computer in the store, it was more than I could comprehend, and he did not even blink as he gave them his card.

And none of that matters, not now. My heart pounds like a drum in my chest. I want to let the towel fall, I want to tell him to show me how to make love to him.

My hands shake as I grip the towel where it is rolled tight around my chest. My thighs tremble, and I remember how I shook and moaned when he touched me there, kissed me there between them. I want him to do that again. I want to beg him, *please touch me, please kiss me.* When he kisses and touches me I am not so afraid, and I can forget the horrible darkness that was my life...my existence.

I need it. Need it. Need the forgetting that exists only when I am in his strong arms.

My tongue is frozen and my words are stuck. I cannot speak. I try, move my lips, but nothing comes out. Actions are the only way I can ask him to give me what I need.

I make my feet move, and suddenly I am standing next to him. He is on the left side of the bed, wearing only a pair of loose red and black underwear like shorts, but not. *Boxings*, I think he called them. I can see his hardness making a tent of the fabric, and there is a gap in the material, showing me glimpses of his manhood. I want to touch it again.

My breasts rise and fall in short, sharp breaths, making the towel tighten and loosen. I am not afraid of him seeing me naked; he has before. I am afraid of truly giving in to my desires, because then I will need him completely. Being able to resist how much I want to feel him and touch him is the last of my independence. It is a small thing, a foolish thing. I want him, and he is my husband, so it natural that we should share this thing we both so badly want. But I need him.

I have never needed anything but money for food and somewhere to sleep.

Now, I need this man.

"I need you," I whisper in Arabic. "That is why I am afraid."

He does not answer. He sits up, swings his long, thick legs off the bed, and frames my knees with his. He puts his hand on my thigh just beneath the edge of the towel.

"I need you, too," he says in Arabic. "And that is why *I* am afraid."

The knowledge that he has the same fears I do comforts me, erodes the paralytic grip on me.

Now I can smile at him, a true smile. I am not trying to be seductive, because I know he wants me. His hands are curling around the backs of my thighs, pulling me closer. I look down at his soft, loving blue eyes and find the courage to tug the end of the towel free. His eyes widen, and he licks his lips. His hands tighten around my thighs.

I think he can hear my heart beating so hard my ribs shake.

It is done. The towel is billowing open around me, falling to the floor, and I am naked before him. There is no going back now. I could hyperventilate, but I do not. I keep breathing, forcing myself to take long, slow breaths, lift my chin, and gaze down at him.

His chin brushes my navel as he looks up at me between my breasts. "Tell me what you want, Rania. Tell me what you want, so I can give it to you."

I can only shake my head. "I do not…I do not know."

"Yes, you do."

He is right. I do know. I tangle my fingers in his hair and pull his handsome, rock-chiseled face against me, against my belly. I back up a little, and his face is lower. He turns his head sideways slightly, looks at me, grins.

"Say it, Rania. I know what you want, but I want to hear you say it."

"Why? I am embarrassed. I cannot say it."

"Yes, you can." His voice is soft and confident.

His lips touch my belly, hot and moist on my flesh, which pebbles with need. Between my legs I am wet and warm and trembling. I know now how his lips and tongue feel, pressed there, moving there, and oh, by Allah and Mohammed his holy prophet, I want it so badly. I feel a rush of guilt for swearing so, but then I no longer care. Blasphemy or not, I no longer believe in Allah. He did not rescue me; Hunter Lee did.

And I want Hunter's mouth on my privates.

"I want you to kiss me…down there." My words are whispered so low, so soft and hesitant I can barely hear myself.

Hunter hears me. His mouth touches one of my hips, the right one, tongue tickling and trailing heat. Then my thigh, the crease of skin where my leg joins to my hip. I widen my stance, legs spreading farther apart. His kisses trail down my leg, and his arms wrap around my waist so his strong hands can cup my bottom. He pulls me closer, and I gasp when his tongue laps against my entrance.

"Oh, god," he says, "you taste so fucking good."

I blush furiously at his words, but cannot speak my embarrassment. My back arches and my head falls back. He does not give me immediate satisfaction, but draws it out. Oh, what excruciating joy his game gives me, his tongue darting into me, lapping at my flowing juices, flicking at my sensitive little nub of nerves.

One of his powerful hands stays cupped on the half-globe of my buttock, and the other roams around, caresses my thigh next to his face, and then I am gasping again because his fingers are probing into me, moving into the soft wet folds, then farther in, curling to graze that sensitive little spot inside me.

My legs do not want to hold my weight, but Hunter's arm curls under my bottom to hold me up, and I am gripping his hair so hard it must hurt, but he does not protest.

Fire billows inside me, centered on my hot, quivering feminine core. Oh, this feels so good. This is heaven. His fingers sweep inside me, his tongue brushes my clitoris, and then he presses his lips around me and sucks, tonguing me. I cannot stop my moaning and do not try to. I do not care who hears me. My legs continue to give out beneath me, and then I find my strength again and stand up. This turns into a rhythm as he licks me, kisses me, fingers me.

I am on the edge of the abyss again, and this time I go willingly into abandon. A storm overtakes me, sweeps me into shivering ecstasy.

Hunter pulls away at the peak of pleasure, and I look down at him in panic.

"Please, do not stop now," I say. I am begging, and I do not care. "Please, do not stop."

Hunter licks at me, but it is not enough to drive me over the edge. "Say something for me, baby."

"Anything."

"I want you to say 'I'm going to come.'"

"Come?"

"It's the word we use in English. It means orgasm." He licks me again, slowly, so slowly.

I sink down almost into a crouch at the glacial slowness of his tongue against my womanhood. "Please, Hunter. I am going to come. Please, make me come."

He growls against my folds. "Fuck. I'm gonna make you come so hard, Rania."

He moves his fingers inside me, brushing that special spot swiftly now, and his tongue circles my clitoris and I am bowing my legs to get closer to him. I do not know when, but at some time he sank to his knees in front of me. He is on his knees in front of me. This makes me want to cry, although I do not know why.

I explode without warning. I am on the edge, wavering, closer and closer, and then I am falling against him, unable to support my weight. I am gasping, making high-pitched whining noises as he sucks and licks and flicks my clitoris, driving me into explosion after explosion.

Then I know I cannot stand any longer. "Please, Hunter, catch me. I cannot stand up anymore."

My legs give way, and his arms are around me, under my neck and my bottom. He lifts me effortlessly. I could be held by him like this forever. So content, so safe in his arms, against his chest so I can feel his heart beating. He lays me down on the bed and leans next to me. He does nothing but look at me for a moment.

"You are so beautiful," he whispers. "Do you know that?"

I shake my head. "I know that men think—"

He cuts me off with a kiss. "Man. One man. Me. I'm all that matters. No one else can have you. You're mine."

I shiver at his words. "Do you promise me?"

"Yes, my love. I promise." He kisses my jaw, then my neck, and I am still trembling from the force of my orgasm.

But he is not done with me. He kisses my shoulder, then my chest, then the underside of my breast. One of his hands is roving my body, brushing my waist and my belly and my other breast, grazing my face, then down to my leg and up my thigh.

He is leaning not quite against me, but close enough that I can feel his manhood nudging my hip.

"I want to touch you," I say. "I want to make you come."

"You will," he whispers, his mouth around my nipple. "I promise, you will. First, just let me kiss you."

And he does. He spends an eternity just kissing me. He kisses every inch of my body, my arms, my hands, my fingers, my knees, the soles of my feet; he rolls me to my stomach and kisses my spine, my buttocks, the backs of my thighs. He kisses me until I cannot bear it any longer.

I stop him, push him to his back, and strip his boxings off him. I am not sure that is the right word. Before I toss them to the floor, I hold them up.

"What is the word for this kind of underwear?" I ask. "Boxings? Something like that? I cannot think of it."

He laughs hard. "Boxings? Oh, god, Rania. That's funny. Boxers. They're called boxers, sweetheart."

I frown at him. "Are you making fun? I do not know all the right words yet."

He takes my face in his and draws me into his embrace, still laughing. "No! No, baby. No. I'm not making fun of you. It's just funny. I mean, 'boxers' is a funny word now that I think about it, but for some reason, 'boxings' is funnier."

He stops laughing, and suddenly we're gazing at each other. His eyes, the thing about him that first arrested my attention, they are impossibly blue in the light from the bathroom.

He puts his palm to my cheek. "I love you, Rania Lee."

I gather my courage once more, and tell him what I want. "Make love to me, Hunter."

I touch his manhood, find it hard as stone and leaking fluid from the tip, yet when I grasp him in my hand, he is softer than soft, and I love that wonderful contradiction, as I love the way he arches his body when I touch him like this. As I love his lips on me, as I love his voice when says my name.

I love him.

It is so unbelievable, even still, in this impossibly luxurious house he calls a "condo" that a man such as Hunter could love me, a whore.

But I am not, am I? He would be upset with me for thinking that. I must not think it. I am not a whore.

I am not Sabah.

I am Rania Lee, and I am Hunter's wife.

Hunter kisses me, and I lose myself in his lips, his body hard and strong next to me. I am ready. I settle onto my back, such a familiar position, and ready myself for him. He kisses me, plants his hand next to my face, moves slowly above me.

I cannot help the panic that hits, the feeling of memory overtaking me, of so many other men moving above me. My fingers curl into claws on his shoulders and I fight it, fight so hard, but I cannot, and my breath comes in short sharp gasps. My eyes are squeezed shut tight, my knees pressed together, and Hunter is whispering in my ear, but I cannot hear him, cannot understand him.

Then, motion. Hunter's hands are on my waist and I am rolling, lying on top of him. I bury my face in his shoulder and weep.

"I am sorry, Hunter. I—I cannot. I thought I could, but—"

He touches my lips. "Hey, it's fine. I'm so sorry, I didn't think, I didn't know it would have that effect on you. It's fine."

I cannot stop crying. I have let him down, and I cannot do what so much of me wants to, what I know he wants. "I am sorry, Hunter." I move to get off the bed, to get away from him, from his disappointment.

"Hey, wait a second," he says, and does not let me move. "Look at me."

I lift my face, and his thumb brushes away my tears. He kisses me, and for a moment I am lost once again in the heaven of his kiss. I begin to forget myself, and grow hungry for him, kiss him desperately.

He pulls away and meets my eyes. "That's not the only position, you know."

"What?" I am not sure what he means at first.

"I mean…look, I'm not trying to rush you or pressure you. If you can't, if you're not ready, that's totally fine—"

I shake my head. "I want to. But…that just was so frightening. There were so many things in my head and heart that I could not breathe. But I do not want to let you down."

He takes my face and draws me close. He moves me up higher and now I am sitting on top of him, straddling his waist like he is a horse and I am a rider.

His eyes blaze. "You could never, *ever* let me down, Rania. If you're not ready, that's okay. I want this to be something you want. When you want. How you want. *Only* what *you* want. Do you understand? You can't and won't disappoint me. Don't ever think that."

"I *do* want this. It is confusing, Hunter. So much of me wants this, wants *you*. But…another part is afraid, and that part feels afraid when you are above me."

He smiles and rubs my thighs. I sit straighter at his touch. His hands slide up my legs, closer to my core, and my desire burns hot. I can feel the liquid evidence of my need for him heating up within me, filling me.

"I don't have to be above you," he says.

"No?"

"No," he whispers back, smiling.

He runs his hands up my torso, fondles my breasts, slips his hands over my shoulders and down my back before sliding his hands beneath my buttocks and lifting me up. I lean forward and brace myself with my hands on his chest. My privates are hovering above his body now. He moves, shifts slightly beneath me, and then I feel the soft, thick tip of his manhood probing at my entrance, just touching, just brushing.

I gasp in a sharp, surprised breath. "Like this?

He rubs his hands in comforting circles on my back. "Just like this, my love."

My love. The words hit me deep in my heart, spearing into the most secret places in my soul. I am his love. How can that be? How could I be worth his love?

He waits. Watches me. Hunter never does anything unless he is sure I want it. He is straining, tensed, needing me. I can feel it in him, taste it the air. I kiss him, taste his need on his lips, in his saliva, on his breath, on his tongue.

Does he feel my need? I need him. I want him. But he is not moving, just waiting, and I think he will not do this for me. I must do it.

My throat is clenching tight, so dry, and I am sweating, trembling on him. My thighs are around his hips, and his taut, muscular stomach is beneath my core, and his arms are around me, his hands on me.

"Kiss me, so I can do this," I say.

He closes with me slowly, eyes on me until the last moment. I watch his eyes slide shut as our noses nuzzle against each other and our lips touch, and then I am lost, so sweetly lost. I reach between our bodies and grasp his manhood, guide him to my entrance and in, then pause.

He knows the words I need to hear: "I love you, Rania."

He is inside me. I could burst, split open at the seams, for he fills me completely. He is motionless, his hands on my waist, blue eyes wide, soft, loving, fixed on me in that soul-searching way he has. He is not fully immersed in me, only part of the way. I swallow hard and lean over him, slip my hands beneath his head and clutch his hair, press my lips to his throat.

I am shaking like a scrap of paper in a long wind.

I move my hips, withdrawing, and a whimper slides out from my throat. Hunter groans deep in chest and his hands tighten on my waist, but he does nothing to urge me faster or deeper.

When he is nearly slipping out of me, I gather a deep breath into my air-starved lungs—making me realize I had been holding my breath—and then I slide down his body, driving him deep, fully into me, exhaling as he impales me.

"God," Hunter says, but the word is drawn out into many syllables, a groan as long as his exhaled breath, matching mine.

"Please, touch me," I whisper. "Tell me what you are feeling. Your voice…I want to hear your voice as we make love."

His hands drift up my sides to caress to my breasts, taking their weight and treasuring their softness. "You feel so good, Rania. Being inside you like this is…it's fucking heaven, baby."

I move again, draw my hips high, so only the soft, broad head of his manhood remains in my privates, and then I pause, waiting for him to speak, for I heard him draw breath, heard the scrape of air past his vocal chords. My eyes are shut tight, and every other sense is tightened like a string across a sitar. I can smell him, sweat, faint cologne, deodorant, soap…and me, my scent mixed in with his. His body is beneath me, filling my sense of touch. There is nothing to feel but Hunter, his hands on me, his legs like flesh-covered stone, his manhood within me, his breath on my cheek as he speaks.

"I love this so much. I love your skin." He moves, just a little, his hips ever so gently drifting up and then back down; the slight motion sends rockets of delight bursting in me, and I let myself slide down so his hips bump mine, driving him deep, deep into me. "I love your eyes. I love your breath on my lips."

And then I move again. I let myself slide up his length and back down, not just with my hips now, but with all of me, my whole soft body on the hardness of his. He moves with me, just one sweetly slow thrust, and it feels so good I have to claw my fingers into his shoulders and whimper.

"Move with me, Hunter."

He groans. "Thank fuck. Holding still like this is the hardest thing I've ever done."

He scratches his nails down my back and I shudder, writhing on top of him and driving him deep. A small, fluttering explosion billows through me when he is all the way inside me, and now…

Something breaks open inside me when he begins to move, slow gliding strokes into me. There is no fear anymore, no worry, no memory, nothing but Hunter and the incredible sensations he gives me.

"Oh, god, you feel so good, so fucking good." Hunter's voice is a low growl in my ear, driving me to move faster.

I love that I make him feel good. I want more.

I kiss his lips, hungry and needy. Now his thrusting is a little faster, and I match him. I cannot help but move in sync with him. His manhood slides into me, fills me, stretches me, and now I come to a realization.

He does not just fill my body, my womanhood. He fills me. My heart, my soul. He fills the horrible emptiness that has gaped inside me all my life. The moment that he slid into me, I knew. It has just taken me this long to understand the strange feeling flowing in my veins in place of blood:

Happiness.

I let the tears flow, let myself sob. I never stop moving, and now I take control of the pace, collapsed on top of Hunter, my love, my husband, my fullness, and I move like a madwoman, like a woman possessed. I am sliding and slipping on top of him, driving him into me and pulling up and away until he has almost pulled out of me, and then he is deep again.

Our bodies crash together in a perfect symphony, my cries of pleasure growing louder and more desperate, more passionate. Hunter's voice joins mine, and I love the sound of his voice raised loud in pleasure, ecstasy given to him by me, by my love.

"I love you, Hunter. Please do not stop. Not ever."

"I won't, I promise. Never. I'll love you forever. I'll make love to you until there's no me and no you, only us together like this forever."

"Yes, please! I want that, always. Only us. I love this. I love this." My words are spoken to the rhythm of our body's union, crashing together, gliding and sliding away, rhythm like a song, and my thoughts are disjointed poetry, my words are pidgin of English and Arabic, and all I can do is sob above him and move above him and kiss him where my lips drag along his skin and grasp him and claw him.

Heat blooms and curls inside me, crushed hotter by Hunter's body within me, and now the heat is exploding and spreading and my entire body is convulsing and I am curling into a ball on top of him, weeping helplessly. The way he made me come in the past had seemed earth-shaking, more intense than anything I could have imagined. This...this is beyond those orgasms by several degrees of intensity. I come, and I come, and still Hunter is moving into me, becoming desperate himself now, and I can only cling to him as he crashes into me, ungentle and furious, and I would not want him to change it or stop or be gentle.

"Yes, Hunter!" I prop my hands on his chest and move my hips to meet his, and he is driving so deeply into me I think he cannot go deeper, and then he pushes me upright, gently leans me backward, and I lift up with my legs and he drives up with his hips and he is even more completely inside me and I come yet again, and I have an errant, lucid thought. That phrase of his, *to come* in reference to orgasm, it is perfect, so right for the experience of reaching orgasm with the man you love. You are not merely finding a physical release, you are coming into a new realm, coming into heaven, coming into him, becoming him.

And then he comes, and I think I have truly lost myself in him. He explodes, and I feel his seed fill me, hot and wet inside me and I love that, too. I love the way he groans wordlessly, almost yelling, plunging hard and hard and hard, and I fall onto him, wrapping my arms around his neck and weeping, weeping onto his shoulder, body-wracking sobs.

We are still now.

"Why are you crying, Rania? Are you okay?"

I gasp, shuddering with aftershocks and receding sobs. "Yes. More than yes." I lift up and roll over so I am cradled by him, palm his cheek and let him see into my soul through my eyes. "I am crying because that was so wonderful, so good that I do not know the words for it in my language or yours."

He sighs deeply and lets it out, clutching me close. "For me, too. That was the most amazing thing I've ever experienced."

"Do you remember asking me if I have ever been happy?"

"Yes."

"I am happy now. You have given me happiness."

I see his eyes shine and shimmer, and his arms tighten around me and I see a tear streak down his face. "You've made me happy, too, Rania, and I didn't think I could ever be happy again after my parents died."

"We can be happy together."

"Yes, please," he whispers. "I'd like that."

Hunter

We sleep after making love, and I wake up with the most raging hard-on of my life. Rania is nestled against me, spooning me, her back to my front, and her ass cradles my achingly hard cock. She is so soft in my arms, so warm, so fragile and small, yet I know she is strong, so unbelievably strong.

I don't care who she has been, what she has been. I know some guys wouldn't be able to get past the fact that she was a prostitute, but that doesn't matter to me. What matters is she loves me so completely, and she doesn't hide it or hold back.

I thought I would die of sheer ecstasy when she slid down my body and pushed my cock into her hot, wet pussy. I did die, I think. I died and went to heaven, and to remain still while she found herself, while she learned to let herself feel, that was the hardest thing.

Like, ever.

I wanted to plunge into her, hard and wild and desperate, but I couldn't. And I am so, *so* glad I didn't. It took an age, it seemed, for her to understand the joy of making love, for her to open up her heart and her mind and her body and let me love her truly, but she did, and she rocked my world.

And now I want to do it again.

My palm slides of its own volition up her thigh, then in across her belly, up to her breasts. Dim gray light streams in through the window and gives us a gentle glow of lightening dawn. I cup her breast, gently toy with the nipple. She moans in her sleep, shifts. I slide my hand down between her thighs to the tight triangle and she moves, just a little, loosens her clamped legs.

I'm not sure I should push this, but I can't help touching her, wanting her. My middle finger reaches the top of her cleft and slides in. Now she is waking up, her eyelids fluttering to grant me glimpses of her chocolate eyes.

"Hunter?" Her voice is thick and sleep-muzzy.

"I'm sorry," I say. "You're just so sexy when you sleep, I couldn't help touching you."

She smiles, brushes a stretching hand across her face, groaning as she flexes and tenses her muscles languorously, like a cat. Her breasts arch up and out, and I slide my hands across them, and then, when she is at the peak of her stretch, I lean in to suckle her nipple, flicking it with my tongue.

She moans, an impossibly erotic sound. I snake my fingers down to her slick pussy and slide my fingers into her, sudden and without warning. She giggles and writhes, pulling me over onto her. The sound of her laugh, true, innocent laughter…it's the most amazing thing I've ever heard.

I'm above her, poised between her thighs, weight on my elbows, lips inches from hers, and her laughter fades. I hadn't meant to land on top of her; it just accidentally happened. My cock nudges her entrance, and I have to tense every muscle in my body to keep from plunging into her.

Her eyes are wide, her laughter gone, but her hands are on my shoulders, still and not trembling. I move to get off her, but she shakes her head.

"No, please. Just wait." Her voice is so gentle, so hesitant, so innocent.

I wait. While I wait, I kiss her. She seems to find some kind of courage, some kind of solace in my lips on her skin. I begin at her shoulder, the round arch where arm meets shoulder, and then move to her clavicle, her throat, the hollow between throat and chest. She whimpers but does not move, does not speak. I venture a risk, kiss the swell of her breast, one and then the other, then take her nipple in my mouth and tongue it erect, one and then the other.

Her arms slide around my neck while I kiss her breasts. Then I move up to kiss her lips, and her hands glide ghost-soft down my back to cup my ass.

"Look at me," she says.

I look at her eyes. She is afraid again, but I see determination in her expression.

"Rania. You don't have to prove anything to me."

She shakes her head. "Not to you. To me." She caresses my ass, small, hesitant circles. "This was Sabah's place, on her back. I want to make it mine, Rania's. Ours. I do not want to let Sabah steal my pleasure."

We share the silence for a long moment, and then she pulls at me, gently urging me closer. Her small, warm hands on my ass urge me into her. I pause before entrance.

"Are you sure?" I ask.

She nods. "Yes. Just…slowly. And kiss me." She touches my lips with hers, and then says, "I need your kisses to make the memories disappear."

This time, it's me. I have to make this perfect, make it right.

I breathe in her scent and kiss her sweet lips. I kiss her with all the tenderness, all the bone-deep love, all the soul-shaking passion welling up in me for this woman. There is so much. I had no fucking clue I could feel this way, this much. It's like some deep well opened up inside me, and now all the love in all the world is being poured through me into her.

She pulls at my ass, insistently now, and I adjust my weight, spread my knees slightly, and move into her. I enter her with a slowness at once excruciating and delightful, so slow it is almost not motion at all. She whimpers again, high in the back of her throat, and as I slip deeper her whimper is drawn into a moan.

Our bodies meet and her back arches as I bury myself to the hilt inside her, and now it's my turn to groan. "God, Rania…you feel so amazing. I love being inside you."

"Please, more," she whispers. "More, more."

I give her more, but slowly, gently. I try to make love to her as softly as I kiss her, not as if she's fragile, but with tenderness. I go so slowly that each slide in, each slip out seems to take an eternity, an infinity of heaven.

She clutches my ass, pulls me against her, and I move a little faster, a little deeper. I alter the rhythm of my thrusts, a slow thrust in, a slightly faster withdrawal. She moans, gasps, and clutches me, breathing harder and harder. I feel a sheen of sweat slick across her body, mingling with my own sweat.

"Hunter," Rania gasps, "I love this, with you. Don't stop. It feels so good, so right. Please, give me more, a little more."

Something about her words strikes me as unusual, and it takes me a few beats to figure out what: she used a contraction.

I don't bother saying that I couldn't stop if I wanted to. I can only move with her, feeling her sweet, lush body slipping like yards of the softest silk beneath me, tasting her lips, her breath. God, I love her. Love her so fucking much it should be impossible, and I love her more with every breath I take, with every delve of my cock into the heaven of her pussy.

I love her more, and more, and I wonder how much I might love her in ten or twenty years. I try to imagine it, and my head spins.

Her nails claw down my back, and she whimpers, cries out, and now her legs curl around my ass and she pulls me in, and in, and in, harder and harder. It's heaven, it's sweet glorious perfection, angel of love made flesh, made woman, whose name is Rania.

Her breasts are crushed against my chest, firm but giving, and her breath is on my ear, erotic moans, the soundtrack of sex, of love. Her inner muscles are clenching around me, clamping down as I drive in, releasing as I slip out, and goddamn I didn't know a girl could do that. It feels like her pussy is grabbing me and letting go, and it's the hottest thing I've ever fucking felt.

I slip my arms beneath her neck and kiss into her oblivion, into breathless abandon; I kiss her until she's gasping for breath and bucking into me, flung by passion into wildness. She's an animal suddenly, arching her back, clinging to me with her arms and legs, with her whole body, screaming my name as she comes, and I can't hold back, can only come with her, and oh, my fucking god, it's the most intensely purifying experience of my life, my whole body is plunged into fire, into ecstasy.

"Rania..." I gasp her name.

It's the only word I know, in that moment. All I know is her. Her name. Her body, her love. Nothing else has ever existed.

The war, the goddamned awful memories, the death, Lani's betrayal...it all is vanished, gone, subsumed in the river of Rania's love.

She's still holding tight to me, clinging to me like I'm a spar and she's shipwrecked, her breath coming in long, deep, ragged gasps, breasts heaving against my side. Her palm rests low on my belly, inches away from my cock. Her leg is thrown over mine, and she traces circles on my skin with her finger, then reaches down to touch my cock, rubbing her palm along its length, toying with the tip.

We don't speak, and she plays with me, and then I'm hard and she's climbing astride me and riding me.

She spears herself onto me and sits with me deep inside her gorgeous body, and she rises up and falls down and her long bottle-blonde hair is in her face and across her shoulders and brushing her nipples. I take her hips in my hands and lift her up, crush her down. I kiss her belly. I kiss her breasts.

I hold back, tensing, until she comes for the first time, and then I sit up and guide her legs around my back and move with her, sitting up, face to face, kissing, making out as we glide into each other, and I feel the river widen, deepen, her love filling me and making me love her yet more.

THE END

EPILOGUE

Dyeing

Des Moines, Iowa, 2005

A WOMAN STANDS IN FRONT OF A MIRROR FOGGED WITH STEAM. She has a robin's-egg-blue towel wrapped around her chest. She wipes a streak across the mirror with a slim palm, cleaning a swath in which to see her reflection. She smiles, a sweet curving of red lips. She unwraps the towel and cleans the mirror the rest of the way.

She smiles at her reflection again, her expression surprised, almost as if seeing someone familiar, someone not seen in many years. She drags her fingers through her hair, cut to brush the tops of her shoulders.

A man enters the bathroom, murmuring in appreciation of her naked body. He slides his hands down her sides to her hips, then over her slightly rounded belly and up to her breasts, which he cups in tender hands.

He rests his chin on her shoulder and takes in her reflection with her. He lifts a hand to run a tendril of her freshly dyed ink-black hair through his fingers. "I love it, Rania," he says.

"You do?" She turns to look at him, kisses his nose.

"Yes, I do. I really, really love it. It looks so perfect. So you."

"So I didn't look like me, before I dyed my hair?" Her voice holds a note of teasing.

The man just snorts. "You know what I meant."

She laughs. "Yes, my love. I just enjoy teasing you."

He chuckles with her, then moves his hand from her breast down between her thighs.

She smacks his hand away. "We don't have time for that, Hunter. We have to be at the doctor in half an hour. Or don't you wish to know if our baby is a boy or girl?"

He backs away, but not before giving her backside a playful smack. "Well, then, you'd best get moving, shouldn't you?"

She snorts, turning to slap his arm as he dances out of the way. When he is gone, she turns to look at herself again, running her fingers through her hair. Her expression is distant, as if seeing a young girl in the mirror, young and innocent.

The woman shakes her head, and the girl is gone, replaced by her own face once more.

But for weeks afterward, she sometimes sees that little girl in the mirror, sees her in the flash of hair so black it is almost blue, in the wide, dark brown eyes that now hold love, happiness, and completion.

About the Author

JASINDA WILDER is a Michigan native with a penchant for titillating tales about sexy men and strong women. When she's not writing, she's probably shopping, baking, or reading. She loves to travel, and some of her favorite vacations spots are Las Vegas, New York City, and Toledo, Ohio. You can often find Jasinda drinking sweet red wine with frozen berries.

To find out more about Jasinda and her other titles, visit her website: www.JasindaWilder.com.

Printed in Great Britain
by Amazon.co.uk, Ltd.,
Marston Gate.